"Za

Ivy worked her gaze from his head down to his toes and then back again in a slow and silent perusal. "Is it you?"

He stared at her, struggling to find his voice.

"Yes," he managed to force out. "It's me."

"What a surprise," she breathed, swiping a muddy hand across the front of her lavender-colored skirt. Her long eyelashes whispered down over those eyes of hers. "I barely recognized you. It's been—"

"S-s-six years." He cleared his throat, and his stomach convulsed at the way he could've rattled off the months, the days…maybe the hours since he'd last seen her.

But he was more disgusted with the way the one syllable had suddenly become three.

The sound of his broken speech raked over his hearing like a hundred pricking barbs. Surely it was a mishap. A blunder. There was no way, after all of the labor, sweat and fortitude he'd poured into overcoming his stutter that it'd descend on him again.

No way.

Books by Pamela Nissen

Love Inspired Historical

Rocky Mountain Match
Rocky Mountain Redemption
Rocky Mountain Proposal
Rocky Mountain Homecoming

PAMELA NISSEN

loves creating. Whether it's characters, cooking, scrapbooking or other artistic endeavors, she takes pleasure in putting things together for others to enjoy. She started writing her first book in 2000 and since then hasn't looked back. Pamela lives in the woods in Iowa with her husband, daughter, two sons, a Newfoundland dog and cats. She loves watching her children pursue their dreams, and is known to yell on the sidelines at her boys' games and being moved to tears as she watches her daughter perform. She enjoys scrapbooking weekends with her sister, coffee with friends and running in the rain. Having glimpsed the dark and light of life, she is passionate about writing "real" people with "real" issues and "real" responses.

Rocky Mountain Homecoming

PAMELA NISSEN

Love Inspired

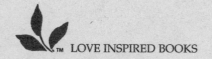

LOVE INSPIRED BOOKS

Recycling programs
for this product may
not exist in your area.

ISBN-13: 978-0-373-82884-5

ROCKY MOUNTAIN HOMECOMING

Copyright © 2011 by Pamela Nissen

www.LoveInspiredBooks.com

Printed in U.S.A.

It was for freedom that Christ set us free;
therefore keep standing firm and
do not be subject again to a yoke of slavery.
—*Galatians* 5:1

For my loving son, Noel Kas Nissen
~A young man beyond his time
in wisdom and understanding~

Thanks go to my husband, Bill: for loving me
and giving me the freedom to create.
To my son, Elias: for being a whimsical source
of joy in my life. To my daughter, MaryAnna:
for overcoming and loving life. To my
critique group, Jacquie, Diane and Roxanne:
for your sincere dedication and cherished friendship.
To my wonderful friends and family:
for your profound influence in my life.
And to my dad: for carrying on where Mom left off.

Chapter One

"Make way! Big load comin' through," Pete O'Leary, the local grave digger, announced as he plastered his tall lanky form against a row of mercantile shelves. "Zach, you must be half ox, with the way you're lugging those heavy crates."

"Ahh…they're not all that heavy. I'll be fine." Adjusting his grip on the two jam-packed crates, the ranch foreman ducked under a display of bridles that had been hung like moss from a tree.

"I think Conroy here's scairt of ya, Zach." Pete dragged his pet ferret, its long-whiskered nose twitching, from his shoulder and held out the critter to Zach. "Feel how the little guy's jest shakin' up a storm."

Pausing, Zach eyed the lanky critter, a purchase Pete had made from a traveling salesman a year ago. The cute weasel-like animal was Pete's constant companion, except at church, which Pete had often mourned, saying that attending might do the ferret's *thieving soul* some good. Zach was pretty sure that if he didn't take the time to alleviate Conroy's *apparent* fear, he'd wound Pete's feelings.

Easing the crates to the floor, he took the ferret from

Pete, chuckling at the way the animal draped over his arms like a wet cloth, peering up at him with those mischievous marble-like eyes of his. "Well, aren't you a cute little guy," Zach said, if for no other reason than to placate Pete. "See, I'm as harmless as a newborn pup. I wouldn't hurt a soul."

"I don' know 'bout that," Pete contradicted. Blowing out a big breath, he stirred up tiny particles of dust on a nearby shelf that sashayed on his hot air to some other shelf. "Conroy and me...*we* wouldn't want to cross you—that's for sure."

"I'm slow to rile," Zach reasoned, recognizing that with the long hours of hard physical labor he worked on the Harris ranch, he'd come by his size honestly. "But when it comes to defending what's right and looking out for loved ones, I don't back down." Zach wore the trait proudly.

"Yer jest like yer brothers," Pete stated with a tight wink. "Every last one of you Drake boys is cut'a the same sturdy, God-fearin' cloth."

"I count myself a blessed man to have them."

His brothers meant the world to him. He'd do anything to help them out, and they'd do the same—that is, *if* he let them.

Zach swallowed a generous gulp of pride as he recalled just how often his brothers had said that he needed to stop taking on the world by himself. And more than anything...that he needed to find his way to trusting God again instead of trying to be the Almighty for himself.

He was trying. He'd even felt God's gentle tugging, but time and again, it seemed Zach was better off carving out his own path. He had too much to prove after living in his brothers' long successful shadows. Now, he was determined to forge his own way in life. Or die trying.

The rhythmic jangling sound of a wagon rolling down the street filtered into his hearing like some patent reminder to get a move on. The way his boss, Mr. Harris, had seemed under the weather recently, Zach had stepped up his duties a notch.

"I've got to get going, Pete." He returned Conroy to Pete's arms and hefted the crates again. "See you around."

"See ya later, Zach," Pete said, observing Zach as though he was carrying a big old pine tree down the aisle.

Craning his neck around the bulky load, Zach headed toward the door, the bolts of colorful calico to his right. Turning, he nudged the unlatched door with his backside. When it stuck, he gave it a hard shove.

"Get off!" a female voice yelped from the mercantile platform outside.

He whipped his head around just in time to see a flourish of hands flailing, skirts ruffling and wings flapping.

"Go!" she hollered, waving her hands madly.

A barn swallow bolted from the woman's fancy feathered hat into the crisp September air. She spun around and backpeddled, stumbling toward the edge of the four-foot boardwalk.

Dropping the crates with a clank and clatter, Zach bolted into the late afternoon sun. Snaked out a hand to grab her. Missed.

As she tumbled to the mud-slopped ground with a delicate splat, he shot off the platform, landing on his feet beside the woman. He hunkered down at her side. "Are you all right, ma'am?" He touched her shoulder.

"I'm fine. *Just dandy,*" she sputtered, her mouth a resolute line and barely visible from beneath her wide-brimmed, dirt-splattered hat that had been knocked askew. She struggled to lever herself from the mud's sloppy grasp.

"Here, let me help you." He pulled the woman up to a sitting position then retrieved her small handbag, and after wiping the mud from it onto his breeches, held it out to her. "Here's your bag, ma'am."

She hunkered down and whispered, "Where's that horrible bird? Is he still here?" A heavy thread of desperation flashed through her words even as a wavy lock of rich auburn hair tumbled from beneath her hat.

"He's gone." Zach scanned the rooflines. "Flew the coop. At least for now, anyway."

"You mean he's likely to *return?*" she yelped. She ducked her head between her shoulders as though she was about to be swooped down on by an entire flock. "Because I'm scared to death of birds."

He didn't believe he knew this woman, hadn't even gotten a good look at her with that pretentious hat draping over her face, but the fact that she was so obviously unsettled by a harmless bird struck a chord of compassion in his heart.

He settled a protective arm around her shoulder and angled a glance at the mercantile overhang where the barest makings of a nest had been wedged onto a strut. "I hate to break the news to you, but with that nest he has started up there, he'll likely be back."

She gave a muffled screech, and with muddy hands, shielded her hat-draped head as if she was being pelted by egg-size hailstones.

"It's all right. Don't be afraid." He gently grasped her arm. "I'll protect you if he returns."

With the wagons clattering by and horses plodding through the streets, he almost missed the long breath she inhaled right then. But he couldn't miss the way she stiffened, her spine growing straight and unyielding, as though she'd been jarred to her senses.

She pulled away from him and with mud-caked fingers, primped the ruffled white shirtwaist beneath her fashionable silken wrap. "I can manage just fine by myself."

He shook his head at her show of stubbornness. Something about this woman was vaguely familiar. Her voice... with its rich lilting tone, and her slender fingers...the way they tapered to a delicate end, and then there was the almost prideful way she'd diverted his concern.

Angling his head down, he tried unsuccessfully to peek at her from beneath the mud-wilted brim. When he took in the bedraggled state of this spritely stranger, and her seemingly unconcerned attitude about her condition, he couldn't help but be slightly amused. The hat she wore, big and looking more like a small garden of frippery than a head covering, dwarfed her petite frame.

The sound of wildly flapping wings broke through his musings. She must have heard it too, because the woman balled herself up tight as the bird braved another approach.

"Go on, bird. Shoo!" He waved off the curious winged creature with one arm and folded the other around the trembling woman. His heart skipped several beats as she burrowed against his chest, her warm breath seeping clear through his shirt.

He could've stayed right here with this little lady in his arms for the next hour. Maybe more. Even in spite of the noticeable way a gaggle of older women had gathered outside the hotel, their lips tight disapproving lines as they stared in his direction.

He'd never quite felt like this before. He'd never gotten close enough to know what this felt like. In years past, his annoying stutter would crop up, unbidden, chasing him away from the very idea of love. And once he'd been made foreman, he'd been too focused on doing the best job he could to spend any kind of thought on a woman.

Scooping her into his arms, he lifted her from the mud and crossed over to the walkway, giving little notice to the dark slime that now caked his arms, hands and down the front of his shirt.

But the soft gasp that came from her lips just now…he *definitely* couldn't ignore that.

She scrambled to free herself from his arms, jerking him from his temporary lapse of wits. "What in the world?" she sputtered, irritation sharply framing her words.

"I said I'd protect you if he returned, and that's what I was doing," he defended, a little put out by her abruptness.

"*Please*…put me down!" she demanded, breathless.

He grinned at her endearing grasp for control, and held on. "You might want to take that thing off your head if you're planning on protecting yourself." He settled her feet on the boardwalk. "With all those feathers and leaves and whatnot, I'd say it's a little too tempting for that nesting bird. He probably thinks he's discovered a perfect fall and winter home."

Stomping mud from her fancy buttoned boots, she tugged the brim of her hat down all the more, hiding her face nearly completely. "I'll leave it on, thank you."

"Suit yourself." With unabashed curiosity, he looked on while she brushed at her skirt. With the delicate way she was going about it, she may as well have been trying to remove a smudge of innocent dust, not a thick layer of reddish-colored mud. He could hardly blame the spirited woman for being so on edge. After all, her entire backside was coated in a slimy layer of mud. She was probably mortified. Humiliated. Downright mad.

With that silent acknowledgment, he drew his neatly folded handkerchief from his back pocket and held it out like an olive branch. "Here. Take this."

Clutching the front edge of her hat, she lifted it into place with more dignity than he'd expect, given her filthy condition.

"This might help a litt—" His words died on his tongue as she tipped up her face and met his gaze.

His breath whooshed from his lungs. He stared, wide-eyed, his vision pulsing black. White. Then splotching in an array of colors as he took in the woman standing before him.

Ivy. Grace. Harris.

He blinked hard in the hopes of producing some other image than her.

The one and only love of his childhood heart.

His boss's daughter.

And the *sole* reason he'd suffered years of humiliation.

She stared at him for a long and lingering moment. Her lips parted and then fell open as wide as her sparkling eyes.

Zach's blood thickened in his veins as he met that beautiful, memorable spring-green gaze of hers. He'd never forget it—with just one glance his knees used to grow as flimsy as a blade of grass bent by the wind—just like they did now. Nor had he forgotten the adorable way her pert little nose turned up ever-so-slightly. Or the way her full lips formed the most perfect Cupid's bow, begging to be kissed.

He worked a swallow past the lump that had knotted his throat. Battled back that familiar, thick, tongue-tied feeling that strangled him even now. Struggled to keep all six feet of his work-hardened body from trembling.

For over a year now he'd been foreman on John Harris's ranch, and for the first time since childhood he'd felt secure. Confident.

But now...

Now with this girl—this *woman's*—appearance, he was catapulted back to nearly twelve years ago all over again.

He blinked back the apprehension she was sure to find in his gaze. Swerved his focus a block down the street where he spotted Beatrice Duncan beelining toward them, her short legs eating up the walkway with surprising swiftness as she aimed an overly eager, almost giddy look in his direction. He clenched his jaw at the woman's clear intent. But it was the woman in front of him that gave him pause.

"Zachariah Drake?" Ivy worked her gaze from his head all the way down to his toes and then back again in a slow, silent and wholly discomforting perusal. "Is it you?"

He stared at her, struggling to find his voice.

"Is it *really* you?" The buoyant sound of her voice disconcerted him all the more.

"Yes," he managed to force out. "It's me."

"What a surprise," she breathed, swiping a muddy hand across the front of her lavender-colored skirt. Her long eyelashes whispered down over those eyes of hers like tender branches bending to kiss the fresh green of a beautiful spring landscape. "I barely recognized you. It's been—"

"S-s-six years." Clearing his throat, his stomach convulsed at the way he could've rattled off the months, the days...maybe the hours since he'd last seen her.

But he was more disgusted with the way the one syllable had suddenly become three.

The sound of his broken speech raked over his hearing

like a hundred pricking barbs. Surely it was a mishap. A blunder. There was no way, after all the labor, sweat and fortitude he'd poured into overcoming his stutter that it'd descend on him again like some dark and stormy day.

No way.

"It has been, hasn't it?" She lifted her chin in that stately way of hers. Fingered the wilting blue fringe dangling from the navy wrap that was now plastered by mud to her back.

He nodded, shoving his hands into his pockets as he hauled in a deep, deep breath, something he'd learned to do when he'd faced his stutter head-on. Dragging his hands out of his pockets, he unfurled his tight fists one finger at a time. "What are you d-d-doing here?"

What in the name of all that was true!

There it was again.

He'd defeated this thing. Hadn't tripped up more than once over the past couple years. He could speak clearly. Wasn't given to stumbling. Or even pausing overly long.

He was *fine.* Just *fine.*

She tipped her head slightly. Furrowed her graceful brow.

Zach held his ground, even when part of him wanted to flee from her presence and from the haunting impediment. But he'd come too far over the past six years to let her shake his confidence, even if it was quite a shock to see her again.

His boss hadn't said a word about Ivy coming for a visit. In fact, Zach had only heard the man speak of his daughter once since he'd been working at the Harris ranch.

She lifted her hat from her head, exposing those silken auburn curls he'd stared at for hours on end when he was in school. "As you can see, I was stopping by the mercantile. That is until that bird—"

"What I mean is...*why* are you in B-B-B-Boulder?" His face muscles tensed.

She set a quivering hand to her neck. "I was stopping by to see if I could find someone who might be able to drive me to the ranch," she measured out as though he had a miniscule understanding of the English language.

Her placating tone grated his nerves. In school, he'd been ridiculed. Teased without mercy. Treated as though he couldn't read, write or add two plus two.

He hadn't been able to speak one sentence without stumbling over the words. And all because of this beautiful woman standing in front of him now.

She glanced around as though there might be a fancy carriage waiting to do her bidding. "My visit...it's *unexpected.*"

He'd rather flinch beneath that stubborn stance of hers that he'd glimpsed just moments ago than to writhe in the obvious pity seen in her gaze at this moment. He sure as shootin' *wasn't* going to allow her to strip away all the confidence he'd worked for. No matter how beautiful she was—even more stunning than she'd been six years ago. No matter how often her perfect face had sneaked into his dreams.

He thought he'd overcome the strange hold Ivy once had on him, but one look at her and his traitorous heart had begun beating a wild-stallion rhythm.

And the sight of Beatrice Duncan invading his peripheral vision didn't help matters one bit. The woman, as benevolent as she was at times, seemed to glory in drama.

"*Ivy Harris?* Is that *you?*" Mrs. Duncan's shrill voice pierced the noise of clattering wagons. "What in the world happened to you? You look a sight."

Ivy glanced at him, that heart-stopping gaze of hers undermining the core of his resolve as Mrs. Duncan tramped over the last few feet and came to a sudden stop.

"Don't tell me you knocked this poor girl off that platform there, Zachariah Drake," she scolded, a stiff gust of wind blowing wisps of bright orange hair into the woman's round face.

Scrambling to gain control over his slipping confidence, he drew in a deep breath as the memory of Ivy fearfully ducking for cover from a harmless bird flashed through his mind.

Ivy sighed, perching her hat on her head again. "He didn't—"

"It was my fault," Zach confessed, meeting Mrs. Duncan's scorn, face-first. He gulped back his pride, knowing that the woman would pick the situation apart until Ivy would have to admit to being terrified of a harmless bird, and he just couldn't allow that to happen.

He set his back teeth, annoyed that he somehow felt it was *his* responsibility to leap to her rescue. He'd learned the hard way—the long, painful, life-altering way—that following his heart like he had twelve years ago, was a *very* bad idea. At least where Ivy Harris was concerned.

"I had my hands full c-carrying those crates." He nodded up at the platform, where the crates lay on their sides, the contents having spilled out like some bountiful cornucopia. "I wasn't looking where I was g-g-going and startled—"

"It was an accident, ma'am." Ivy sliced him an admonishing look, mortifying Zach by refusing to let him take the blame.

Beatrice Duncan slid a doubtful gaze from the front edge of the platform then down to the patch of mud created by the recent rains and constant run of horse hooves and wagon wheels. She jammed her fists on her doughy waist. "I don't know how many times I've said to my Horace, 'Horace, you need to get out there and fasten a railing to the front of this platform before some soul or another gets hurt!'" She gave her round head a decided shake, huffing and puffing in a gratuitous show of frustration. "But that mule-headed man of mine insists that it stay like it is. Says it makes loading wagons easier."

The corners of Ivy's mouth tipped up the slightest bit. "The platform is just fine the way it is, Mrs. Duncan. I was—"

"Oh, never you mind the platform. You come here, girl, and give me a big ole hug." She started for Ivy, flinging her arms wide open and then shutting them up just as suddenly, as if realizing she'd soil her go-to-meeting dress. "Oops, that won't do at all now, will it? How about a friendly nod for now? Land sakes, you were just a girl when you up and left Boulder, but *now* look at you." She slid an approving look all the way from Ivy's toes to her head. "If a body sees past the mud, I'd say she's turned into quite a beautiful young woman. Hasn't she, Zach?"

He met Ivy's stunned expression, unwilling to appear pathetic or indecisive in front of her, as he had when he was younger. "Yes," he confirmed, struggling to drag himself over to some distantly objective viewpoint. "Yes, she has."

"What brings you back to these parts, anyway, Ivy?" Mrs. Duncan folded her hands in front of her. "Why, I just saw your daddy the other day and he didn't mention one thing about you journeying out here for a visit."

"Violet sent for me." The momentary look of bravery crossing Ivy's face pricked Zach's heart. "My father doesn't know I'm coming."

"Well, why in the world not, child?" the woman challenged. "He'd be happy to know of your visit. He'd probably roll out the red carpet for you, if he knew you were here."

When Ivy's focus drifted down the road where her father's ranch stretched across the foothills, Zach had to wonder just how long she planned on staying. Three weeks? Two? Maybe one…if he was lucky?

She met the older woman's intense stare, a certain sadness dimming her bright eyes. "As ill as he is, I didn't want to cause him any undo worry. It wouldn't be good for him in his condition."

"What do you mean?" Confusion furrowed Mrs. Duncan's ruddy brow. "What *condition* are you talking about?"

Had Zach not worked closely enough with Mr. Harris to notice otherwise, he would've echoed the woman's query. But maybe there was even more cause for alarm than what he'd observed. Mr. Harris's housekeeper, Violet Stoddard, had worried many a path in the kitchen floor. Was there a new path, deeper than just *a little under the weather?*

Distress flitted featherlight across Ivy's fair features. She tugged her wrap together at her chest, worrying her bottom lip.

"When I saw him the other day, he looked fit as a fine-tuned instrument. Why, he dismounted his horse with almost as much vim and vigor as Zach, here," Mrs. Duncan announced, poking Zach in the arm. "But that daddy of yours is a proud man. He'd probably prefer going to his grave without a soul knowing he was sick than to show weakness."

Ivy's wide gaze grew even more troubled. "Probably."

"I suppose you didn't want to cause him any worry

with you traveling all the way out here, and it's good of you to be concerned, mind you." Mrs. Duncan primped the white ruffles meandering down the front of Ivy's shirt. "But honestly…the careless way you young'uns go gallivanting all over the country, these days, us parent-folk are bound to fall face-first into an early grave."

Zach clenched his jaw. With Ivy's mother dying shortly before Ivy had headed east, Mrs. Duncan's poor choice of words was downright irritating. "Ivy is exhausted, Mrs. Duncan. She probably j-j-just wants to get home and settle in. I'd better g-g-get her loaded up."

"What in the world is *wrong* with you, Zachariah Drake?" the older woman demanded, pivoting to face him. "Are you tripping over your words again?" Despite the generous serving of concern coating Mrs. Duncan's inquiry, Zach squirmed.

"It's nothing." He clamped his lips tightly together.

"I thought you had that thing licked," she persisted.

"I did."

The woman gave a halfhearted harrumph and squared her shoulders. "Well, if you're headin' that way, Zach, then you may as well take this poor girl home with you before she catches her death of a cold."

"With you?" Ivy's petite features creased as she peered at Zach. "I'm not sure I understand."

He wasn't about to let her opinion of him strip away his hard-earned confidence. He'd tripped all over himself one too many times for her. Never, *never* again would he be so weak, so vulnerable. He'd just steer clear of her. Keep busy until she went back to where she belonged.

"Why, girl, don't you know?" Mrs. Duncan blurted, obviously way too eager to bear the untold information she'd stumbled upon. "A year ago your daddy up and promoted Zach here to—"

* * *

"Foreman," Zach interrupted, the news taking Ivy by complete surprise.

"Foreman?" she echoed, struggling to swallow her shock. Violet hadn't mentioned a thing in her letters.

She peered at him. Maybe she shouldn't be so surprised. He was nothing like she remembered from school. Nothing. *That* Zachariah Drake had been skinny and lanky and awkward. But *this* Zachariah Drake was tall and powerfully built, strikingly handsome with his crystal-blue eyes and strong jawline. This Zachariah Drake was...

Her father's *foreman?*

"What happened to Cliff?" she finally managed to say, her mind racing with a plethora of questions. "He's been foreman as long as I've been alive."

"Cliff passed on last year," Mrs. Duncan commented. "Poor soul. That man was as trusted as your daddy, himself."

"I had no idea," Ivy breathed, clutching her handbag tight.

It wasn't as if she'd had a close relationship with the man, but he'd always been a fixture on the ranch. Always. He was honest and solid and had years of wisdom in that silvery head of his.

Being the stubborn man of detail that her father was, he'd often driven home the fact that time-earned experience was a priceless commodity on the ranch. That there was no substitute for the strong lines on a cowboy's face carved by years of sun and hard work.

Zach was young. Twenty-three. Twenty-four in two short weeks. From the monthly church dinners and collective birthday celebrations she fondly recalled from her childhood, she couldn't forget how his birthday fell two days before hers.

Still, as she peered at him, all six feet, work-hardened muscle of him, she knew she would not soon forget the warm and comforting feel of his arms cradling her as he'd carried her to the boardwalk mere moments ago, either. He'd grown up. But had he grown up enough to handle the grueling responsibilities that come with running a ranch? And for that matter, *when* had Zach grown from the scrawny fence post of a boy she recalled from school, to this inarguably strapping man? And why did she suddenly find that so attractive?

Back in New York she'd mostly encountered men in suits, cravats and handsome boots that shined. She certainly hadn't forgotten her ranch-style roots here in the west, but perhaps, standing at the precipice of womanhood six years ago, she'd been too young to take notice of a man who'd been chiseled by hard work, fresh air and physical labor.

A man like Zach.

All good sense had seemingly left her the moment he'd wrapped her in his strong arms, shielding her from that wayward bird—and she'd *never* felt that before. But just as soon as he'd taken it upon himself to pick her up and cart her like a sack of potatoes to the boardwalk as though she was a helpless newborn babe, she'd been jerked out of her silent reverie.

When their gazes had finally met she'd scrambled to hide her shock. She'd been caught completely off guard, especially by the news of his position as foreman. For six years, she'd clung to her well-ordered world as a matter of survival, and she'd flourished. Change—especially change that involved an exceedingly handsome young man who now managed her father's greatest interest—

was not something she navigated through with much confidence. She'd expected to come home and tend to her father and his ranch.

How was she ever going to maneuver through the next few weeks?

Chapter Two

When Ivy glimpsed her father's ranch anchoring the long and winding lane, she willed herself to relax. But her heart—it was beating right through her chest. She'd figured she'd be nervous returning home after all these years, but the trepidation that threatened to loosen her tightly wound control caught her *completely* off guard.

Especially after she'd discovered that her father's health apparently wasn't as tenuous as Violet had inferred. She didn't think that the woman was given to telling tales, so why had the letter sounded so urgent? From the way Mrs. Duncan had reacted, it seemed that her father wasn't heading to his grave, after all.

The thought of him suffering had nearly broken Ivy's heart in New York. She'd rushed back to Boulder right away. But was she needed here after all?

Struggling to ward off the chill and raw emotion quivering her body, she clutched the wool blanket Zach had stubbornly insisted on wrapping around her shoulders.

While he steered the wagon down the lane, she inched her gaze over the broad expanse of well-maintained buildings and new barbed-wire fencing that hemmed in plentiful acres of grazing land. The homestead looked good, probably better than she remembered.

Being here now and seeing the ranch, smelling the familiar scents of hay and cattle and the beginnings of fall, she could almost feel the memories struggling to escape from where she'd buried them deep inside her heart. Memories of a carefree childhood spent scampering behind her daddy as he took care of the chores, of learning to ride her first pony with him at her side, of swinging from the rope he'd looped around an enduring arm extending from one of the Ponderosa pines.

There'd been a time when she'd envisioned working alongside her father into his old age, but once her mama had taken ill, he'd changed. Her father's adoring focus had shifted to a desperate, almost frantic search for some kind of medical help. The more time that ticked by without a cure, the more agitated he'd become. The ranch had been his only solace, and along with tending to her mama, he'd poured himself into making it the best and most respected in the region even when it seemed he could do nothing to help his wife.

Warding off the gloom of that memory, she dragged in a long breath of crisp late-September air, seasoned with the musky scent of drying foliage. She had a hard time believing that she was actually here, days away from New York, and years away from life as she'd known back east. Six years ago, she'd vowed never to return to Boulder— not after her father had sent her away with such cruel finality.

Her father had blamed her for her mama's death— surely he'd never forgive her.

And she felt horribly responsible. Alone, she'd carried guilt's heavy burden for the past six years, wondering if she'd ever be able to forgive herself. As desperate as she sometimes felt to climb to God's open arms of love and acceptance, she felt stuck in a deep hole of guilt and shame.

When the wagon lurched to the side, she was jerked from her painful thoughts. She grabbed hold of the thick wood seat, steadying herself as Zach guided the team off the path to avoid a big tortoiseshell tomcat, intent on maintaining his sunny spot in the middle of the lane. *Tortoiseshell cat...?*

"Shakespeare?" She scrambled to peer over the side of the wagon. The big cat's eyes squeezed shut and his ears twitched in her direction.

"That's him," Zach confirmed with a cluck of his tongue. "He thinks he owns the p-p-place."

"Oh, my. He's grown so much." She wrenched around in her seat, tears stinging the backs of her eyes seeing how Shakespeare had grown into the noble looking tomcat he was now. "He was just an undernourished litter runt that Mama and I bottle fed. He was nowhere *near* this big when I left."

After Zach eased the wagon to a stop just beyond the furry road block, he swung down from the seat and crossed to where the cat lay, content as could be. The delicate state of her heart grew even more fragile when Zach appeared a moment later, holding out the enormous cat for her.

"Shakespeare," she cooed, pulling her arms from the blanket and hugging him close. She burrowed her face into his thick, sleek fur. "You're absolutely enormous. What have they been feeding you?"

"An egg every d-d-day, beef fat—and Lord knows what else." Zach pulled himself up to his seat, settled the blanket around her shoulders again then sent the wagon lurching forward. "Your father sees to Sh-Shakespeare's feeding."

Her father had never shown Shakespeare one bit of interest in the past. That he had obviously spoiled her kitty tugged at her heartstrings.

The cat's loud purr and the way he stretched to touch the tip of his pink nose to hers was almost her undoing.

But she couldn't afford to weaken. Not now. She was already over half unraveled and she hadn't even set foot inside the house.

Sitting a little straighter in her seat, she drew her focus toward the house as she gently raked her fingers through Shakespeare's soft fur. Although this place had been home for the first seventeen years of her life, it could never be home again.

There'd been too many changes in her life. And likely too many changes in her father's life, as well.

Like Zach being her father's foreman...

When Zach slowed the wagon to a halt at the edge of the yard, she snagged a look at him from the corner of her vision. The sure way he handled the reins, his hands, large and work worn and yet so very gentle, had caught her attention off and on throughout the trip. The noticeable way his arm muscles bunched beneath his shirt as he swung down from the wagon captured her focus all the more. She didn't know if she'd *ever* forget the warm feel of his comforting touch.

A million questions had streamed through Ivy's mind during the silence-saturated wagon ride home. The foremost being, *when* had Zach changed into the solid and confident man he was now?

While he crossed in front of the horses, her focus flitted to his manly jawline. How was it that a feature so strong and sure looking could fumble so with the English language? She recalled the agonizing way he'd struggled through school, the relentless way the teacher had chastised him for refusing to stand and recite his lessons, the harsh way he'd been laughed at by some of the schoolchildren. And, to her shame, the cowardly way she'd giggled right along with them—at times.

Diverting her focus from his steadfast gaze as he approached her side of the wagon, she struggled to tug her composure back into place. But when he carefully lifted the cat down then circled her waist with his large and calloused hands, she couldn't seem to maintain a coherent thought. His touch, the lingering feel of his hands around her waist, gave her a heady feeling, even after he set her feet on the ground. A very real and unwanted quiver worked its way straight up her spine.

She'd seen what sickness and death had done to her parents, and had decided that loving just wasn't worth the pain. She'd been so careful to guard her heart when it came to men, but felt that resolve already slipping from her unrelenting grip. She didn't need anything or anyone tying her down here in Boulder. Certainly not Zach Drake.

"Here we are," he voiced, his words coming slow. His throat visibly convulsed as though he'd just swallowed one gigantic bug.

"Home…." Gathering in a steadying breath, she took in her surroundings.

"Has it ch-changed much?" He reached over the wagon bed and grabbed two of her four valises.

She tugged the blanket tighter around her shoulders, trying to keep from trembling as she slid her gaze around the homestead. "It looks better than I remember."

When he set the back of his hand featherlight to her cheek, she nearly startled.

"You're cold," he said, his voice low, his gaze direct.

"I'm quite comfortable." She turned her head from his debilitating touch. In truth, the weighted chill of mud drying on her garments had seeped clear though to her bones and she didn't know if she'd ever warm up, but she wasn't about to let this man direct her steps like she had no fortitude about her.

He gently pressed a hand to the middle of her back, guiding her to the front steps as he cleared his throat. "We need to get you inside so you c-can change into something warm and d-d-dry."

Drawing her mouth into a grim line, she forced one foot in front of the other when all she really wanted to do was to dig her heels in deep, delaying going inside until she was *good and ready*. And not a minute before.

Being home after so long was far more difficult than she'd ever imagined, and the control she'd embraced as her nearest and dearest friend for the past six years had exacted an outright betrayal, leaving her stranded back at the mercantile.

Regardless of Zach's tender show of good manners, she shrugged out of his reach, hurrying across the grass-sprinkled ground. She came to an abrupt stop, glancing at the second-story windows, suspended half-open, the same delicate white curtains she remembered her mama stitching years ago, hanging inside, whispering about in the breeze as though to welcome her home.

"Is something the matter?"

For a brief second, she almost wished that Zach would pull her into his arms and ease away her fears and uncertainties.

What was she thinking?

"No. Of course there's nothing wrong." Ivy hugged

her arms to her chest, fracturing small chunks of dried mud from her garment, just like the crusty shell that had started breaking from her heart the moment she'd arrived in Boulder. "I'm just struggling to understand what, exactly, Violet meant by her desperate language regarding my father. Quite honestly, I was under the impression that he was very ill."

"He's not a mmmman to show weakness, but I have caught him feeling poorly a couple of t-t-times." His jaw visibly tensed. "Maybe Violet has been witness to more."

Stepping up to the yawning porch that stretched in a lazy fashion at the front of the house, she tentatively padded over to the corner where the old porch swing hung.

"Your father sits there sometimes, after a long hard d-d-day." His voice was low and laden with certain respect. "It's a p-perfect place to see the sunset."

Reaching from beneath the blanket, she ran her fingers over the weathered wood. Gave the swing a soft push. The familiar, faint creaking beckoned memories. She couldn't even begin to count the times when her father would sit here and snuggle her close on crisp fall days. Like today.

"I'm surprised it's still here, after all of these years," she whispered, picturing her father sitting there reading to her from many a book or telling her a fascinating tale of honor, love, bravery. She'd developed a deep appreciation for literature because of him.

Zach cleared his throat, easing her from the memory. And for some very tangible reason, having him standing there, right beside her, gave her a solid sense of comfort.

"I d-d-did a little repair work on it a few months ago," he forced out, the strained and determined way he worked to speak piercing her heart. "It's as good as new."

She swallowed past the emotion clogging her throat.

She'd wept a spring-flooded river of tears right on this swing when her father had announced that he was sending her to school in New York. Despite her protests and her insistence on staying, he'd stubbornly, almost angrily, ignored her request, saying that he knew what was best for her. The startling sting of that on the heels of her mama passing, and the blame he had cast Ivy's way, had been indelibly written on her heart. No matter how much she'd prayed, it seemed the guilt only grew deeper and wider.

Pulling her hand from beneath the blanket, she willed herself to stay strong. She'd stick around for a while and make the best of the situation. When the time was right she'd return to New York, where she'd left behind friends, and the assistant editor position that was awaiting her at *The Sentinel,* and Neal—a gentleman she'd gone on several grand outings with.

"I'll see you inside then g-get the rest of your things," Zach said, easing her back to the moment. "Violet will have dinner ready shortly."

She could do this. Surely after six years, her father would be pleased to see her.

Wouldn't he?

The few letters he'd written over the years had been short and to the point, and after a time she'd found it easier to author the same kind of correspondence. He'd kept her bank account stuffed full, but he'd never once come to visit, nor had he suggested that she travel home for a stay.

She was very likely the *last* person he ever wanted to see.

At the moment, Ivy was grossly unsure of herself. She'd learned to live with her guilt, and had spent the past years abiding to every aspect of life with the tightest of reins. She'd been successful, and had flourished with strength and perseverance she didn't even know she possessed. She couldn't allow her fears and misgivings and guilt to override her good sense—not when she'd come so far.

"Let's g-go inside, Ivy. Your father will want to see you." When Zach gently grasped her arms and began directing her toward the front door, Ivy wrenched free from his touch, and from his misguided statement.

She pinned him with an admonishing glare, and from the way his brow creased in confusion, she knew she'd overreacted. But she was scared to death that if she softened to the comfort of his strong and sure presence, she'd crumble in the face of her guilt, losing the woman she'd become in order to survive.

Scared even more that, if she denied herself the comfort she yearned for, the comfort she found in his touch, she'd never make it through this homecoming.

Chapter Three

Zach had only just left Ivy in Violet's care and stepped outside when a sharp whistle from the wide barn entrance caught his attention. "Zach!" Hugh Bagley, one of the ranch hands, yelled. "Come quick!"

Hugh didn't worry about much, so the frantic way he was waving, his long arms flapping about like wind-whipped flags in the early evening, gave Zach pause.

Zach took the porch risers in one leap and raced out to the barn, each step a weighty reminder of the responsibility he carried on this ranch.

"What is it?" He pulled up beside the lanky man, scanning the solid structure, half expecting to find some horrible disaster awaiting him inside. "What happened?"

Hugh swiped a chambray sleeve across his mouth. "I was checking over the stalls when I found Mr. Harris down on all fours, heaving." His thin lips grew rigid as he turned and stared down the long corridor.

Zach yanked the man that direction. "Where is he now?" The earthy scent of fresh hay and dank hard-packed ground filled his senses the moment they entered the barn.

"The last stall." Hugh stopped midstride at the hub of the three rows of stalls, dimly lit by day's waning light and several lanterns hung securely on rod-iron hooks. He blanched a sickly white, pointing down the row to the right. "I'm no good when it comes to others being sick, Zach. Honestly, I've never been able to handle that sort of thing. I'll be down on all fours with Mr. Harris, if I stick around."

Zach struggled to hold his frustration in check at the way Hugh was nearly gagging just talking about it. "I'll see to him. You go and fetch Ben. Just make sure you don't let this slip to others, do you hear?"

Zach's stutter was all but gone—at least now that he was nowhere near Ivy. Ever since he'd dragged her from the mud a good hour ago, he'd tried to reason that his broken speech was a coincidence appearing at the very same moment he set eyes on that little lady. But the fact that he was speaking clearly now screamed otherwise.

She was the cause of his stutter.

And the sooner he shoved her tempting image from his mind and grabbed hold of his flailing confidence, the better off he'd be.

That task would be manageable, too, if not for seeing the moisture that had rimmed her eyes when she'd held Shakespeare. Or the vulnerability etched into her gaze when he'd pulled the wagon into the yard.

"You sure you want me to get your brother?" Hugh angled a questioning glance up at Zach as the low moo of cattle sounded in the distance. "The boss probably won't want a doctor involved. He was furious that I was going after you."

"If he's sick, then he needs to see a doctor," Zach reasoned. Mr. Harris had to be worse off than he'd thought if he let a ranch hand see him in that condition.

Hugh draped his arms about his chest. Nudged up his chin. "Your call, boss," he measured out in a that's-not-what-I'd-do-if-I-were-foreman kind of way that stuck Zach like a big prickly burr.

"That's right." Zach held Hugh's challenging gaze, unwilling to look weak in front of the man—not when Hugh had played a big part in the years of struggle Zach had faced when he was young. "This is my call."

Mr. Harris was sure to object to the matter. The ranch owner was an unyielding strength on this spread and abhorred looking weak in front of anyone. But as foreman, it was Zach's responsibility to make sure Mr. Harris was taken care of. Zach had been humbled when the responsibility of foreman had been handed to him after only a year of employment as a hired hand. He wasn't going to let his employer down.

"Well, I don't want the big boss throwing any blame my way when your brother shows up carting his black bag." Hugh arched one blond eyebrow beneath his brown wide-brimmed cowboy hat.

"Just get Ben." Zach shrugged off his impatience, turned and ate up the rest of the corridor with long resolute strides.

Slowing, he entered the dimly lit stall to find his boss hunkered down against the wall, his arms wrapped tight around his middle. "Mr. Harris? Are you all right?"

The man angled a glance up at Zach. "Never better."

Zach knelt down next to him, his concern heightened at the way perspiration beaded the man's pale face. "That's not what Hugh seemed to think. And now that I've seen you—"

"Hugh should learn to keep his observations to himself, and that flap of a mouth he has shut." Mr. Harris tipped up his black Stetson, his squared jaw set in that steadfast way of his. "It's nothing."

"This appears to be more than just *nothing*," Zach carefully challenged. To see how gaunt, tired and out-of-sorts he looked made Zach almost feel guilty for noticing.

With an irritated huff, Mr. Harris yanked his hat from his head. "I told Hugh not to make a fuss about this."

He stuck his boss with a narrowed gaze. "By the looks of you, it was a good thing he did."

"I'll be fine." When Mr. Harris slowly inched himself up the wall to standing, Zach had to resist the urge to help. Despite the favorable working relationship he shared with the man, there were just some boundaries he knew not to cross. "Like I told Hugh, this is nothing more than a bad case of stomach cramps. That's all."

"This isn't the first time this has happened, though, is it?" Zach stood face-to-face with his boss, noticing the frequency with which Mr. Harris swallowed, as though fighting off another bout of nausea. "If there's something more going on with your health than what I've noticed up to now—"

"There's been nothing to notice," Mr. Harris defended in a nonnegotiable kind of way as he stuffed his hat back on his head. "Listen…if I thought it was something to be worried about I'd be the *first* one to let you know. Do you think I'd keep something like that from my foreman?"

Zach contemplated, snagging Mr. Harris's pain-pinched gaze. "I'm worried. If you're feeling—"

"Snap off that worrying branch, Zach! It brings out the worst in me." Fishing in his back pocket, he pulled out a wrinkled white handkerchief. "It always has."

"Maybe you need to let someone worry over you now and then," Zach encouraged, not at all surprised at the way the man drew his shoulders back in a stubborn show of pride.

Just like a certain young woman, cut of the same cloth.

"It'd be a good thing to have Ben come out and check you over, don't you think?" He braced himself for a fight.

"Absolutely not. It'd be a waste of Ben's time." Mr. Harris jammed his hands at his hips and peered at Zach. "And just in case you already sent for him, I'll tell you right now that he won't be looking me over. You can have Violet send him home with a healthy dose of dessert for his trouble."

With an uncharacteristically wobbly hand, the man drew the cloth over his forehead and neck. When he gave an abrasive cough then wiped his mouth, Zach noticed a small splotch of red.

His concern kicked up several notches. "Mr. Harris, is that blood?"

His boss glanced down at the cloth then stuffed it into his pocket. "I must've bit my lip."

Zach studied the man. "Are you sure about that?"

"Yes, I'm sure," his boss roared, taking Zach aback.

"All right." He held up his hands as though surrendering. Silently, however, he vowed to keep a much closer eye on the man's health—especially with Ivy being here now.

Zach's chest tightened at the thought of her.

"I'll decide when someone should worry." Mr. Harris clenched his jaw. Gave the slightest wince. "Besides, Violet—as good as that woman is—is about to drive me half mad with the way she flutters about like I'm knocking on death's door."

"She obviously cares about you."

"Well, Violet cares too much, then," Mr. Harris dismissed, as he straightened the worn suede collar of his dungaree jacket.

If his boss had a problem with Violet pampering him and fussing over him then surely he'd be mad as a snake that Ivy was back in town…and all because of his health.

"Now, tell me where things are with the stock," his boss said, strategically shifting to another topic. "We need to make sure we put away plenty of feed and hay before winter comes nipping at our toes."

"It's done," Zach assured, wondering how that monumental task had escaped the man's keen attention. "We put the last of it away yesterday."

"Good man." He clapped Zach on the shoulder and stood a little straighter, his coloring still uncharacteristically pale.

"In fact, with the banner hay crop we brought in this year, we'll have more than we'll need." Zach nodded up above at the sturdy loft floorboards where hundreds and hundreds of bales of dried hay had been stacked. "Unless it's a long hard winter, that is."

"Hopefully, we'll be sitting just fine to help out if other ranchers run low." Mr. Harris exited the stall and started down the long corridor in that purposeful, albeit slower, stride of his that closed a conversation.

"Mr. Harris," Zach called, shoving his hands into his pockets as he stepped into the aisle. Zach felt it only right to tell the man about Ivy's arrival. If there was tension in their relationship, then having some forewarning might help ease the shock.

The man turned around. "What is it, Zach?"

"I thought I better inform you…there's someone who'll be joining you for dinner tonight." His heart beat a little faster just thinking about the young woman.

Mr. Harris reached out and grasped a thick beam as

though to steady himself. "It's not a good night for company, Zach. Tell them to come around another evening."

A silence fell between them, and for some unexpected, hair-raising reason, Zach just knew that Ivy being here now was every bit as much providential design as it was Violet Stoddard's.

"It's not that easy," he began, searching for the right words as he caught movement coming from near the center of the barn.

Mr. Harris's jaw ticked. "Why in the world not? Who is it?"

"Father…" Ivy called, willing the tremor from her voice. She hugged Shakespeare tightly as she peered around the corner down the west-facing row of stalls.

When she spotted her father, halfway down the corridor, she had to will one shiny, booted foot in front of the other in his direction. She'd known it would be difficult returning home, but she'd had no idea just how unnerved she could be at the sight of her very own father.

Violet had tried to ease her distress minutes ago, but there was no dispelling Ivy's apprehension. The day she'd left for the east coast six years ago had been a bitter taste of life, indeed.

He'd not so much as offered her a goodbye hug.

He turned to face her, his long legs braced in that familiar way that had always made Ivy think that he was ready to ride at any moment. His thick shoulders were every bit as broad as she remembered—and yet his dungaree coat seemed to hang bigger than usual.

Violet had hurried her through a hot bath and had laid out a fresh shirtwaist and silk taffeta skirt from one of Ivy's valises. Though Ivy's hair was still damp and her skin still pink from scrubbing, the woman had all but shooed her outside, as though she was a small child again, to surprise her father.

Well, he didn't look surprised—at least not in the way that made a heart glad.

One look at the taut expression on his face and her heart sank.

She should've stayed put in New York where she belonged. Her mama had wanted her to spread her wings in the big city, where culture and opportunity hung like big ornate doorways into another world, and Ivy had promised she would do just that. There were so many reasons why she should've stayed.

But her father...

"Ivy?" He yanked his black hat from his head as she neared. Six years of life had scattered shards of silvery gray through his dark hair.

"Hello, Father," she breathed, trailing her fingertips down the cat's broad back, thankful to be holding something warm and soft and receptive to her love. Struggling to drag a tenuous smile to her face, she met her father's unreadable gaze.

Haunting dark patches shadowed his brown eyes. "You're home...."

"I was about to tell you, sir," Zach put in as he stepped out from the shadows. Her father had always appeared larger than life, but seeing Zach standing beside him now, she realized that this new foreman was even brawnier than her father.

For a brief moment, she found herself suffering with an unexplainable yearning to have Zach wrap her in his strong arms. She gave a small sigh, shoving that stray thought away as though it threatened her very existence. Setting her focus on her father, she struggled to steady herself.

"I didn't realize you had plans to visit." He wore indifference like some stage mask.

"It was a last-minute decision," she responded, carefully choosing her words as Violet had instructed.

The housekeeper had cautioned her to skirt the real reason for her visit. She'd said it would anger her father to no end if he were to find out Ivy had come all the way here because of his health.

"Everything's all right, isn't it?" He turned his hat in his big, work-worn and slightly trembling hands. Hands that had comforted her when she'd been sick. Steadied her when she'd learned to ride her pony. Smoothed the hair from her face as she'd buried her nose in a compelling book. Pushed her away in those last days, darkened by blame and grief.

The idea that she'd lost his trust and his love had cut her to the very core. And as much as she had tried to ignore the wounding effects of his blame, she couldn't deny her longing to have his love once again.

She scrambled away from the memories as though they threatened to eat her alive. "Everything is fine."

"You have enough money, don't you?" Reaching to the side, he grasped the top rung of a stall door, his knuckles blanching white. He dragged in a long slow breath.

"Of course. You've been very generous." She was saddened at the way he was trying to maintain his strong, virile image. And saddened, too, that he would think her only reason for returning would be due to a lack of funds.

Besides, she'd done well for herself, and had not so much as touched the account for over two years now.

Clearing his throat, he peered just over her shoulder. "The job is going well?"

"Yes," she answered as Shakespeare pressed his big paws against her chest in an effort to get down. "In fact, when I return they are going to be promoting me to the assistant editor position at *The Sentinel*."

He coughed, his focus falling to the hard-packed dirt floor. "Your mother would be proud."

Ivy nearly choked on emotion. Her mama would've been thrilled to know how well she'd done in New York.

But her father...was he proud?

He withdrew a handkerchief from his back pocket, then wiped at the perspiration beading his upper lip. The evident way his hand trembled tugged a tear to Ivy's eye, but she quickly blinked it away, determined to stay strong.

Setting Shakespeare down, she watched for a moment as her cat darted off after something he'd spied in that familiar, playful way of his.

Some things never changed. Like her room, where nothing—*not one thing*—had been moved from where she'd left it six years ago.

Violet had said that sometimes, right before she'd retire to her quarters at the backside of the house, she'd find Ivy's father standing inside the door to Ivy's bedroom. Seemingly unaware of Violet's presence, he'd stay there for the longest time, his arms folded at his chest, his head bent low, and the barest whisper of a prayer wafting to her hearing.

That small bit of knowledge had nearly uncapped the well of tears and pain Ivy had hidden away.

But crying wouldn't change a thing. It hadn't six years ago, and it wouldn't now. She had only to keep her head about her as she tiptoed into the depths of her past.

And somehow, she'd have to find it within herself to smooth over the rough edges with her father because the idea of returning to New York without some kind of closure was more than she could bear. He was sick. That was more than apparent. And, by the obvious way he was struggling to appear strong, Ivy would have her hands full trying to offer him comfort and care.

He grabbed for the railing. "What brings you back then?"

Her faltering courage was bolstered a little by the warm look of encouragement Zach aimed her direction. "I decided that a visit was long overdue." Swallowing hard, she barred her heart from getting hurt as she peered at her father. "And I thought that maybe you and I could—"

"It's a busy time of year, Ivy. I don't know that you'll be seeing much of me." His jaw tensed. He shoved away from the stall and started toward her, and just when Ivy half wondered, half hoped that he'd open his arms to embrace her, he strode right past her. "Besides, I'm sure you're going to be itching to get back east before long," he said, his voice echoing in the barn and clear down into the jagged recesses of her soul. "Back to where you belong."

Chapter Four

Zach stole another glance at Ivy from across the dining table. Though he couldn't shake his frustration at the debilitating affect she had on him, his plan to avoid her had been completely discarded. For now, at least.

Despite his discomfort in her presence, something about the wounded look he'd glimpsed in Ivy's gaze when her father had declined joining them kept his back end firmly planted in the thick pine chair. That, and the forlorn thought of Ivy sitting alone at this long trestle table, her only company being the memories contained within these four walls.

Mostly, though, a strong chord of compassion had been strummed deep in his heart when her father strode right past her out in the barn…without so much as a welcome-home embrace. That all-business, unaffected manner Mr. Harris had shown Ivy had been unsettling.

Zach had the utmost respect for the man, but he had a hard time figuring this response. He'd never known Mr. Harris to be anything other than fair. Dedicated. Loyal. Reasonable. What had transpired between him and his only daughter—his only *child*—to drive such a wedge between them, Zach could only imagine.

Contrary to all that he'd vowed regarding Ivy, he felt compelled to be a safeguard, of sorts. *Her* safeguard. Just long enough to ease the stinging effects of Mr. Harris's rough edge.

With a gentle clank, Ivy set her knife and fork across the far edge of her fine bone china plate. She dabbed the white cloth napkin to her lips, her gaze never once straying to him.

"D-d-did you get enough to eat?" he asked, annoyed by his stutter that cropped up like some ungainly weed. With anyone else, he could talk up one side and down another without a single pause.

But with Ivy…

"Plenty." She folded her napkin then set it next to her plate.

He peered at her nearly untouched food servings. "You barely ate enough to keep a bird—" He shot up his focus to find her beautiful eyes wide and peering at him as though he'd just tossed a feathered foe her direction.

"Really?" She locked an irritated gaze on him. "Could you think of *nothing* else?"

"All right then, a *p-puppy* alive," he amended on an innocent wink.

When one corner of her mouth tipped ever-so-slightly, he couldn't miss the way his heart skipped a beat.

Zach dragged in a steadying breath. He'd have to keep his head about him if he planned on being any kind of a buffer for her, especially when she seemed determined to put up a strong front.

"I don't want to p-p-put my nose into someplace it doesn't belong, but is there something wrong?" he braved, setting down his utensils and willing his throat muscles to relax. "B-b-because, earlier when you saw your father—"

"It's a very long story, Zach." She traced a single fingertip around the delicate flower pattern framing the plate, her wary gaze flitting to him momentarily. "One I'm fairly certain you won't want to hear."

"T-t-tell me, anyway." He rested his forearms on the table and leaned toward her. As awkward and irritating as his stutter was, he couldn't allow himself to be absorbed by its effects.

A silence, broken only by the gentle ticking of the hall clock, filled the room. He held her gaze, struck by the expert way she instantly cloaked any hint of vulnerability.

Perhaps it was just as well. He had no business rifling through Ivy's past, present or future. If he knew what was best for him, he'd keep his distance.

But what was best for her?

She raised her chin a notch, her expression an unreadable mask.

"Well, if ever you want to talk…" he began, sidestepping his resolve yet again. He couldn't seem to help himself when it came to Ivy. "I'd be glad to listen. I'm pretty good at that, you know."

A dim smile inched across her face. "And how did you get so good?"

Leaning back, he draped an arm over an adjacent chair. "B-b-brothers who insist on communication when things get tough. Sisters-in-law who talk circles around them," he added, keeping his words slow and steady in the hopes of limiting his stuttering. *"And,"* he continued, holding up his index finger, "I spent plenty of time not t-t-talking when I was younger."

She pinned her gaze to the table. Fingered the tatted edge of her napkin. She opened her mouth as if to say something, but then stopped herself with a jarring suddenness.

He searched her expression. Did she remember—was she even *aware* of just how difficult things had been for him then? "Just know that the offer st-stands," he finally said, refusing to bend to any amount of self-pity. "All right?"

"Thank you," she breathed.

When the sound of footsteps came from the long hallway leading from Mr. Harris's office, Zach glanced up to see Ben coming to a stop at the dining room entrance.

"Come join us." Zach motioned his brother in.

"Hope I'm not interrupting dinner." Ben set down his bag at the end of the long table.

"We just finished." Standing, Zach shook his brother's hand. "Thanks for c-c-coming out. I know how busy you've b-been."

His brother's brow crimped for a brief, questioning moment, as though caught off guard by his stutter. "I was just finishing up for the day when Hugh found me at my office."

As the oldest Drake brother, Ben had done all he could to encourage Zach in those years when Zach's stutter had been so bad. But Zach had refused to be mollycoddled. His brothers had never known what, exactly, had transpired to cause the impediment. So they'd never known how closely connected it was to Ivy Harris. And that every beat of his childhood heart had been spent on her.

"D-d-do you remember Ivy, Ben?" Zach motioned across the table to her.

Ben grasped the back of the chair and slid a confused gaze at her. "I do. It's good to see you again, Ivy."

She pivoted in her chair to face Ben, the gracious tilt of her chin commanding Zach's attention more than he cared to admit. "And you, as well. Should I call you *Doct—*"

"*Ben* is fine." He held up a hand. "So what brings you back to Boulder?"

Ivy swerved her gaze to her plate as though unsure of what she should say.

"Violet sssss—" The word got stuck somewhere between his head and his mouth.

"Violet sent for me," she finished for him, the gesture grating his pride. "My father's been sick."

He hated when he couldn't speak clearly. Loathed even more when others, well-meaning though they may be, completed his sentences for him.

"Well, as far as your father's concerned, there's nothing wrong." He pulled a hand over the shadow of a beard darkening his face. "As far as *I'm* concerned, with the dark circles under his eyes, the hollowness of his cheeks and a few other symptoms I noticed, he has to be fighting some kind of sickness. But he flat out refuses to let me check him over."

"That comes as no surprise," she murmured with a frustrated shake of her head.

Ben crossed his arms at his chest. "I'll say one thing for him…he's—"

"Stubborn," she supplied, her eyebrows arching. "He always has been."

"A family trait," Zach put in on a muffled cough. He gave Ivy a quick wink, half surprised and pleased that he could hold his own with her.

She pushed up from the table, her scolding focus set on him in halfhearted chastisement.

Zach bit back a grin and casually swung his gaze to his brother. "Sorry you made the trip out for n-n-nothing, Ben."

"Oh, it's never a waste of time." His brother tapped the top of his bag with hands that had eased many a patient's pain—even his own wife's, after she'd shown up on his doorstep, half frozen and nearly drained of all hope. "After all, Violet said she'd wrap up a pie for my trouble, *and* it's not every day I get to see my baby brother."

"Baby?" Zach challenged on a sigh. Clasping his hands behind his back, he stretched, unable to miss the wide-eyed way Ivy's attention flitted to him. "Are you sure you want to ssstick with that?"

Though there'd never been a pecking order with his brothers, they'd all teased about it as though a certain hierarchy was well-established. In truth, Ben had been the family's saving grace after their parents had both passed away when Ben was just seventeen. He'd raised his brothers, and Zach was grateful. But that didn't mean he'd let Ben get away with treating him like he was still a young child.

"I'd think he'd be used to the title by now." Ben directed his words to Ivy. "But for some reason, it ruffles his feathers every time."

She gave a restrained smile, veering her cautious gaze to Zach. *"Feathers?"* she mouthed.

A grin tugged at the corners of Zach's mouth. Poor thing. She hated birds, and yet it seemed she couldn't get away from them. She was sure never to step foot in the barn again if she knew that Zach's pet owl, Buddy, resided in the rafters.

"So, how long are you here for, Ivy?" Ben buttoned the front of his dark brown coat.

She slid her chair into the table. "I haven't decided yet."

"Maybe you'll get to meet my daughter, Libby, and her friend, Luke, in a couple days." He shoved a hand into his coat pocket.

The eager smile that tipped her full lips seemed to brighten the room. "I'd love to."

"That's right," Zach commented, remembering how much he'd enjoyed the last time Libby and Luke had visited. "They're c-c-coming out this week, aren't they?"

"Once every two weeks, that's what you said, right?" Ben pulled a hand over his shadowed jawline.

"Absolutely," Zach put in, nodding. "It was fun having them t-tag around with me last t-t-time."

Ben's low chuckle rumbled quietly in the room. "After those two begged me like a pair of unmannerly pups, I finally relented and asked Zach if he'd mind if they came out every now and then and helped around the ranch."

Her quizzical gaze hadn't left Zach. "That certainly is nice of him."

He grasped the chair, trying to remain unaffected by her rapt attention as he willed his throat and mouth to relax so that his words could come out whole. "I'll mmmmake sure to find some tasks for them to d-do." He took a long deep breath to settle himself. "That is if they sssssstill want to come out."

Obvious concern flashed momentarily in Ben's gaze, but he seemed to know not to bring it up right now and for that Zach was inordinately grateful.

"Are you kidding me? They talk about their time here, nonstop." Ben lifted his hat and raked a hand through his hair. "But you really don't have to pay them this time."

Zach scowled. "A good man is worth his wage. It's a g-g-good lesson for them to learn."

After a long pause, Ben gave his head a single nod. "All right. You drive a hard bargain. If you insist on paying them, then go ahead."

Zach wouldn't have it any other way. He loved his seven-year-old niece and Luke, an eleven-year-old boy Ben had taken under his wing two years ago. The boy's mother had lived a harlot's lifestyle. Ben's caring influence on the boy had gone a long way in giving the child a chance. When a fire had nearly taken the boy's life, and his mother's, she'd made a dramatic turn for the good. She'd even worked alongside Ben and his wife, Callie, to get the Seeds of Faith Boarding House, a refuge for women in need of a fresh start, off the ground.

Ivy cleared her throat. "If you'll excuse me, gentlemen, I am so tired I think I may fall over."

Jerked out of his discomfort, Zach stepped around the table to stand beside her. He'd caught her in his arms once already today. He'd catch her again, if need be.

"You'll have to come over and have dinner with my family when you're feeling rested," Ben remarked.

The smile she gave Ben had Zach wishing for one himself. "Thank you. I would love that," she replied.

Ben nodded her way. "You'll let me know if your father needs anything. Right?"

"Yes, of course." Her eyelashes whispered down over her eyes.

"G-G-Good night, Ivy," Zach said, keeping his voice low as he ushered her to the stairway. He would've walked her on up to her bedroom door just to make sure she was all right, but in no way did he wish to appear overly eager. Nor did he want to seem at all inappropriate.

"Good night, Zach," she responded, the hint of jasmine wafting to his senses as she ascended the generous staircase.

As her footsteps faded, Zach turned to face his brother.

Ben gave a long sigh as Zach walked back into the room. "All right. Tell me what's going on."

"What do you mean?" Zach braced himself. Ben's big-brother demeanor wasn't all that comforting, seeing as how Zach was the focus.

Ben jammed a hand on his bag. "I mean with her. With *you.*"

Crossing to the table, Zach stacked Ivy's plate on top of his. "She came home to see her father. That's what. And he insisted I have dinner at the main house tonight—not that that's uncommon. I eat here more often than not," he added, grasping her napkin as visions of her pressing it to her lips ricocheted through his mind. He thumbed the linen fibers, half tempted to breathe in any lingering scent of her there. "I couldn't exactly disregard a sick man's request, could I?"

Ben gave his head a slow shake. "That's *not* what I'm talking about and you know it."

Zach swallowed hard, struggling to gather himself as he tightened his fist around Ivy's napkin. It wasn't Ben's fault that Zach couldn't seem to abandon his confidence-shattering feelings for Ivy.

When Ben rested a hand on Zach's shoulder, his sympathetic manner had Zach squirming. "What is this with you stuttering again? I haven't heard you stumble over your words in a very long time."

He met his brother's worried gaze. "I'm just fine."

"*Now* you are. But just a few seconds ago, you were stuttering almost as bad as you did a long time ago." Ben's brow cocked in concern.

"Do you think that that fact escaped my notice?" Resisting the urge to shrug from his brother's touch, he willed his feet to remain planted. "I am *painfully* aware of the fact."

"Why now? Why all of a sudden?"

"It's not that bad," Zach defended, knowing, even as the words passed his lips, that it wasn't that *good,* either. He might not be stuttering every sentence, but it was there, bold and sure. When Ivy was around, he seemed to have no control over his tongue, just like before. "See, I'm fine now. I haven't stuttered for several minutes."

"But you haven't had a problem for a long time," Ben argued, withdrawing his hand from Zach's shoulder. "Why now?"

"I *don't know*," Zach threw back, inwardly cringing at the lameness of his response. He picked up the dinner plates and headed toward the swinging door leading to the kitchen.

Ben followed and grasped Zach's arm, bringing him to a halt. Ben cleared his voice—something Zach and his brothers had defined as a this-is-serious sign. A growing sense of panic swarmed Zach's waning confidence. He didn't want to discuss the topic. Not now. Not ever. "Did something happen? I mean something *bad?*" Ben queried, dipping his head to grab Zach's attention. "Listen, I know you've never really talked about what happened when you first began stuttering…and I can understand why. You were eleven. A raw age for something so traumatic."

Any age was a raw age when it came to that. Sometimes Zach wondered if the devastating impact of that event would ever lessen. Once he'd grown tired of the effects beating him down, he'd fought back. Hard. But as much as he battled for confidence and wholeness of speech, a cavernous place in his heart still gaped wide open.

"What happened back then isn't up for discussion."

"The most we ever found out is that you got separated from the group of school kids you were with," Ben continued, ignoring Zach's declaration. "And that somehow you fell into an abandoned mine shaft. Isn't that right?" Ben probed, obviously hoping Zach would seize the opportunity to rehash the past.

Struggling to keep his breathing even, Zach dragged in a lungful of air. He braced a hand on the doorknob as images from twelve years ago flashed through his mind.

He'd been head over heels in love with Ivy from the first grade, falling over himself to carry her books. Her lunch pail. Helping with any task, big or small, she'd allow him the privilege of doing. He'd dreamed of her more nights than not, of whisking her away from evil captors, of braving the worst of elements to carry her to safety. His whole life had hung in the balance as he'd been on the ready, waiting for any opportunity to garner her coveted attention.

She'd never shown him the slightest interest.

But when he'd tagged along with a group of kids into a cave just to be near her, and when he heard her screech in fright, he'd seized the moment. It'd been his chance to shine. To prove himself worthy of her affection. The moment he'd dreamed of.

Ivy had laughed in his face. The brilliance in her eyes sparking in the lantern's light had grown almost brighter than the noonday sun as she'd made it clear that she didn't *need* his gallant gesture.

Hugh Bagley's riotous laughter had echoed off the cave's dank dark walls, along with the other kids. Zach had utterly embarrassed himself. Hugh had hung back long enough to warn Zach to keep his *paws* off Ivy. Then he'd given Zach a rough shove, sending him stumbling backward, falling hard and long into an abandoned mine shaft.

Zach had hated confined spaces—still did. Loathed the unknown elements that hung like a mire of webs in the obsessive darkness. Still, he'd been too prideful to call for help, at first, anyway. But after Hugh and the others continued on, leaving Zach swallowed up by a darkness he'd never imagined, he'd called. Prayed. Yelled. Screamed until his voice had turned raw.

No one came.

It seemed that even God hadn't been listening.

He'd remained trapped for two whole days, and by the time he finally found a way out—scratching and clawing at the walls until his fingers bled, the soles of his boots were worn to shreds and his words refused to come out as anything other than a stutter.

Desperate, Zach scrabbled his way back to the present, his face flaming hot. His blood boiling. And his heart somehow growing colder and harder after reliving the memory.

"I'll say it again...this subject is not up for discussion," he measured out.

A slow sigh escaped Ben's mouth. "I can't make you talk about this," he began, his tone saturated with concern. "But know that if you don't deal with what happened, it *will* continue to haunt you. It'll affect you in ways you won't be able to ignore. Like now. I know it's been a deep dive taking on the role as foreman. Ask for help if you need to, because if you're having a hard time keeping up out here, your stutter could've shown up as a direct result."

"No," he ground out, irritation now joining the other raw emotions flapping around like broken shutters in his soul. "I told you I'm fine. Things on the ranch are fine. I'll work through this alone, just like I do with everything else. I can handle it, Ben. Just like I have everything else."

Chapter Five

The next morning, Zach sat across from Mr. Harris in his office just like he'd done every single morning from the day he'd taken over as foreman.

While he waited for his boss to finish reading something, he peered at the man's well-built, handsome desk—just another mark of Joseph's expertise. Joseph, the second in the line of Drake brothers, had been building furniture with Aaron, the third in line, for several years now. Joseph's legendary, satin-smooth finish didn't suffer one bit from his lack of sight. Thoughts of his brothers' successes filled Zach with pride—but also determination to do just as well, to work just as hard for his own success.

Mr. Harris shifted in his generous leather chair, grabbing Zach's attention. "I need to discuss something with you, Zach."

"I'm listening." Zach grasped the scrolling chair arms a little tighter, unable to shake the grim feeling hanging over him. "Is everything all right?"

The forced look of concession inching across his boss's face wouldn't have seemed a bit out of place if he'd been held at gunpoint. He grimaced. "Violet thinks that I should be more up front with you than I have been."

"About…"

"About my health." The half defeated way the man's head hung for a brief moment strummed a deep chord of compassion in Zach.

The idea that Mr. Harris would admit to this confirmed its severity. And that he'd take *anyone's* advice on the matter took Zach by complete surprise. He knew that Violet cared deeply for her employer, and had a way of saying things to Mr. Harris that no one else would think to say, but still…

There'd been times over the past months when Zach had wondered if Mr. Harris and Violet cared for each other beyond a working relationship, yet had been unable to recognize the signs. It was a comfort to know that Mr. Harris had Violet to rely on, but Zach was committed to doing his part, too, to help his employer.

Mr. Harris yanked his hat from his head and slapped it on the desk. "Violet thinks that I should probably let you know—" He shifted in his seat again. Turned and peered out the window with a certain amount of longing, as though freedom stretched beyond these walls. "I've been feeling more poorly than I've been letting on. Violet's been worried sick about me even though I've told her that I'm going to be *just* fine. But that ornery woman threatened to spill my health woes to the town if I didn't at least let you know."

Zach worked furiously to bat down his outright shock. Mr. Harris was a proud man, and the last thing he'd want was sympathy spooned out to him. "Boy, she means business, doesn't she?"

"You're telling me." The man rested his elbows on his desk and leaned forward, steepling his fingers in front of him like he often did when he was faced with a tough situation. "It's hard enough knowing that my health is the reason Ivy is back."

Zach propped his right booted foot above his left knee. "You know about that?"

"I'm no fool, Zach." He raised one dark eyebrow over an eye in that studious way that instantly brought to mind a petite, auburn-haired young woman. "I know good and well that Violet had to have penned a letter to Ivy. But just between you and me...we'll let those two ladies think that they're getting by with something."

A grin tugged at one side of Zach's mouth. "All right."

"Good man." Mr. Harris winked on a nod.

Zach breathed a little easier for a moment, but not for long. His boss's health was shaky, at best. The fact that Violet had threatened him like that said as much. The woman could be almost as headstrong as her employer.

"I'm sorry about all of this, Mr. Harris."

"Don't be sorry." He held up his hand. "I'll be fine. It's nothing more than a sour stomach now and then, maybe some cramping, too."

Zach clasped his hands between his knees. "How long have you been sick, anyway?"

Mr. Harris pinned Zach with one of his don't-press-too-far gazes. "A few months."

Zach's mouth hung open in rebellious shock. "A *few months?* Why didn't you say anything?" he probed, frustrated and yet, he could hear Ben's voice from last night, challenging Zach in a similar vein. "I could've done more to help out."

Mr. Harris leaned back in his chair again. "It's probably just a passing illness, and all of Violet's fussing will be for nothing," he dismissed, tapping his knuckles on the wide chair arm. "Besides, if I wasn't able to get out on the ranch, well then, I might as well just dig my own grave right now."

"Is there *something* I can do to help?"

"Just keep doing what you're doing. You're a good man out there, Zach." His boss's intense gaze bore into Zach. "A lot like I was at your age."

Zach swallowed hard. "What about Ben? Don't you think you should let him look you over? He could help."

"Take no offense," he replied on a wince. "But I learned, a long time ago, that doctors just poke and prod. They don't know much more than their patients do."

"But I know that Ben would be glad to—"

"Zach, I carted my wife all over creation, looking for a doctor who'd help. And what did it get me?" His knuckles grew white as he gripped the arms of the chair.

Zach had only heard bits and pieces about just how sick Mrs. Harris had been. He'd learned this much…Mr. Harris had loved his wife, but no amount of love or care could heal her. Her suffering had been long and great.

"So," his boss continued, perching his hat back on his head. "I'm feeling fine today. I'll probably be feeling better tomorrow, and who knows…the next day I might just be feeling like myself again."

Zach sat up straight, looking his employer in the eye. "I'm glad you said something."

The man chuckled with a definite amount of irony as he pushed up to standing. "Son, I didn't have a choice. Violet's holding my feet over a fire and I don't care to get burned."

The clumsy way he grabbed for the desk, as though he was unsteady on his feet, sent alarm shooting straight through Zach. He stood, keeping an eye on his boss's every move in case the man toppled over. "You've been good to me, Mr. Harris. Is there anything else I can do?"

The man slowly crossed to the window and braced his hands on the wide golden pine trim. For a silent moment he peered outside at where the sun had inched up a little higher, christening the day with brilliant light. "You want a job?" he asked, his back to Zach. "Because this one won't be easy."

Zach pulled his buckskin gloves from his back pocket. "I'm up to the task."

Turning, Mr. Harris kept one hand on the window trim as he eyed Zach. "First, you need to know that there's quite a lot of water that's run under the bridge between me and Ivy. Things are strained between us," he admitted, his gaze shrouded with the kind of hurt a man rarely showed. "You may have noticed."

He'd noticed all right. That's why he'd already decided that he'd try to be a buffer for Ivy. The hurt look that had flashed across her hopeful expression yesterday in the barn had nearly broken his heart.

And the sorrow drifting over his boss's expression just now gave him equal pause. Zach had no idea what had transpired between Mr. Harris and Ivy, but having lost his brother Max to a sordid lifestyle which had led to his death, Zach would do whatever he could to help heal the torn relationship.

He'd be a listening ear. A voice of encouragement.

And he'd pray. In spite of his floundering relationship with God, he'd pray that God would do that which Zach was fairly certain *only* God could do. He'd seen God work miracles in Ben, Joseph and Aaron's lives. God could work a miracle here, too. Couldn't He?

"I know she's found a place for herself out east just like her mama wanted for her, but if something happens to me, then all of this, every last inch of this ranch, must fall to her." Mr. Harris reached out and grabbed Zach's arm in an uncommon show of desperation. "She *needs* to fall in love with this place again, Zach. I need her to love it just like she did when she was a little girl—before things changed. Do you hear me?"

"I understand." Zach gulped back a lump of uncertainty. He'd do whatever Mr. Harris wished, but this would require him being in close quarters with Ivy, and he'd already discovered that her very presence incited his old insecurities and fears. Having her back here was one thing, but could he go to this extent without losing the man he'd become and the confidence he'd worked so hard to gain?

"With the way you love this place, you're just the man to help her with that." Mr. Harris's grip on Zach's arm tightened. "If things take a bad turn for me, then she's going to have to stay here. I want you to lead her heart home."

Ivy's first night back at the ranch had been fraught with every emotion imaginable. She was grieving, still, her mama's death. Sorrowful for her father's cool, uninterested greeting. Overjoyed to see Violet.

But the stomach-fluttering thrill she felt at the mere thought of Zachariah Drake had sent her into an outright tailspin. He'd knocked her control off-kilter without doing a thing. Last night, she'd even dreamed of the man. His broad, burden-bearing shoulders. His chiseled, masculine jawline. His crystal-blue, secret-bearing gaze.

She tipped her head back and breathed in deep, wishing she could get the man out of her mind.

Back in New York she'd gone on a few lovely little outings with Neal Smith, and *never* had she had such an all-encompassing response to the man. *Ever.* Oh, Neal was handsome in a very pristine way. And he was as agreeable as a man could possibly be. Kind. Respectful. But he'd never once made his way into her dreams. In fact, he'd barely even interrupted her thoughts.

She threw her chestnut-colored paisley wrap around her shoulders and headed down the front steps for a breath of fresh air, if for nothing else than to clear her head of Zach Drake. She could only hope that, perhaps, she'd find her wayward common sense and self-control out here, because it had escaped her last night. Completely.

She'd likely not had it in her possession from the moment she'd stepped foot off the train.

When she caught sight of Zach out by the barn, talking with one of the hands—Hugh Bagley, a former classmate and old friend—she stopped in her tracks. Shielding her eyes from the bright morning sun, she saw Zach jam one hand to his waist and jab his pointing finger toward the barn, his brusque litany of words falling just out of reach. But his stern expression…it was readable from here, a good hundred feet away.

When Hugh caught sight of her, his defeated stance shot upright. "Ivy!" he called as he started jogging her way, leaving Zach glaring after him.

"Hello, Hugh." Smiling, she waved and hurried over the hard ground to meet him.

"If you aren't a sight for sore eyes then I don't know what is." Catching her up in his long-armed hug, he squeezed tight then grasped her arms and held her away from himself. "It's good to see you, Ivy. *Really good.*"

Her frustration regarding Zach's behavior all but vanished at Hugh's warm greeting. "How wonderful to see you, too, Hugh."

"I heard whisperings from one of the hands that you were back. I've been looking for you all morning."

"Surely you had better things to do." She stepped away

from him, her arms aching from his tight hold. He always had been like a grown but playful pup that hadn't yet learned the word *gentle*.

"I thought you'd never come back." A grin stretched the width of his long and narrow face.

"Well, believe it or not, I am here."

"That, you are," he confirmed with an appraising look.

Readjusting the scarf around her shoulders, she gently rubbed where his hands had been and planted a smile on her face, even when she felt confused by everything that had happened since she'd been home. She didn't need Hugh digging into her heart. They'd been friends years ago, but she'd never thought to parcel out the deepest secrets in her heart to him. He couldn't seem to be serious enough to handle that kind of information.

"Boy, have I ever missed you, Ivy. All of the fun we had…" He raised his eyebrows. "Things just aren't the same as they were back then."

"I wouldn't imagine they are." Memories of the fun adventures they'd shared flitted through her mind. "So, you're working here, too?"

"Too?" His heavy brow furrowed beneath his brown cowboy hat.

She angled a quizzical look at him, then slid her gaze over to where Zach stood, jamming a shovel into the earth with enough force she'd have thought he was planning to dig all the way to the other side of the world. "You know…Zach."

His eyes rolled back for a brief moment. "Oh, yeah… the *big boss*."

Ivy fingered the delicate wool fringe edging her scarf, recalling how Hugh had never much liked Zach. "I had no idea he was my father's foreman. Can you imagine my shock? He's changed so much."

"He sure has changed." Hugh gave a huge sigh. "And he's foreman here, whether I like it or not."

"What happened out there just a minute ago?" She passed a quick glance toward Zach. "He looked quite mad."

"Enough to spit iron stakes." With a mutinous manner about him, Hugh looped his arms at his chest. "Screamed at me like I was some no-good criminal sniffing around for trouble."

"He wasn't *screaming* at you," she admonished with a wry grin.

He hung his head. "All right. Maybe not screaming. But if I'm not working my fingers to the bone or wearing my boots thin like he does, then he figures I'm being a regular old slough."

"Oh, he can't be *that* bad." Certain Hugh must be exhibiting that dramatic flair of his just for show, she gave a delicate laugh.

But when the image of Zach, speaking with Hugh just minutes ago ricocheted through her mind, she had to wonder. Was Zach merely holding to her father's standards? Her father never had tolerated laziness.

She'd never known Hugh to be lazy.

He'd never been rushed, either.

"He oughta stay focused on what's been happening right under his nose." Hugh raised his brows over his small eyes.

"Why? What happened?"

"Oh, it's nothing." He dug a boot heel into the reddish soil. "I should've just kept my mouth shut."

"Come now, Hugh. You know you can't drop hints like that without delivering on them." She had to question whether Hugh was right. "Are you being territorial again?"

"Again?" His narrowed his gaze on her.

"Perhaps your memory needs a little refreshing," she prodded. "Back when we were in grade school, you would target any boy who dared cross you or be better than you at something." Or any boy who dared speak with her. She never could quite figure out why, either. She'd never shown an inkling of interest in him as anything other than a friend. "Does that ring a bell? I would expect that it's hard to have a former classmate, namely Zach, as your boss. Am I right?"

"Oh, I'd gladly work for someone if I had confidence in them."

Uncertainty suddenly pricked deep at his words. She took a hesitant step in Zach's direction. Hugh had been doing ranch work from the time he was thirteen. He was probably fairly seasoned, for his age, especially now that he worked for her father. So why would he doubt Zach's capability?

She came to stand in front of him again. "Do you mean to say that you don't have confidence in Zach?"

"I think he's green—it shows in the way we're always coming up short on supplies." He narrowed an uncharacteristically serious gaze on her. Craned his head around, looking the direction of the corral where Zach was still shoveling with intense ferocity.

"Short? On supplies?"

"Things keep coming up missing. And when I ask if I can look at the books, he gets as mean as a bear with new cubs."

"Doesn't he know you're just trying to help?"

"I don't think he sees it that way, no." He ran a long-fingered hand over his sparsely whiskered chin. "Half the time, I don't agree with his decisions. He's headstrong. And way too proud, if you ask me."

She dropped her focus to where Shakespeare had appeared and was doing circle eights at her feet, his big thick tail swishing across her dark rust-colored taffeta skirt. Scooping up her hefty cat, she held him close, recalling how easily Zach had brushed her the wrong way with his headstrong manner.

"Zach's a lot like your daddy." Hugh's overly eager nod only served to annoy Ivy. "Only your daddy has a good handle on things here, being so experienced. But with the cattle theft that happened a week ago not far from here," he said, slicing a breath through his long teeth, "we need a foreman who knows what he's doing, leading the way."

"Cattle theft?" An ominous chill crawled down her spine.

Hugh hooked a thumb through his belt loop. "The theft has the ranchers around here sitting at the edge of their saddles."

"I can imagine." She draped Shakespeare over her shoulder like a baby—just the way he'd like it.

"As experienced as your uncle Terrance is," Hugh said, reaching out and brushing a hand over her arm, "I wish that he was the one leading the charge instead of Zach."

Ivy patted the cat's back, provoking a loud purr from the feline as she recalled how her mama's brother, Terrance, had worked for her father for years. "I don't think I ever recall a time when he didn't go about his business without a cheerful whistle. He was raised on this ranch."

"Honestly, Terrance never gets much of a fair shake around here." He fingered the brim of his hat. "But…he takes it in stride. He's devoted to your father, that's for sure."

At every turn, her uncle Terrance had talked her father up as though he owned the entire state of Colorado and then some. So, it never quite made sense why he was the only person in the world her father didn't seem to like.

"Terrance has years and years of experience, and a real head for business. But for some reason—" He yanked his hat off his head and slapped it against his long leg. "Why in the *world* are we talking about this, anyway? I haven't seen my Ivy in six years and I'm rambling on and on about the ranch." When he poked her arm, she had to bite back a wince as she silently calculated just how long it would take before a bruise would appear. "How's the big city been treating you, dolly?"

The city had been wonderful.

But here... Ever since she'd been back, she'd been scrambling for a foothold. Struggling to maintain a strong front.

Until this moment, she'd felt inclined to keep her distance, since it was clear her father was eager to send her back east. But now she had no choice. If there were problems on the ranch, it was her responsibility to see to them, with her father unwell. She'd have to make sure that Zach was making the best decisions and that he wasn't putting the ranch in jeopardy just because he was headstrong.

"Grand. I love it there." Suddenly and strangely wary, she glanced past Hugh to find Zach staring right at her, his face set in a distinct scowl. Beads of perspiration glistened over his muscle-roped arms as he jammed his shovel into the ground again and brought out a chunk of dirt.

"Mama was right," she went on to say, trying her best to ignore her father's foreman. "There are so many opportunities to be had out east."

Zach didn't look happy, that's for sure. Was this just one of his ways of throwing his weight around?

After a long yawn, Hugh snapped his jaws, jarring her nerves. "Your mama always did push for you to go, didn't she?"

At times, her mother had been almost desperate for Ivy to leave the ranch. "Even when I was young and talked of owning a ranch of my own someday, Mama would push me that way."

Ivy swallowed hard. The guilt and shame that had hung over her mama's passing had seized any joy to be found in journeying toward her mama's dreams.

At the sound of the front door slamming shut, Ivy glanced over her shoulder to glimpse Violet hurrying down the steps, two small braided rugs draped over her arms. And a clear look of intent on her round face.

"Good morning, Violet," Ivy greeted as the petite woman scurried toward them, clad in an attractive gray-blue calico dress that matched her eyes perfectly.

"Hello, Ivy, dear." She swiped at her brow then laid a veiled scowl on Hugh. "Hugh."

Ivy's heart warmed at the sight of the lively woman. Violet, nearly her father's age, had been with the family for years. "Is everything all right?"

"Oh, yes, just fine." The woman pulled up beside Ivy and patted the colorful braided rugs. "Just thought I'd get these out on the line to breathe for a while. Since it's such a lovely day."

Ivy slipped her focus to the rugs, sure she'd seen them hanging on the line yesterday when she'd arrived. "But they were hanging out yesterday, and the clothesline is in the back of the—"

"Well, would you look at that!" Violet shielded her eyes as though the morning sun had suddenly taken to blazing straight from the west. "Isn't that Zach out there working up a sweat digging something or other?"

When Ivy peered in that direction, she instantly regretted it. Zach was working hard, all right—while she'd been standing around chatting with Hugh. The sight of Zach's back muscles straining against his shirt, and the image of his forearms tensing with every movement provoked a flutter in the base of her stomach.

"Just look at him go. He's as resolute as they come, I tell you." Violet smiled over at Ivy as though expecting a response. "He's such a dedicated worker…Zach. Out there every single day doing every chore under the sun. Just like your daddy."

Ivy's heart squeezed inside her chest.

Just like her father…

She loved her father—had *always* loved her father. But the stubborn, stoic ways that had formed when her mama had become ill nine years ago, contrasted so sharply with the loving patient daddy she'd known. She'd been so confused.

His long run of patience had grown eerily short. His ready smile had hardened to a look of anger. And his faith-filled outlook on life had seemingly dissipated like a puddle on a hot dry day. He'd been driven by some unseen force, and everything—everyone—standing in his path seemed to disappear as he put his hands to task after task after task, as if to somehow make up for the fact that he couldn't seem to help his own wife.

On that fateful day when Ivy had finally bent to her mama's desperate plea to ride out and see the rich stand of yellow aspens blazing across the landscape, the raging anger her father had shown when she'd returned had been almost more than Ivy could bear.

From the moment her mama had passed away two short days later, Ivy had carried the condemning weight of her father's grief. And the heartrending load of her own deep sorrow.

She'd longed for the comfort of her father's arms.

He'd barely been able to look her way.

She'd had to be strong in order to survive—keep things in order so that *nothing* fell through the cracks. Once she'd found her place out east, she'd made the best of things. And now…*now,* she couldn't imagine ever living on the ranch again. But she still cared about the place, still wanted it to thrive.

Was Zach really the right man to serve as foreman? He worked hard, yes, but he was inexperienced. Hugh's opinion surely counted for something. After all, Hugh worked with Zach day in and day out.

She jerked her focus back in time to notice Violet, her hand perched at her narrow waist, staring at Hugh until he finally looked her way. The smile she gave him didn't even begin to reach her gray-blue eyes.

Hugh puffed a big breath of air through his cheeks and stood a little straighter, his razor-sharp Adam's apple protruding a bit more. "I suppose I better get back to work before the big boss-man loads me up with extra chores." He gave an inordinately long yawn, as if to annoy Violet. "Just to keep me in line."

"Hugh Bagley," Violet scolded, her rosy lips pursed in her ivory face as she turned and tramped off toward the house again, rugs in hand. "That kind of talk borders on heresy," the woman added, as she neared the steps.

Hugh raised his eyebrows in challenge as Violet clomped up to the porch. "I wouldn't put it past him," he murmured under his breath. Stepping forward, he wrapped his lanky arms around Ivy, without so much as a friendly forewarning. This time his touch was accompanied with a bit more gentleness, but still, he almost squished her face into his armpit. "I can't tell you how good it is to see you again, Ivy. I'm glad you're home."

The urge to pull away from his embrace overwhelmed her almost as much as the ripe odor coming from under his arm. For some odd reason, she had the distinct feeling that this hug was meant for more than just her. Was Hugh making some kind of statement?

He wasn't like that, was he?

"I'll be seeing you around, dolly. Look for me," he added, his voice low and laden with a healthy serving of possibility.

Her skin crawled with the mere thought as she tried to wiggle her way out of his arms. They were friends. That's all. Friends.

When he finally let her go, she gave a small gasp as her gaze met Zach's.

He was standing right behind Hugh, his mouth a grim line. The muscles at his jaw tensed as he came around to stand beside Ivy. His eyes glinted hard as steel as he stared at Hugh in a way that could make a man shrink in his boots.

For a moment, as the intensity of his focused gaze slid to her, Ivy was overwhelmed with the most wonderful, cared-for, protected feeling she'd ever experienced. The raw masculinity that infused the air around Zach Drake could easily sweep a girl right off her feet.

But when he shoved his focus to Hugh, his eyes snapping with untapped anger and impatience, she shuddered deep. She may be undeniably attracted to Zach, but in *no way,* did she plan on acting on one ounce of that attraction. She'd been warned by Hugh about the man. She'd be stepping into very dangerous territory if she let her heart wander too close to the tender flame that had sparked for him.

Chapter Six

"Uncle Zach!" The distant, albeit exuberant, sound of his niece's voice tugged a half grin to Zach's mouth.

He gladly left the barn where he'd been going over the past few months of ranch records with Ivy. She'd been eager to see the day-to-day operations, and he'd had every intention of reacquainting her with things, but the suspicion with which she'd asked…that had jerked his goodwill right out from underneath his feet. Did she think he wasn't up to the job?

"Uncle Zach!" Libby squealed as Ben drove the wagon up the lane. "We're here. Luke and me…we're here."

Zach waved, his all-out smile cracking the scowl that had been there for the past day. Ever since he'd seen Hugh embracing Ivy yesterday, as though they were ready to traipse down the marriage aisle, Zach had been in one sour mood. He'd not said a single word about the incident to either of them, although he'd wanted to say plenty.

But the prospect of his words falling out in a jumbled mess right in front of Hugh had stopped him dead in his tracks. Back in grade school, Hugh had been the ringleader when it came to teasing. It had seemed a warped lesson in consequence that Hugh had never answered for his cruelty. The moment the teacher, or Zach's brothers, were nearby, Hugh would slither away, completely avoiding getting into trouble.

Because Zach feared more teasing, he'd never retaliated, instead he'd kept quiet about the constant string of taunts. His brothers had seemed to know that something was amiss. But when they'd tried to protect him early on, he'd quickly fend off their concern. He hadn't wanted them embarrassing him further by hovering about like a flock of mother hens.

Working with Hugh these past two years had been a thorn in Zach's flesh. But Hugh was a good horseman, and intuitive when it came to working with the cattle. Zach could put up with the smug, dismissive attitude. Putting up with the man's attention to Ivy would be…more difficult.

"Uncle Zach, here I come," Libby squealed again as Ben lifted her from the wagon. As soon as her feet hit the ground, she bounded in his direction like a playful kitten, her light green calico dress swishing around her with each giant step. "We're here. We're here!"

Zach caught his niece as she launched into his arms. "Hey there, pumpkin," he said, returning her eager hug.

"I couldn't hardly wait to get here," Libby announced.

"You couldn't, huh?" Out of the corner of his vision, Zach watched Luke climb down from the wagon, exercising adultlike restraint as he walked toward them, when Zach was sure the boy would've liked to run just as hard and fast as Libby.

"Libby barely got a wink of sleep last night knowing that she'd be coming out here today," Ben said as Libby tightened her hold around Zach's neck. "And Luke's ma said he's been up since before the crack of dawn."

"Hi there, Luke." Zach gave the eleven-year-old boy a nod. "Glad you and Libby could make it again."

"Howdy." Luke nodded right back at Zach with restrained excitement.

When Zach had passed the idea by Mr. Harris of having these two out, the man had said that it'd been too long since this place had seen a youthful heart. The idea had actually put a smile on his boss's face, and that was worth something.

"We're ready to work." Luke's left hand drifted to the makeshift bolero he'd tied around his neck—a smooth, flat, oval rock he'd wrangled with string then attached to a long piece of braided twine.

"Nice bolero you have there," Zach commented, giving the boy an approving look. "Looks almost like the one Mr. Harris wears."

Luke angled a wide-eyed glance down toward the piece.

"Luke made that himself." Wriggling her way out of Zach's arms, Libby sidled up next to Luke. "Didn't you, Lukey?"

"Sure enough. Wasn't nuthin'—anything," Luke amended, tapping the correction into his mop of blond hair as he stood up a little straighter. "So, what do ya want us to do, Mr. Zach? Give us a job."

"Not so fast, partner." Zach and Ben exchanged amused glances. "I picked up something the two of you will need if you're working for me."

Libby's instant and delighted gasp made Zach laugh. "Oh, Lukey…he got us a present." The enthusiastic way she clapped her hands beneath her chin, more than made up for the cash he'd spent. "What is it? What is it?"

"You'll see. I'll be right back," Zach promised, jogging back to the barn. When he entered his small office where

Ivy was sitting at his desk, camped out over bookwork as though she was determined to catch a mistake, his light-hearted mood grew heavy.

But the sight of her there, deep in concentration, her fiery auburn hair blazing in the sun's glowing rays streaming through the small window, made his heart skip a beat. Two.

Just when he felt himself drawn by that unseen force that surrounded her, he jerked himself free. He had a job to do with this lady and he'd never be able to manage it if he was intoxicated by her presence. Besides, he was trying hard not to feel offended by her suspicion.

"Did you need something?" she dared to ask, as though this was *her office. Her desk. Her paperwork.*

He bit back a surly retort and retrieved two cowboy hats from his desk. "Just these." Setting his back teeth, he turned to leave.

"Who are they for?" Her amiable inquiry pulled his exit up short.

Staring down at the hats, he remembered how good he'd felt purchasing them. "They're for m-m-my niece and her friend, Luke. They're here if you'd like to meet them." The invitation fell from his tongue with far too much ease.

Turning, he witnessed the faintest bit of relief in her gaze. Maybe she really didn't relish pouring over boring records for hours on end…. Maybe he'd read her wrong.

"I'd love to." A little timid, she rose from the desk, the sunlight gleaming through the window outlining her shapely figure in an ethereal glow.

He slammed his attention down to the scarred wide-plank flooring, pondering over her suspicion earlier. What did she hope to find, anyway? The only records stored out in the barn were related to supplies and to the cattle—their birthing records, health reports, genealogy....

"Well, they're ready and w-w-waiting..." Standing to one side of the door, he let her pass in front of him, the cloying scent of jasmine teasing his senses.

When they reached the entrance, Ivy hung back while he rounded the corner to meet his eager entourage. He held a hat out to each child. "Here you go. Now you're official."

Libby's gasp brought a wide grin to his face. He looked at Ben. "How do you do it...fathering such a delightful little girl?"

The clear look of pride in Ben's gaze pricked Zach deeply. Zach yearned for a wife and children, someday, but the chances of that happening were slim to none. Having kept a journal since he was fifteen, he could pen a verse about love, but he doubted he'd ever know its abiding virtue for himself. Even though he'd tried his hardest to get Ivy out of his mind, he'd never quite been able to get her out of his heart.

"Oh, Uncle Zach! My very own cow hat," Libby exclaimed, her delight creating a stir among the small cluster of corralled cattle.

"*Cowboy* hat, silly," Luke corrected with a self-important shake of his head. While a chorus of low moos infused the morning air, the boy held out the hat, eye level, inspecting it as though it was some costly treasure. "Cows don't wear hats."

"Yes they do." She jammed her black felt hat over her auburn braids.

"When?" Luke challenged, perching his hat on his head then angling his focus to the brim that projected over his face.

Libby gave a triumphant smile. Clasped her hands behind her back. "In my drawing book."

"Doesn't count." Luke gave an indifferent shrug.

The instant look of disappointment on Libby's face as she peered at her friend could make a hardened criminal change his ways.

"But that don't mean you can't keep drawing hats on yer cows, Libby," the boy added with a bit more sensitivity. "That's fine by me. Is it fine by you, too, Mr. Zach?"

"Absolutely."

Libby launched into Zach's arms again, squeezing the air right out of him. "Thank you for the hat. I love, love, love, love, *love* it."

"Thanks, Mr. Zach. I never had a cowboy hat." The innocent way Luke anchored his mouth off to the side tugged at Zach's compassion.

"I promise I'll take real good care of it," Libby vowed.

"Me, too." Luke gave a vigorous nod.

"I'm glad you—"

"Ummmmm, Uncle Zach..." Libby measured out.

"Yes?" he responded, amused by how she'd just way-laid the conversation.

"Who's that pretty lady back there?" Libby pointed over his shoulder toward the barn.

Zach swallowed hard, yanking his resolve into place as he struggled to keep his head about him. If he let himself be affected by Ivy, he'd be stuttering in front of his niece. Why couldn't he seem to talk clearly around the woman like he did anyone else?

Pivoting, Zach glimpsed Ivy standing near the corral, hugging her arms to her chest. Her glistening gaze penetrated right through him. Her lips curved in a warm smile. "That's Miss Ivy." With a nod, he motioned her over. "She's here from N-N-New York. She's Mr. Harris's d-d-d-daughter."

Libby turned her attention fully to Zach. "Is somethin' wrong with you, Uncle Zach?"

Zach willed his words to come out whole. "What do you mean, p-p-pumpkin?" He forced himself to meet Libby's distraught gaze, but not before he caught Ivy's expression crimp with something akin to pity.

The very thought set his blood to boiling. He didn't *want* her pity. Didn't *need* her pity. And he *definitely* didn't care for her to be adding to Libby's concern.

Just when he was about to set down his niece and get on with his day, as though nothing was out of the ordinary, Libby braced his face between her small hands, squaring his focus with hers.

"Why are you talking like that?" Libby implored.

The weight of worry in Zach's niece's sweet voice nearly broke Ivy's heart.

She forced herself to smile as she came to a stop next to Zach. Seeing him with his niece brought back memories and raw emotions she definitely hadn't expected. Memories of times long past, when her father had held her with such tenderness. Of when he would delight in her unabashed show of excitement. Even the time when he'd purchased her very first hat…made of black felt and almost identical to the ones Zach had purchased for these children.

"It's nothing to worry about, sweetheart," Ben answered, nodding a greeting to Ivy as he smoothed a hand over his daughter's shoulder.

"Yep." The forced smile Zach gave his niece stabbed Ivy's half-gaping heart. "Nothing t-t-to worry about. I'm fine."

"But you never talked that way before. Are you sick?" Libby tenderly prodded.

"Ben could help if yer feelin' poorly," Luke put in, staring up at Ben with a healthy dose of awe. "He's as good a doctor as I ever seen."

"Thanks, b-buddy." Zach gave the boy a manly kind of pat on the back. "But, really, I'm j-j-just fine."

Libby brushed a hand across Zach's freshly shaven cheek. "Well, I've never heard you talk that way. It makes me sad."

It made Ivy sad, as well. Especially realizing that his speech wasn't always broken by a stutter. She had to wonder what would cause him to stumble all of a sudden. From the moment he'd made eye contact with her at the mercantile, he'd seemed to have a problem. Yet, in spite of tripping over his words, he'd plow right on through conversations. And that she found admirable. Very admirable.

"Libby," Zach began, holding her hand in his, his throat convulsing. "There's not *one thing* f-f-for you to be worried about. Do you hear?"

When Libby finally nodded, he gave her a peck on the cheek then set her down. "Luke. Libby. Say hello to M-Miss Ivy."

"Hello, Miss Ivy," the children said in unison.

She shook both of their hands. "Nice to meet you, Luke. Libby."

"My dress is green…just like yours." Libby peered down at her dress.

"It certainly is," Ivy agreed, amused by the girl's candid sincerity. "And I might add that it's lovely."

"My shirt is green…." Luke plucked his button-front shirt out. With a certain amount of fanfare, he lifted his hat and tipped his head in Ivy's direction like some gentleman cowboy.

Giggling, Libby scrunched her shoulders clear up to her chin. "Papa, did you see him do that with his head?" She demonstrated then peered up at Luke. "You looked just like Uncle Zach when you did that, Lukey."

"Sure looks like you're a fast learner, Luke." Ben grinned. "You'll be winning more hearts than you can count if you keep that up."

"That's for sure," Zach agreed, his hearty chuckle curling the tips of Ivy's toes. "Though tipping my hat to the ladies has g-g-gotten *me* nowhere."

Ivy could thank God that Zach hadn't ever tipped his hat to her. It would've sent her stomach into a flurry of activity that would directly threaten her resolve. But she couldn't deny that she found herself watching...and wishing for his deep and lingering gaze.

Ever since Zach witnessed Hugh hugging her yesterday, he'd been painfully quiet—especially after she'd asked to go through the records in the barn. She couldn't just ignore Hugh's concerns. She'd be remiss if she were to leave well-enough alone and not investigate. With her father being sick, surely it would ease his mind to know that she was keeping tabs on the ranch. But she hoped she hadn't offended Zach.

Libby grasped Ivy's hand again. "Do you live here?"

Ivy bent down eye level with the girl. "I used to."

"Well, are ya gonna stay?" Sidling up to her other side, Luke jammed his hands into his pockets.

On a faint sigh, Ivy met his hopeful gaze, a small trickle of regret trailing down her spine. "I'm just here for a visit, Luke. My home is in New York."

"Well...*maybe* you could stay," he persisted, his eyebrows scrunching together in a worried line.

"Yeah. Maybe you could stay," Libby echoed. She crossed over to Luke and rose to her tiptoes, whispering in Luke's ear. *"She could be Uncle Zach's wife."*

"Libby," the boy halfheartedly scolded. He set a hand to his mouth as though to hide the grin that had sparked all the way to his blue eyes.

Brushing her fingers down her off-white shirtwaist, Ivy tried to feign innocence, but she was certain her attempt fell painfully short. From the way Zach's eyes grew wide, she hadn't been the only one who'd heard the girl's words.

"Who wants to help f-f-feed the chickens?" Zach rubbed his hands together, clear embarrassment ticking his jaw.

"Me! Me!" Libby yelped, jumping up and down.

"Ya gotta settle down if yer gonna go into the chicken pen, Libby," Luke cautioned, settling a hand on the girl's shoulder. "They'll get scared if you're hoppin' around like that."

Instantly, she nailed her feet to the ground and her arms to her sides. "I won't step on them. I promise, Uncle Zach." She peered up at him from beneath the brim of her plain black hat.

Just then Ivy had an idea. She tugged out the long off-white ribbon from where she'd bound it around her hair, sending her curling waves spilling over her shoulders. She held up the grosgrain ribbon. "Would you like for me to add a nice feminine touch to your cowgirl hat?"

"Cow*girl* hat?" Libby grasped one of Luke's hands in both of hers. "Is that the same as a cow*boy* hat? Because I wanna be just like my best friend, Luke."

"Trust me…it's the same," Ivy assured, struggling to bite off her amused grin as Libby removed her hat and handed it to Ivy. "I had a cowgirl hat when I was a little girl, too, and my mama tied a pretty bow around it just like I'm doing to yours." Ivy wrapped the ribbon around the hat's base and tied it neatly on the side.

"That's *beauty-full*," Libby breathed, clearly pleased.

Ivy's gaze drifted to Zach's and the unveiled tenderness and warmth she saw there as he watched her nearly stole the breath from her lungs. His mind-numbing attention had a blinding affect on her focus.

Her return to New York could not come too soon, as far as Ivy was concerned, at least not if she hoped to keep the barrier around her heart intact. But she wouldn't leave until she knew that her father was going to be all right. Or until she'd reached some kind of reconciliation with him. Right now, however, both prospects seemed a far reach.

Chapter Seven

Day's fading light bathed the barn's west side in a warm glow. Zach breathed in the earthy and pleasing scent of fresh hay tucked away in the mow, enjoying the much-needed moment of reprieve. He'd been working from sunup, doing early morning chores, working with Luke and Libby and then spending several more hours replacing old fencing along the north pasture.

On a slow sigh, he draped one boot over the other. Staring down at the page in his leather-bound journal, he searched his heart for a strand of words to weave into the poem he'd started earlier.

A poem about Ivy.

It'd been all he could do not to wrap her in his arms and hold her close this morning when she'd so thoughtfully dealt with Libby and Luke. The warmth and openness he'd seen in her gaze in that moment had struck a tender chord in his heart. In the past, when he hadn't been able to clearly iterate what he saw or heard or felt, he would write, the words flowing from his pen with grace and fluidity. Though he had no intention of acting on his rebellious emotions, he'd learned that penning his feelings helped him to move on.

And he definitely needed to move on regarding Ivy—for good.

"What do you think, Buddy?" He angled his gaze to his pet Great Horned Owl perched on his shoulder. "You're supposed to be all wise. Do you have any good advice for this last strain?"

The owl shuttered his eyes for a second, then moved his head from side to side as if shaking his head *no*.

Zach chuckled, tapping the end of his pen against the page. "A lot of help you are."

He'd raised Buddy from a puff ball of downy feathers last spring, and instead if flying away, the owl had taken to him with a definite amount of fondness.

"Zach, are you in here?" Ivy's sweet voice lilted from down the aisle of stalls straight to his heart.

"Over here." He struggled to protect his heart as he capped his ink well. Pushing up from the fresh mound of straw, he tucked his journal back into his saddlebag as her footsteps came closer.

"She might scream when she sees you, but don't take it personally," he whispered as the owl gave him an affectionate, preening peck on the cheek. In spite of Buddy's long, sharp talons and beak, Zach had never once been gouged. It was as if the owl innately trusted him, treating him with a gentleness that belied reason.

"There you—" she gasped. Hunkered down, grabbed an armful of straw from the barn floor and threw it at him with a shriek. "Get away! Leave him alone. Go!" she screeched then snatched a pitchfork from over by the wall. "Don't worry, Zach. I'll help you."

"Whoa… Wait!" He shoved out a hand as she brought the pitchfork above her head.

When she stopped midair, the owl shuddered, fluffing his feathers free of the straw.

"Not so fast there, city-girl," he warned, shaking his head and running a hand over his face to remove stems and dust.

"I am *not* a city girl," she defended through clenched teeth. Her gaze glistened with raw fear as she stared his direction. Her chest rose and fell with every shallow breath.

"It's all right," he assured, stroking the backs of his fingers down the owl's soft chest. "D-don't worry."

"You're telling me not to worry?" Dropping the pitchfork at her feet, she hunched down to nearly half her height, as if she suddenly remembered to be scared now that she was no longer on attack. Covered her head and clambered out the stall until she ran right into the opposite row of stalls. "When you know that I am *deathly* afraid of birds, you're telling me not to worry?"

Zach stepped slowly in her direction, trying not to scare her any more than she already was. "He's my pet. He lives out here in the barn, the way some owls do."

"Wonderful!" Flinging her hands to the sides, she edged her way down the row. "You could've at least had the decency to inform me, Zach. I wouldn't have stepped *foot* in this barn."

On a frustrated sigh, he peered at her. "I am d-d-*definitely* sorry I didn't let you know about him, then."

"And why is that?" Her gaze flitted from challenge to fear as she looked from him to the owl.

He dragged in a long, calming breath. If there was one time he wished he could address her without stuttering, it was now. "Maybe then you'd have b-b-been less inclined to go pawing through my p-papers."

With a stubborn tilt of her petite chin, she gave one side of her shawl a rough yank, sending it trailing like a waterfall off her shoulders to the ground.

He would've expected any other woman to rush head-long out of the barn about now. But not Ivy. She was bent on standing her ground even when extreme fear undermined her comportment. And for some reason, that only increased his attraction to her...luring him in like a bear to honey.

"Do you have something to hide?" she challenged, stooping to get her shawl and whipping it around her shoulders in one long lump. In the midst of all of her huffing and puffing as she struggled to smooth out her shawl, she caught sight of his owl, dipping its head from side to side. Ivy grew stone still. "Zach?"

"Yes?"

"Why is he looking at me like that?"

"Like what?"

"Like *that*," she forced from her fear-frozen jaw.

"I don't know." He didn't even crack a smile, but boy did he ever want to. Buddy wouldn't hurt her, but she didn't know that. He peered over at his owl. "Buddy, w-why are you looking at her like that?"

"Oh, for land's sake!" Clutching her wrap at her chest, she stood a little straighter. "You've probably trained him to attack."

He gave a long irritated sigh. "That's ridiculous."

"Is it?" she dared.

"Of c-course it is." Zach's fingers continued down the owl's belly, enamored, as always, with how bonded he'd become with the owl. "He's as gentle as can be. Unless, of course, you're a m-m-mouse—then you don't stand a chance."

"Oh, must you?" Her perfect features pinched in disgust. "I'd rather not know."

"You grew up here," he reasoned. "Surely you've ssseen worse."

She threaded her fingers together, and with the way she was growing all quiet and still, he decided that he better steer the conversation elsewhere.

"What did you need me for, anyway?"

Picking small bits of straw from her shawl, her gaze kept veering to his owl. "Violet sent me. She wants to know when you'll be in to eat."

At that, he hesitated. "Hmm… That's odd. Violet's n-never once asked me that question." If he didn't show up when dinner was served at the stroke of six, as always, she'd keep a plate warmed for him in the oven.

"Well, maybe she's feeling particularly generous to-night," she spat, clearly irritated.

Zach was beginning to wonder if Violet had other mo-tives. He hadn't missed the way the woman had all but fallen over herself, half running out into the yard to draw Ivy's attention to him when he'd been digging fence-post holes by the barn two days ago. He'd been mortified, but couldn't exactly fault the woman for trying, although she'd be better off finding out now that her labors were in vain.

"T-T-Tell her I'll be in within the next hour." When Ivy turned on one heel to leave, he added, "Ivy, maybe you'd like to meet my friend, here?"

She drew to a graceful halt, pivoted and faced him. "I don't think so."

"Come on." With a nod, he gestured her over as he relocated Buddy to the top edge of the door. The owl stepped sideways across the wood as though to stay as near to Zach as possible. "I p-p-promise he'll be good. With all of your fussing and then showering him with that straw, he must be c-close to perfect. He hasn't even f-flinched."

She held her tightly fisted hands to her mouth and

inched a bit closer. "I can't help it," she whispered, eyeing Buddy as though he had his talons poised, ready to stab her clear through. "I told you...I'm *really* afraid."

Zach felt instantly bad for having teased her. "Come here." He stepped over to meet her halfway when she seemed to get stuck in her tracks. Holding her hand in his, he gently pulled her to his owl. "There couldn't be a better opportunity for you to decide something d-d-different about our feathered friends."

"But what if I don't really *want* to form a different opinion?" she breathed. The vulnerability apparent in the slight quiver of her voice pricked his heart.

"Why are you so scared?" He dipped his head to grab her attention. Tugging her to his side, he kept his arm secured around her even when he knew he risked flattening his resolve to keep his distance in doing so. But he couldn't very well offer her nothing in the way of support. "Did ssssomething happen?"

She angled her distressed gaze up to him. "Again...a long story you will *not* want to hear. In fact, I've never told a soul."

"What happened?" he prodded, hoping that she'd trust him enough. Because it nearly broke his heart to see her so intimidated and panic-stricken.

Her wary gaze darted to the owl perched a mere three feet away. She hugged her arms to her chest. "I'd been climbing a tree in the apple orchard when I found a nest."

He secured a hand on her shoulder as he turned to face her. "Were you very young?"

"Younger than Libby. I was five." Her brow crimped. "The nest was so perfect and the eggs so beautiful and delicate that I couldn't resist holding them. I thought I'd take the whole thing home to raise the birds myself."

Her entire body quivered as though a wintery breeze had just blasted through the comfortably warm barn.

In that moment, Zach longed to pull her close and soothe away her fears and sorrows, but letting her go... now *that* would be hard.

"I started back down to the ground, holding the nest with one hand and hanging on to the tree with the other when—" She dropped her gaze. Swallowed hard. "When a bird started attacking me."

Compassion overwhelmed Zach. He slid his hand down her arm and grasped her fingers. "That had to be horrible for you."

She nodded, her distraught expression made his heart hurt. "I tried to hang on to the nest and the tree. I screamed, but the louder I screamed the more the bird attacked."

"She must've b-b-been the mother." He grasped both of her hands in his in spite of the caution flagging in his soul.

When it came to others hurting or in danger, he seemed to have an endless well of compassion. Maybe because he'd been through so much himself. Or maybe because God had given him a double dose at birth. Whatever the reason, he'd learned the hard way that the well-meaning light of compassion could be stomped right out if he wasn't careful.

Sometimes, though, he just couldn't help himself.

She drew her mouth into a tight line and peered up at him. "That's what my father said—that the bird was the mama. Later that day when he went out to investigate, he found the nest lying on the ground and the two eggs shattered." Her pinched gaze directed to the floor, she grew still, as though playing the whole thing over in her mind.

"I honestly don't remember dropping the nest, but I must have."

"I'm sure you didn't mean to," he assured, longing to bring her some kind of comfort.

"My father had always cautioned me not to touch a bird's nest. That I could look, but not touch." She pulled in a fractured breath. Stood a little straighter.

"It's all right, Ivy." He smoothed the pads of his thumbs over her delicate hands, moved by her sensitivity. "We've all done something or other like that."

"Like what?" She jerked her hands free and gripped her shawl closed at her chest. "Have you killed innocent baby birds, Zach?"

He tried not to react to her sudden show of anger, knowing firsthand how desolate it could feel to have gone through something so impacting. Alone.

Pulling up her chin a notch, she pushed elusive tendrils of auburn waves from her face. Straightened her shawl around her shoulders. Brushed a trembling hand down her evergreen-colored skirt.

It broke his heart to see the frantic way she seemed to grasp for control over herself—as though she regretted having let him in on this memory.

"It was the first time I ever saw my father mad," she confessed, her voice eerily even, the vulnerability in her eyes shuttered as she faced him. Quiet. Strong again. And very much shut off. "It was the first time I was responsible for a death."

The raw pain seen in her beautiful face and heard in her voice cut Zach to the quick, and he decided that he would do whatever he could to ease her heartache.

"We've got a bad situation on our hands, Zach," Ivy's uncle Terrance called as he dismounted from his horse outside the barn along with Brodie Lockhart, a U.S. Marshal and former schoolmate. "They're sick. Several of 'em."

In spite of the seriousness of the news she'd just overheard through the small window in Zach's office, Ivy's heart soared at seeing her uncle. She hadn't seen him once since she'd arrived four days ago, and though she would like to run out and throw herself into his arms right now, she thought better than to interrupt.

Zach ate up the distance from the house with his long legs. "What is this about? Who's sick?"

"The cattle." Her uncle stripped off his gloves and swiped a sleeve over his brow in that unhurried way of his.

"I rode out there just yesterday and they looked perfectly healthy." Zach's jaw muscles visibly bunched as he reached out and gently ran his hand over the horse's sleek neck.

The two horses nickered softly, nibbling at the sparse grass as Ivy's thoughts found their way clear to yesterday. To the utter tenderness in Zach's touch. She would not soon forget Zach's compassion when he'd coaxed the haunting memory from her. She'd been so caught up in the fear of his owl that she'd allowed him to undermine her composure, and had spilled one of her biggest secrets at his feet. It seemed as though she'd had no control over herself, and when her vulnerability had grown in unstoppable waves, he'd offered her a lifeline out of the pain.

In retrospect, she'd rather have drowned in regret.

Almost.

If not for the warmth and gentleness of his touch, the compassion in his gaze and his genuine concern...

Shoving her thoughts from the get-her-nowhere musings, she made a neat stack of the pile of papers she'd been organizing.

"What do you mean, they're sick?" Zach probed, snagging her attention again. His large hands formed fists.

"They're coughin' up a storm. Runnin' at the nose." Yanking his trail-worn hat from his head, her uncle slapped it against his thigh, sending a cloud of dust filtering her direction. "They're even heaving now and then."

"That's not sounding a bit good, my friend," Brodie cautioned, a slight Scottish brogue woven into his words. "What can I do for you, Zach? You name it."

Zach frowned on a heavy sigh as he fixed his gaze toward the corral where a couple dozen cattle were moseying about in the sunshine. "Not a thing. I'll take care of it."

Ivy doubted he needed another thing to worry about with her father being sick. Not to mention the constant tension that hung between her and Zach. Was he up to the task of foreman?

Hugh didn't seem to think so.

But the way Violet spoke of him at least two or three times a day, Ivy would've thought that Zach had hung the moon, painted the stars into the sky and christened the sun in its place. The woman doted on him like he was her own beloved son.

When Zach pulled off his hat and raked a hand through his light brown waves, hanging to just above his collar, Ivy's fingers ached to do the same—to him. She wrung her hands in a vain attempt to get rid of the odd and rebellious sensations. She needed to concentrate on what they were saying, not get distracted like a schoolgirl at the thought of a handsome boy. If she was going to keep an eye on the ranch, then she needed to be aware of what was going on.

"Have you gotten wind of any other herds taking ill?" Zach asked Brodie.

"I haven't heard a thing." Brodie gave his head a decided shake.

"How many cattle are sick, Terrance?" Zach jammed a hand at his taut waist, narrowing down from those broad, burden-bearing shoulders. "Is it the entire herd we have grazing in the north pasture?"

The couple of times he'd wrapped her in his arms, providing shelter and protection, she'd felt a tug at the very base of her heart. An odd sense of providence. As if her very existence was somehow dependent upon him.

But that was nowhere near the direction she was willing to let her thoughts go—at least when she was awake and aware. Asleep, she seemingly had no control over her insubordinate thoughts.

"I don't know," her uncle Terrance responded with a shrug. "Maybe a half dozen of the eighty that are there— from what I could tell. They were pretty edgy."

"I'd imagine they are." Zach drew his shoulders back, dwarfing her uncle's wiry frame. "We're going to have to herd them to the barn. Cordon them off so that we can nurse them back to health."

A small gasp escaped her lips as it dawned on Ivy how Zach had not *once* stuttered as he'd spoken with her uncle and Brodie. In fact, his speech was confident, unbroken and weighted with absolute certainty. As much as she tried to pay no heed to his stutter since her arrival, it had been difficult. The way his neck would tense right along with his jaw muscles, and the way his eyes would shutter with frustration when he was having a particularly difficult time getting the words out had affected her deeply.

She remembered how distraught and undone young Libby had been yesterday morning, hearing Zach's broken speech. Ivy's heart sank a little at the possibility that he stuttered around her, alone. Did she make him so uncomfortable that he couldn't be himself? The very idea doused her with a cold dose of shame and confusion.

"I'll go for them, boss." With a single nod, her uncle sauntered over to where his horse was grazing. "I'll head out right now."

"I'll bring the sick ones back myself." Zach's firm words brought her uncle to a sudden halt.

"You sure?" His booted foot hung in a stirrup. "I'd be glad to get the job done."

Zach shook his head. "I'll handle the situation."

"Are you sure you won't be needing some help?" Brodie offered, his enormous black stallion, standing probably seventeen hands high, nudging him with the gentleness of a young foal. "Hero and I could ride along. We'd have the job done by supper."

Zach was so much like her father. Take-charge. In control. Do-it-yourself. Her father had to have his hands in everything. He'd built the ranch to what it was today. Said that he shouldn't expect his men to do something he wasn't willing to do himself. Admirable qualities, really.

"I said I'd do it. But thanks for the offer." Worry set in as his gaze drifted to the north. "Listen, Terrance, I know you just returned from being on the range for a few days, but would you mind going out again?"

Her uncle slid his boot from the stirrup. "Sure. I'll load up my saddlebag and be gone before supper."

"I want you to keep a close eye on the other herds," Zach instructed, taking a step toward her uncle.

"Will do." Uncle Terrance grabbed the lead rope and started toward the barn with his mount in tow.

"If you notice anything abnormal, hightail it back here," Zach added.

"Keep your eye open for rustlers," Brodie cautioned, stopping her uncle Terrance in his tracks.

A fleeting look of discomfort passed over her uncle's face. His gaze dropped to the ground as he looped the lead rope once more around his fingers.

Ivy's heart sank at the news.

Brodie mounted his horse in one easy movement. "Along with the strike they made over a week ago due west of here, they've now struck not too far north of this place. Just beyond Gulp's Canyon."

Terrance gave a single silent nod.

"Why can't they just leave well-enough alone?" Zach growled, raking a hand through his hair again.

Recalling her conversation with Hugh, Ivy felt a twinge of dread tighten in her chest. There were a dozen reasons why she should've stayed in New York. Twice as many reasons why she shouldn't have returned to Boulder, but for the life of her she felt absolutely compelled to stay right here.

For her father.

For the ranch.

And for herself.

She could watch over her father's holdings, and hopefully find some kind of reconciliation with him. Some kind of healing for herself.

She'd book passage on the first train east as soon as possible, though. After all, she'd barely even seen her father in four days apart from the brief and nearly silent interchange at mealtime. Either he'd been avoiding her or he'd been seeing to pressing matters. Whatever the case, Ivy's hope for some kind of reconnection with him was fading.

The least she could do was to see to things around the ranch. The past two mornings she'd helped with chores and had gone through files, having found no obvious sign of incompetence on Zach's part. She was beginning to wonder if she'd find anything at all.

"I've got my nose to the ground, Zach." Brodie reined his horse around. "I'll be tracking the thieves."

"All the way to jail, knowing you, Brodie." Zach smoothed a hand down the stallion's massive neck. "Thanks for riding out here to keep me informed," he added as he walked beside the horse toward the lane. "I'll keep watch here."

Ivy turned from the window, confused and a little shaken, but certainly not deterred. When she heard her uncle leading his mount down the barn's main aisle, she rushed out the door of Zach's office. "Uncle Terrance!"

He pivoted, his expression laden with even more shock than that of her father. "Well, if it ain't Little Ivy." He dropped the horse's lead rope and held open his arms. "Is it really you…home at last?"

She rushed over to hug him, wishing she'd been met with those words and equal eagerness from her father. "Are you surprised?"

"You better believe I am. Let me have a look at you." He held her at arm's length, surveying her from head to toe. The approving shake of his head coaxed a chuckle from Ivy as she curtsied. "You're all grown up."

"Six years away from home and life on my own will do that." She tugged at her rose-colored brocade waistcoat, brushed a hand down her matching skirt. "I don't believe you look a day older, Uncle Terrance. Your work on the ranch must agree with you."

When he lifted his hat from his head, that same old scar she remembered angling across his forehead stared back at her. Years ago, she'd heard whisperings that he'd gotten into a scuffle with her father—shortly after her father and mama had married. She'd always wanted to know what, exactly, had happened, but had never had the nerve to ask.

"This business keeps me young, that's for sure," he remarked, stuffing his hat back on his head with an exaggerated wink.

He'd been around the ranch for most of her life. Being five years younger and a decade more youthful than her mama, at times he'd been more like an older brother to Ivy.

"So what brings you back?" Tugging a piece of straw from a lonely bale in the aisle, he stuck it in his mouth.

She explained about her father's health, grateful for the attentive way her uncle listened.

"Yeah, I've not been around a whole lot," he put in, shifting the straw from one side of his mouth to the other. "Just kind of come and go since they keep me out on the range mostly. But last time I was here, I thought I heard one of the hands saying something about him feeling poorly. What's ailing him?"

"His stomach. And from what Violet has said, he suffers with the chills and fever on occasion, too," she added, feeling positively horrible for her father and yet helpless to help him. She fingered the fabric of her brocade skirt. "I'll warn you right now…he doesn't want a big fuss made over him. He's trying to be strong."

"As always." The sharp edge to his voice caught her off guard. "Doesn't surprise me in the least. That's his way."

Having worked with her father for so many years, he likely knew that better than anyone, yet she didn't exactly feel inclined to agree with him. In no way did she want to dishonor her father, though she couldn't help but feeling bad for her uncle. Ivy couldn't understand why her father seemed so contrary when it came to Terrance. It wasn't as if her father had ever been outright rude to him, but he'd never shown him the same kind of respect he did others.

"I suppose it's not easy being back after what happened to your poor mama?" He slid out the straw from between his teeth. "Probably brings all kinds of bad memories."

The haunting image of her mama's last few hours flashed through Ivy's mind. Her mama's desperate gasp for breath… Her gray pallor… That spine-chilling gurgle of death…

Those hours had seemingly lasted a lifetime. And they'd passed by in a second. She hadn't been ready for her mama to die. There was still so much to say. So many memories yet to make.

"I've got to face things at some point. Especially after six years." She'd buried her pain and grief and guilt for this entire time. Her homecoming simply had to provoke some kind of resolution.

Maybe not with her father.

But with herself.

And with God.

"Ivy, listen to me." He grasped her shoulders. "I'm telling you, girl, from your good ole uncle Terrance, this big sprawling ranch just isn't the place for you."

"Right now I need to be here," she defended. She was a little irritated at the way he assumed he knew what was best for her. And at the way his thin fingers poked into her flesh. "I'll be fine. In some ways it's been good being back."

Uncle Terrance gave his head a decided shake and released his hold. "But New York…now *that's* the place for you, sweets." The way he tweaked her nose just then, as though she was a small child, only furthered her irritation. "I've heard all about how well you've done there. Violet can't hardly keep her big mouth shut about it."

"Violet is a dear, isn't she?"

Violet was as pure as a mountain stream. Upstanding, faith-filled, honorable, true. She rarely spoke ill of others. Although, she didn't seem to care too much for Hugh, and with the lack of regard Hugh obviously had for her, it seemed that the feeling was mutual. And Violet could find absolutely nothing unkind to say about Ivy's father. Ivy had noticed a softening in her father's demeanor whenever Violet was around, too. In fact, Ivy had begun to wonder if their affection for each other went far deeper.

"Your mama…she would be so proud of you, Ivy. She had always dreamed of planting her feet in the big city." Removing his hat from his head again, he held it over his heart in a sweet gesture of respect. "Dreamed about it from the time she was a young child."

"Really?" A quiver shimmied up Ivy's spine. "She always talked about me going out there. But I never knew that she'd wanted the same."

"Oh, yes. A day didn't pass where she wasn't going on and on about the prospects for a life in the big city." His eyes narrowed suddenly. "That is until she met your daddy."

"What happened then?" she prodded.

"She loved him so much she decided she'd forego her dreams in order to be with him." His wide mouth formed a grim line. "Even if it meant getting sick and dying on the ranch," he measured out, his words piercing her heart.

She didn't remember her mama loving the ranch, necessarily, but she'd certainly never lamented being here—at least not as Ivy could recall. After all, her mama had grown up here, and when her own parents had passed away some twenty odd years ago, the ranch had gone to her and Ivy's father who'd been working here as a hand.

Uncle Terrance turned and glanced at where the sun

was streaming in through the double doors, lapping up the darkness in a golden glow. "I can just hear her now, praising you up one side and down another for doing what she'd only dreamed of."

Ivy smiled, recalling how life-giving her mama's words had been. "She would be, wouldn't she?"

"You better believe it, sweets." He reached out and snagged his mount's lead rope as the horse started meandering toward the warm sunlight. "Which is *exactly* why you can't let yourself get waylaid here on the ranch. Do you hear me?"

"I hear you," she said, confused. "But for now I know that I'm supposed to be here, Uncle Terrance. For how long, I don't know. I would love to have some kind of closure with my father, but—"

"But he's stubborn."

She'd been called the same…by Zach.

"Believe me…I know all about it." Shrugging out of his duster coat, she had to hold her expression in check as the ripe scent of range and sweat and dirt infused her general area. "Don't hold your breath about making nice with him, sweets…I gave up trying to do that years ago. There's a full life just waiting for you in New York and you need to get yourself back there as fast as you can. You promise?"

She stared at her uncle, the urgency of his words barreling through her mind, knocking her reason off-kilter. Although she wanted to promise him as much, she couldn't seem to find the words to agree.

She swallowed hard, searching her soul for some kind of answer. If ever there was a time when she needed to know God's gentle leading it was now—to feel His abiding, loving presence as she had when she was young. To *know* that everything was going to be all right.

As fast as that yearning filled her heart, her thoughts drifted to Zach, his strong arms, tender care and the way he'd willingly offered her a hand on her journey home.

Ivy peered into her father's study where he was sitting and having his early morning coffee, an almanac in his hand. In spite of the beautiful day, the heavy damask drapes were merely cracked open, leaving two lamps struggling to fill the room with light. Shelves and shelves of books anchored one whole wall, books she'd spent hours paging through, pretending to read....

Long ago, Sundays had been her favorite day, filled with family, friends and neighbors and the comforting feel of Boulder's quaint clapboard church, with windows that stretched to the sky and pews that creaked like a kindly grandfather telling a story.

She hadn't been to church in years. She'd stopped going not long before her mama passed away. Her father had wanted nothing to do with God then. Ivy had no idea where he stood on the matter now, but figured that they both could benefit from finding their way back, even if they were on separate paths.

"Father..." she began, fingering the crisp golden taffeta of her skirt.

"What is it?" The way he barely spared her a glance above his reading glasses did not give her much encouragement.

"It's Sunday, and I was wondering..." Ignoring her uncertainty, she stepped over to stand in front of his big desk, piled unusually high with papers and books. "Well, I was wondering if maybe you'd like to attend church with me."

He lowered the almanac to the cherrywood desk, darkened and made rich by age. "Violet's already asked."

"Oh, she did?" Ivy commented, hopeful. Sweet Violet not only cared for her father's earthly needs, but for his soul, as well. "That's thoughtful of her."

Clearing his throat, his hands fisted. "She asks every Sunday."

Ivy trailed a finger over the wood's smooth edge, recalling all the times as a child when she'd plant herself on top of his desk and watch him work. He'd give her papers to tap into place and books to look through. He'd ask for her advice on ranch affairs as though her five-year-old opinion held an ounce of weight.

"Do you mind if I join you and Violet, then?" she asked, annoyed by the tentative quiver threaded through her voice.

He shifted in his chair. "I've got work to do here, Ivy."

"Maybe you could take some time this morning to go with me. I know I haven't gone in a while and I thought that maybe—"

"Like I said, I've got work to do. You go on ahead." Leaning over his desk, he tapped the ends of his thick fingers against the wood the way he used to when he was thinking.

"Well, maybe we could just stay here and talk, then. We haven't done much of that since I've been home." Emotion rebelliously clogged her throat as she noted just how *little* they'd interacted.

When he hesitated, as though considering, her heart started racing wildly inside her chest. Anticipation shuddered her insides every bit as much as apprehension. She longed for something deeper than just a brushing of formality with her father.

"I'm heading out shortly," he finally said, flattening a palm against the desk.

"It'd mean so much if we could talk through some

things, Father," she persisted, trying to keep any amount of begging from her voice even when she did feel horribly and profoundly desperate. "It's been so long since… well, since I left. And since mama—"

"Ivy…I…" he began. "I can't talk now," he measured out. "I've got to meet with Zach before he heads into town."

"Can't that wait?" she implored, intent to make some kind of headway with her father.

When he stood from his desk, his gaze blanketed by that stern unmoved look of his that gave no room for discussion, her hopes were nearly completely deflated.

"Well, maybe later, then?" she braved, struggling to hide her discouragement when he made his way to the double doors of his office and held them open for her to leave.

He didn't speak one word as she moved across the room. But his gaze…shuttered and empty and firm…his gaze completely doused Ivy's hopes.

Chapter Eight

"**S**urprise!"

Zach scanned the house, an appreciative grin stretching across his face at the sight of his entire family, and then some, packing Joseph and Katie's home.

After he'd run into Ivy exiting her father's office the other day and seen her expression, crestfallen and sorrowful and almost without hope, he'd found himself praying for her. Asking God to ease whatever it was that had weighed that sweet smile of hers down. Surely she had to know how folks cared about her. It seemed he couldn't go anywhere without overhearing some townsperson or another talking about her return, and about how good it was to have her back in Boulder.

"What's all this about?" He set a hand to Ivy's back and ushered her through the front door.

"What do you mean, *what's* this about?" Joseph chuckled and drew his wife close to his side.

"Something must be distracting him these days if he doesn't have any idea," Aaron teased from the front room where he was standing with his new bride, Hope, in front of the glowing hearth.

Zach shot Aaron a barbed look as he latched the door,

closing out the early October chill, but he couldn't hold his frown for long. It was too good to see his brother looking so happy and in love.

After Aaron had suffered the loss of his wife and newborn baby boy over a year ago, he'd vowed he'd never marry again. He was a man to keep his promises, too, but then he'd made a promise to Paul, his dying friend. He'd promised that he'd hold on to hope, not knowing that *hope* was *Hope* Gatlin, Paul's mail-order bride who arrived the day he'd died. Love had walked right through the back door of Aaron's heart and as far as Zach was concerned, Hope and Aaron couldn't be more perfect for each other.

Zach tugged his hat from his head. "I thought this was supposed to be a *nice, quiet* dinner. Not that I mind all of you being here," he added with a smile.

"We can leave if you like." Brodie walked over from where he was talking with Violet in the kitchen. "Though it's sure you'll never be having another birthday celebration if we do, my friend."

"It's your *birthday,* baby brother." Joseph held out his hand to take their coats. "And this is a celebration."

"There they g-g-go with that baby brother bit," he muttered, lifting Ivy's emerald green cloak from around her shoulders then shrugging out of his jacket.

When she smiled up at him, her glistening gaze fixed on his, his heart beat a mutinous rhythm.

"And it's also *Ivy's* birthday," Joseph added.

When Joseph and Katie had invited him for dinner along with Ivy, he'd thought it was nothing more than a nice gesture. But he'd asked if Katie could whip up a cake for Ivy, since her birthday fell in just two days and he wanted her to feel special. As stalwart as she'd been in the face of her father's growing distance, Zach had felt

driven to put a smile on her face. To add some bright-
ness to her day.

Standing on her tiptoes, Katie gave Zach a peck on the
cheek. "Happy birthday, Zachariah Henry Drake. You're
the best."

"The best?" He winked at his sister-in-law.

"Stop your winking at my wife, Zach," Joseph warned
with a mock scowl.

Zach arched his eyebrows, grinning. "Nothing gets by
him, d-does it?"

"Not a thing," Katie confirmed, pressing a hand to
Zach's chest. "You're the best brother-in-law with a birthday today."

When he turned and glanced down into Ivy's enchant-
ing gaze, his good mood extended a little further. "The
only b-b-brother-in-law with a birthday today," he added.

"Like I've said before...I know him all too well."
Joseph clapped Zach on the back. "Happy birthday,
brother."

"Happy birthday, Ivy," Katie said, wrapping Ivy in a
tender hug. "I'm so glad you were able to make it tonight.
We're thrilled to have you."

Ivy fingered the ruffled sleeves of her crisp white
shirtwaist as though she didn't quite know what to do
with herself in the face of all of the attention. "It is very
thoughtful of you to include me in the festivities."

"Actually," Katie put in, "Zach was the one who mentioned something about it being your birthday."

The appreciative look Ivy settled on him in that
moment seemed to add a couple inches to his six foot
frame. If he wasn't careful, his diminishing resolve to
not let himself fall for her again would be stripped away
to nothing.

"Ivy, I don't believe we've been properly introduced." Katie held out her hand.

"I'm s-s-sorry," Zach apologized, thankful that Katie didn't draw attention to his stutter. "Katie, this is Ivy. Ivy…Katie."

She sighed. "Please excuse his *horrendous* manners."

"Have a little mmmmercy, will you? I'm still trying to get my bearings after opening the door to find half the t-t-town of Boulder crammed in here."

"I've never known you to be flustered before," Katie shot back.

"Sure I've been flustered," he argued.

"Don't let him fool you," Katie whispered conspiratorially, leaning toward Ivy. "When Joseph and I had known each other for less than a month, this bad boy bid an enormous twenty-eight dollars and fifty cents on *my* entry at the box lunch auction."

"He did?" Ivy's wide-eyed gaze swept over Zach.

Katie nodded. "Oh, yes, he did—and without the faintest show of remorse. Even when he proceeded to dump the *whole thing* in Joseph's lap."

Joseph pointed one finger. "Let me put in here that I did *not* mind." He wrapped his arms around his wife as he stood behind her. "Well, later I didn't, anyway. At the time I wanted to haul out and hit him square in the jaw for being so bold on my behalf, but I suppose I thought I'd miss or something."

"*I,* on the other hand, was mortified," Katie confessed, setting her fingertips on the new life growing inside her belly and due at the end of November. "Can you imagine? Paying twenty-eight dollars and fifty cents for my box lunch when he had every intention of pawning it off?"

When Joseph kissed his wife's head, Zach felt a sting of longing. He yearned to share the same kind of love with someone, but it just wasn't worth pouring his heart and soul into loving someone who might never love him back. He'd poured himself out for Ivy years ago. It had cost him plenty, and he'd gained nothing.

"You were worth every penny, darlin'." Joseph smoothed his hands over Katie's shoulders. "And more."

"Did you *really* do that, Zach?" Ivy peered at him.

He held up his hands in surrender as a few chuckles sounded around them. "He needed *someone* to prod him along. I was just d-d-doing what any good brother would."

Joseph gave his head a slow shake. "Always the match-maker."

"Never the match," Zach added, his heart sinking at the bleak reminder.

"Oh, Zach…" Katie gently swatted at his arm. "You're some fortunate young lady's fine and noble match. She just hasn't discovered you yet."

He shot her the clearest and most unthreatening look of admonition he could manage, but from the broad smile creasing her face, he was pretty sure he'd failed to get his point across.

"He was shameless about the whole thing, I tell you," she went on to say. "Positively shameless." Folding her arms at her chest, Katie nailed him with a mock glare. "That self-satisfied grin he'd plastered on his face as I watched him saunter across the town square to announce the news to Joseph made me want to crawl into the nearest hole."

"They're being *way* too hard on me," Zach defended as he looked down at Ivy and shifted the overcoats to the other arm. "I was j-j-just giving the situation a little shove, that's all."

"And I thank you for that. I needed the shove." Joseph set a hand to the life growing inside his wife's belly.

"Well, all of that to say, it's good to see you again, Ivy. Can't say as I remember you much since you and Zach are four years younger and my memory for faces is fading, but it's good to have you here, at any rate."

"Thank you. It's good to be here." The tenderness in her voice arrested Zach's attention.

Katie perched her hand on Ivy's arm. "I hope you like chocolate cake. Zach said that it was your favorite."

"I do. I love chocolate." The smallest bit of wonder infused her expression as she asked him, "How did you know?"

As much as he'd tried to forget every little nuance about her from years ago, he couldn't. It was as though the details were permanently imbedded into his mind. He could likely write a book about Ivy. Her likes. Her dislikes. The sure things that could prompt one of her soft smiles or endearing frowns.

But as images flitted through his mind of Ivy assaulting him with an armful of straw—and all because of a harmless bird—his certainty at knowing all there was to know about this spritely auburn-haired beauty was pulled up short. There was more to Ivy than what he'd known. Far more.

The very idea provoked a pure and unwelcome challenge in his heart—and he never could seem to back down from a challenge. He was tempted to delicately mine for those things that were hidden, if only to know her more.

Swallowing hard at the unsettling dare that had snagged his soul, he tried to rip his gaze away from her, but those eyes of hers were so captivating. And that tender look of timidity held him completely rapt.

"How d-did I know?" he lamely echoed. "I suppose I just recall your love of ch-ch-chocolate from years ago."

She studied him, as though searching for something

in his gaze. Well, his former interest in her couldn't be more obvious with the way Katie had dropped *that* clue. Ivy would've had to have been blind not to realize how he'd pined for her way back when. In all those years of falling all over himself for her, surely she couldn't have missed his ardent affection.

Or had she? Had he really poured out his heart for nothing?

"And, Zach, guess what?" The excitement in Katie's voice tugged him from the harsh reminder.

"What?" He struggled to temper his frustration.

Katie clasped her hands beneath her chin. "Callie made you a white cake with that *delicious* whipped icing you like so well."

"Mmmmm... Sounds great," he commented, wondering how he could choke down a morsel of food with the way his mouth had suddenly gone bone dry. "I can't wait to d-dig in."

"I hope you'll like it." Callie slid into the conversation. "I dug through your mama's old recipes, but couldn't find the one for the icing Ben said was your favorite."

His family's kindness helped to shear the edge from his irritation. "So, how'd you come up with it then?"

"Mrs. Duncan. Apparently, *she* was the one who'd given the recipe to your mama in the first place—at least that's what she told me."

"Makes me appreciate the mmmmeddling woman all the more." A grin tugged at the corners of Zach's mouth, easily picturing the woman eagerly taking credit. He remembered how blunt Beatrice Duncan had been that day Ivy had arrived. For all of her frank observations, self-trumpeting and prying ways, a soul just couldn't help but like the woman.

"Zach wanted to make sure we included Violet for you,

Ivy." The artful way Callie had just plated that bit of information only furthered Zach's awkwardness.

He trusted his family completely. But apparently when it came to Ivy, he couldn't trust them as far as the slightly crooked nose on his face.

"By the way, my name is Callie." Callie held out her hand to Ivy. "I'm Ben's wife."

"It's a pleasure to meet you, Callie."

"I feel like I already know you. Libby and Luke have talked of nothing else since they met you." Callie's gaze filled with delight as she peered over where the two children were engrossed by some trick Aaron was demonstrating for them.

"They're delightful," Ivy breathed.

"There's never a dull moment in our home when Luke and Libby are together," Callie noted while Ben moved to stand beside her.

"Never," he agreed, winking down at his wife.

Katie set her hand on Ivy's arm. "We invited your father to be here with us, but it looks like maybe something must've kept him." She glanced at the mantle clock then back to Ivy. "Do you mind if we start without him?"

Ivy slid a hopeful glance over her shoulder, as though he might walk through the doorway even now. "No, that's fine."

Zach's compassion swelled at her obvious disappointment. "I c-could ride out and get him, if you want me to."

"That's not necessary." The calm understanding etched in her expression didn't fool Zach for a minute. He could tell she was let down by the hopeful way she glanced back toward the door again. "I'm sure that, if he was going to be here, he would've made it by now."

"All right, then." Katie clapped her hands in an unsuccessful effort to grab the guests' attention.

When Joseph stuck two fingers in his mouth and gave a sharp whistle, a hush fell over the room. He smiled down at his wife. "The floor is all yours, darlin'."

"Thank you." She faced the room full of folks. "I thought that before we begin our meal we could take a moment to pray."

From the corner of his eye, Zach saw Ivy hug her arms to her chest and edge back a step. The vulnerability in the action made him wonder just where she stood with God.

Zach's own faltering relationship with God stared him in the face. After he'd suffered through being hopelessly trapped and then stuttering as a result, he'd been angry, depressed...he'd cast blame on others and on God. When he'd finally taken his life by the horns, and by sheer determination and a heaping dose of pride had overcome his stutter and straightened his life around, he'd finally come to some kind of resolution. But through it all, he'd remained firm in his insistence on fixing his problems himself, depending on no one—not even God. Was Ivy the same way? She'd lost her mother and been sent away from her home so quickly. Had she felt there was no one she could lean on?

Pricked by her apparent unease he reached back and set a hand to the small of her back, easing her forward a bit.

Zach couldn't control how her father and she got along, but he sure could be someone she could lean on.

The instant Libby moved through the crowd to stand beside Ivy soothed Zach's heart. "Miss Ivy?" Libby whispered. "Are you worried because of your sick cows? Cuz I've been praying for them."

Ivy's breath hitched. "That is very thoughtful of you, Libby."

"They're definitely g-g-getting better," Zach assured, nodding at Libby.

She gave the sweetest smile then drew a little closer to Ivy. "Can I hold your hand, Miss Ivy?"

"Of course. I'd love that." When Ivy took hold of Libby's small hand, a certain warmth spread all through his heart.

Zach peered down at Ivy, moved by the softness and wonder he saw in her tonight. It pleased him.

And frightened him.

Because by not doing a thing, she was shaking everything he'd worked so hard for. At least that's what he'd thought right after his stutter had begun again. But the way his stutter had vanished when she wasn't around, he was beginning to question his conclusions. Did his problem root more inside of himself?

"Who would like to pray?" Katie asked, jerking him from his musings.

Libby's hand shot up in the air, lightning fast. "I will. I will."

"Go right ahead," Katie encouraged.

Libby reached for Joseph's hand and then slid her ever-observant gaze around the room to make sure each person was well connected to the next. "Uncle Zach," she urged, nodding to where Ivy's left arm dangled at her side.

He slung their overcoats over his shoulder then took Ivy's hand in his, the simple touch searing straight through to his heart.

"Dear God, thank You for this day," Libby began, her eyes squeezed tight. "Thank You for all my pets, and please make Uncle Zach's cows all better," she prayed in earnest, her compassion and simple trust hitting him square in the chest. "Thank You for my aunts and uncles.

Thank You for my friends—especially Luke." She popped one eye open and peered at Luke, whose face beamed with pride. "Thank You for changing his mama's heart. And thank You, especially for Uncle Zach and Miss Ivy. Help them to have a good birthday—and God…I was thinkin' that maybe You could help Miss Ivy be Uncle Zach's wife since he—"

Joseph bent over and whispered something in Libby's ear as Zach's pulse slammed a deafening rhythm in his ears. It was by sheer will that he didn't drop Ivy's hand, but the very real possibility that Libby would innocently draw even more attention to the situation kept his hand firmly connected to Ivy's.

"That's all, God," Libby finished with a sweet smile. "Amen."

A chorus of muffled chuckles along with hearty amens followed. But how could Zach add his *so-be-it* to that? He would likely never get married. If he did, well, then Ivy was the *last* person in the world he'd marry. Right?

Releasing Ivy's hand, he felt completely unnerved. And yet, a small part of him, way down deep and hidden beneath years of hurt, championed his young niece's heartfelt prayer.

"Out of the mouth of babes…" Joseph said, arching his eyebrows mischievously over his sightless eyes.

Zach was sorely tempted to wipe the triumphant grin right off Joseph's face. "She's a helpless romantic, just like—"

"Her Uncle Zach, *that's* who," Ben put in, his Cheshire-cat grin wide across his face.

"You two leave poor Zach alone." Katie's grin far from supported her chiding tone. "All right, everyone…time to eat," she announced as the guests started toward where the food had been laid out on the dining table.

Zach couldn't seem to move his feet more than an inch. But no matter how discomforting the moment, he figured that, for all of the prodding he'd done in his brothers' lives, he half deserved their needling. That didn't mean he had to like it, however.

"Libby's t-too young to know better," he commented, turning toward Ivy and feeling oddly pleased by the rosy color tinting her cheeks. "But I'm afraid you're going to have to forgive my b-b-b-brothers. They jump at the chance to t-tease me."

She pinned him with a challenge-laced gaze. "From what Katie said, it sounds like you deserve it."

"Me?" He pulled his head back.

"Don't try placating me with that all-innocence look." Following a brief scowl, her expression softened some as she glanced around the warm and cozy room. "This is so nice of your family, Zach. So very nice. They really didn't have to go to so much trouble. And *you* really didn't have to tell them about it being my birthday."

"Everyone d-deserves to be celebrated." He tipped his head toward her, fighting off the instant longing to wrap her up in his arms. "I just hope you don't mmmmind sharing the day with me. Honestly, I wasn't even th-th-thinking about my birthday when they invited me over."

"Of course, I don't mind." Her wide gaze took in every inch of the gathering as though to memorize the moment. "Mama always made my birthday special, but I can't ever remember having a birthday party with so many people. It was always just the three of us." Her gaze drifted to the chocolate cake displayed on the sideboard like some prized possession. "It's overwhelming," she breathed, blinking hard.

When a sudden vulnerability shifted into her expression, and a faraway look deepened in her gaze, concern for her mounted. "Do you want to step outside for a moment?" he asked.

Ivy peered at Zach, her mind swimming with a million thoughts. From the moment he'd brought her here tonight, she'd felt a tangible yet evasive sense of providence. Like somehow, someway, she was meant to be here. That these people, many of them she barely knew from years ago, not only played a part in this very moment, but somehow played an integral part in her future.

But how could that be? Her future was firmly fixed in New York City. She couldn't very well transport the whole of the room there with her when she returned.

And then there was the sweet way Zach had paid great attention to detail, on her behalf. From Violet being here to help Ivy celebrate, to the chocolate cake… How did Zach know what she liked, anyway? Had he paid her that much attention years ago that he could recall trivial information, like her favorite cake?

"Ivy…" Zach's deep voice tugged her from her thoughts.

"I'm sorry. Wh-what did you say?"

He cocked his head, studying her for a pensive moment. "I wondered if you wanted to step outsssside for a few minutes. You know, with all of the people…"

"That would be nice," she agreed, desperate for any kind of breeze to blow her thoughts elsewhere.

"We'll just get a little fresh air. Maybe we can scare up Boone, Joseph's Newfoundland."

After he settled her emerald green cloak around her shoulders, he ushered her into the crisp and clear night.

"You're so fortunate to have such a wonderful family," she noted, as he closed the door behind him. She followed Zach down the three stairs to the well-maintained walkway leading to the boardwalk. The quaint front yard was hemmed in by a lovely picket fence, gleaming in the moon's pearly-white light. "They are very good people, Zach."

He shuffled to a stop, his head bowed as he slid his hands into his pockets. "I'm a blessed man, that's for sure."

"Do you mind me asking what happened to Joseph?" she asked as a big black mass lumbered their way from behind the house—Boone, apparently. "I don't even remember him having glasses back in school."

Zach hunkered down as the dog burrowed his head straight into Zach's chest. "Joseph lost his ssssight in an accident in his shop about a year and a half ago."

On a small gasp, she knelt across from Zach and touched the dog's soft fur. "How horrible."

"It was," he agreed with a single nod, then scratched his fingers down the animal's wide back. "But I d-doubt you'll hear Joseph say that. He'll probably tell you that, if not for the accident, he never would have met Katie." His studying glance pried at her resolve to stay strong. "Not that he's glad to be blind, but he definitely sees the g-good that has come from it."

"What an honorable attitude to have," she commented, questioning how in the world she could continue to remain unaffected by Zach. He affected her in every possible way. His warm and tender touch. The compelling way he gazed deep into her soul, to where her wounds gaped open. The strong affection he showed for his family, and them for him.

But Hugh's misgivings had kept a foothold, however minute, in her thoughts. Even though Violet had meted out a few unsavory feelings regarding Hugh, Ivy couldn't help but wonder about his concerns.

"I could learn a thing or t-two from Joseph, that's for sure," Zach admitted, his strong whisker-shadowed jaw tensing in the moon's bathing light.

"I don't know if I would be able to see things the way Joseph does."

"I'm *sure* I wouldn't." He swallowed hard. Something she'd seen him do when he was working so hard to speak clearly.

When his intense and confident focus settled over Ivy, a warm rush trickled down her spine. The little she recalled of Zach from her schooldays looked nothing like the man in front of her now. She'd once thought him memorable only because he was the poor boy who stuttered.

But now…*now* he was so much more. In fact, if not for how visibly he seemed to contend with his stutter, she was beginning to barely even notice it was there.

Except for the way he seemed free of the impediment when she wasn't around.

She'd been greatly disturbed by that stark realization. Weighted by the burden of it all and how his stutter seemed directly related to her, she had to wonder if maybe there was something she could do to help.

"Zach?" She tugged her cloak a little tighter and stood up.

He rose to face her, the slight crook of his nose catching the moon's light. "What?"

"Your stutter…does it bother you?" she braved, almost immediately regretting it when the space between them grew stone cold. And when his eyes flashed with an unmistakable look of irritation.

The awkward silence that followed was broken only by

the sprinkling of joyous laughter coming from inside and by the shuffling sound of the dog's feet as he pawed off.

"Does it bother *you?*" he measured out, his intense gaze not shifting from hers for even the fraction of a second.

She held her breath. "N-No. I just thought—"

"You thought wh-wh-what?" he probed, his tone edged with accusation.

On a guarded exhale, she struggled not to shudder against his icy mood. "I thought that maybe I could help."

"I *don't* need your help." His crisp tone pierced deep. Almost immediately the dark shadow in his expression grew a little lighter. "I d-didn't mean to sound sssso—"

"No. I shouldn't have been so intrusive," she meted out, fumbling for composure. She glanced at the party's glowing light spilling out into the night as if to extend a little warmth to the sudden chill. "I'm sorry."

Although every good intention had accompanied her offer, he'd made it painfully clear that he didn't want her help. What should it matter to her whether he *did* or *didn't* want her help? She cared for him as nothing more than an old acquaintance. Right?

Or was she growing beyond just a simple fondness of Zach?

The stomach-fluttering memory of the way his hand had gently folded around hers as sweet Libby had voiced an honest and earnest and heartfelt prayer weakened her already flagging resolve. It was as if Zach had some kind of innate, highly astute sense about her well-being. And that upsetting prospect settled over her like a downy quilt on the most bitter of winter days.

"Ivy…" His warm breath fanned out into the crisp night air. He raised his hand to her arm, but then seemingly changed course and yanked his hat from his head. "I'm ssssorry your father wasn't able to make it tonight."

There it was again. That genuine care and concern of his.

"So am I." She slid away from his reach even when she yearned to step into his strong and steady embrace. "But honestly, I would've been surprised had he come."

Zach raked his fingers through his hair. "I'm sure he probably wanted to."

"I'm not." She sniffed, recalling just how painful it'd been when he'd brushed her off this morning. "He has made it very clear that he doesn't have time for me."

"Maybe he wasn't feeling well." Zach's defense of her father stung a little.

"I should think you'd be more attentive to how your boss is fairing. Especially when he's been ill," she challenged, knowing full well that she could say the same of herself regarding her father.

"He hasn't exactly b-b-been easy to track down." Jamming his hat on his head, his jaw muscle tensed. "He's either out by himself on the range or holed up in his office and d-d-doesn't want visitors."

"Violet has a way of keeping tabs on him," she needled.

His jaw ticked. His guarded expression left her feeling uncomfortably vacant. "Yes, she does, doesn't she?"

"Oh, well, Violet's always had a way of getting what she wants," Ivy quickly reasoned as she peered down the road at the row of warmly lit homes, each topped by a tale-telling chimney. She felt bad for her cutting remarks. She shouldn't take out her frustration over the situation with her father on Zach. It wasn't his fault that her father had no time for her any more than it was his fault that she was starting to develop feelings for him that would make it so much harder to go back to New York, leaving him behind. "Violet knows that he won't leave on horseback without a fresh stash of Uncle Terrance's jerky. I think she uses that to keep luring him home."

On a patient breath, Zach said, "Shhhhhe definitely has a way with him, doesn't she?"

"You've noticed?"

"If I didn't know any better, I'd think they were in l-l-love," he muttered, relaxing some.

She met his keen gaze, a most indefinable tremor shuddering from her head to her toes. "I had the same thought. Violet's always been very caring, but something between them has changed since I was last here. The funny thing is…I don't think they recognize it. They *don't realize* that they're in love."

The hint of a grin that tugged at one corner of his mouth provoked a flurry of activity in the base of Ivy's stomach. "Maybe they need a little help."

Did he have any idea what kind of a trap he'd just stepped into? "Yes, *Mr. Matchmaker*," she measured out, standing a little straighter. "Maybe they need a little help."

Chapter Nine

❧

Mr. Matchmaker...

Zach didn't, for a single second, deny his triumphs in lining things up so that love came easily for others, and he'd do what he could with Mr. Harris and Violet. But when it came to himself, he didn't seem to have a lick of success. He could never seem to get Ivy fully out of his heart or mind, and he'd never felt that fair to another woman.

The irony of Ivy's words still stung as he guided the horse-drawn buggy home across the moonlit road with Ivy at his side. Every jostling movement made by the small conveyance propelled them together, undermining his grasp for a little self-possession. Because from the moment Ivy had realized that the party was in her honor as much as it was his, and that sparkle of wonderment had lit her gaze and her smile, he'd been transfixed.

Moved.

Sent into a tailspin.

How was he *ever* going to navigate through the traps posed by this woman? A warmly tender glance? A radiant smile or an innocent touch? A glimpse of her delightful stubbornness, noble sense of adventure or genuinely caring ways? These attributes were all innocuous enough had they come from anyone else.

But with Ivy...

His throat constricted, noose-tight. Stomach flip-flopped. His mouth went as dry as the dust kicked up by the horse's hooves.

When he braved a glance at her from his peripheral vision, he suddenly wished he hadn't. She was staring at him with the most tender and tentative of expressions, her moist gaze gleaming in the moon's pearly glow.

She rewarded him with one of her heart-tugging smiles. "You're awfully quiet. Do you mind me asking what has you in such deep thought?" Her sweet warm breath whispered across his face.

He swallowed hard. "Tonight, I guess."

The sigh that passed through her perfect full lips seemed to spark something innate in his core. "It really was a lovely evening, Zach. I haven't enjoyed myself like that in a very long time."

"I'm g-g-glad," he forced out, willing his jaw and neck muscles to relax.

The moment she'd brought up his stutter tonight, he'd fought hard not to dip from the deep and dangerous well of insecurity. Shame's assaulting blows had rained down on him without warning, but he'd pulled himself upright as quickly as he'd gone down, reminding himself of every last hour he'd put into overcoming his stammer. The hard work. The sweat. The sleepless nights he'd spent reading aloud from Shakespeare or other classics just to challenge his broken speech. He wasn't about to lose the man he'd become.

Especially not to Ivy, he reminded himself.

When she perched a hand on his forearm, her touch seared straight through his coat and two layers of clothing to his skin. "Thank you so much for thinking of me, Zach. Your thoughtfulness means more than you'll ever know."

Her response meant more than he cared to admit.

He shoved his gaze toward the barn, where an orange flickering glow caught his eye. Tightening his grip on the reins, he peered through the dark night. His blood whooshed at the sight of flames radiating from his office window in the barn.

"Zach?" She gripped his arm. "What? What is it?"

"Look." He pointed toward the barn, over a quarter mile away. "The barn. It's on fire."

"Fire?" Her anguished gasp seized his heart. "Oh, Zach, please we must hurry."

"Hang on tight, Ivy. It's g-going to be a rough ride." He gave her hand a squeeze then he slapped the reins, urging the horse faster over the rutted road. His heart sank at the thought of the livestock stabled inside the barn.

"Please. Go faster, Zach." Her ardent and desperate grip only deepened his urgency. "We've got to get the horses and cattle out."

"Believe me...I'm going as f-fast as I can." He slapped the reins again. "Yee haw! Get on!" he called to the big roan. "Come on, fella. You can do it."

She perched on the edge of her seat, her anxious focus leaping from him to the barn every few seconds. "Do you think any of the ranch hands have noticed?"

"Hard to tell." He shook his head. "M-Most of them go to t-t-town on Friday nights and don't drag themselves back t-till late. And Terrance is out on the range."

"What about my father?" The tears that shimmered in her eyes compelled him to go even faster. "You don't think that—"

"He's all right, Ivy," he assured her even when he

wasn't so certain. He sent up a silent prayer for God's help. Not for himself, but for Mr. Harris. And for Ivy. "I'm sure he's all right."

When Zach pulled into the lane leading to the homestead, the roan packed more power into every galloping step.

"What do you want me to do?" Ivy called over the wagon's jangling noise.

"I keep several buckets by the water pump. Start pumping water into them. I'll get the livestock out. But promise me..." He caught her gaze in the moon's white light. "Promise y-you won't get near the fire. Do you hear?"

"But it's part of my home." She slipped her hands from his arm, her face resolute. "I'm going to do what needs to be done to help save things."

"I don't want you getting hurt. Stay away from the fire," he warned again, his tone a little harsher than he'd intended. "I mean it, Ivy."

The challenge laced in her expression settled like a rock in his gut. "I can't just sit by and watch my father's hard work burn to the ground. Not if I can help it."

"Ivy...filling the buckets will be a great help." Nearing the barn, he scanned the area, searching for signs of his able-bodied men. But the scene was eerily still. Not one holler or determined call could be heard.

Except that of the anxious horses whinnying and cattle calling inside as they beat the stalls with their hooves.

When Zach reined in the roan far enough away from the barn to be safe, he catapulted off the conveyance. Once he had Ivy safely on the ground, he turned and raced for the barn.

"Zach," she called after him, struggling to keep up.

He slowed to a jog and looked back at her, his smoldering fear doused some by the care etched into her expression.

"Please..." She pressed her hands to her heart, her cloak slipping from her shoulders. "Be safe."

He nodded once then sped off toward the barn, peering toward the bunkhouse out back. There wasn't one lamp lit to confirm that the men were up and aware—or even in the vicinity. He glanced toward the main house, but it was as dark as the fear hounding his soul.

He was foreman here. What happened on the ranch was something for which he took direct responsibility.

The sizzle and crackle of flames met his ears as he neared the barn. He unlatched the big double doors and was immediately hit by a wall of acrid smoke. Throwing the doors wide open, he entered and made a quick assessment. The fire seemed mostly contained to his office for now, cordoned off by thick wood walls. Smoke poured from beneath the office door into the large corridor. If he didn't move fast, then within minutes this entire place could be one giant glowing torch.

Before he could think about dousing the flames, he had to get the livestock to safety. The cattle had recovered to such a point that he'd even thought about releasing them into the herd tomorrow. His gut clenched, thinking that tomorrow might be too late.

Racing through the structure, the sound of fearful whinnies seized his compassion. Sprinting to the other end of the barn, he threw open the second set of double-wide doors, then went stall by stall, freeing the eight stabled and frantic horses, including one mare, Mr. Harris's favorite, due to foal in the next week or two. The wild and terrified look in their eyes as he swatted them toward safety sent chills straight down his spine.

He found his way through the smoke to the bigger stable area and herded the cattle to safety.

Thoughts of his owl, Buddy, tugged at him. The owl always stayed close to the barn, his home. As enormous as the barn was, if the owl were to get caught in smoke and not be able to find his way out, he didn't stand a chance.

"Buddy," he called once, then several more times as he raced down the corridor, checking each stall to make sure all the livestock had been freed. He struggled to peer through the thick smoke, listening for Buddy's familiar screeching call over the crackle of flames, but heard nothing.

"Watch over Buddy, God," he prayed, coughing when a cloud of smoke hit him square in the face.

Sick at not knowing for sure if his owl was safe, he forged on and continued to pray. The barn was still aflame and every second was one second closer to an out-of-control fire. A movement caught his eye in the tack room next to his office.

Coughing again, he skidded to a halt at the sight of—

"Zach? Is that you?"

He darted to the side. Peered through the haze. "Terrance?"

"I've got the boss. I saw him here on the ground," he said as he heaved Mr. Harris to his shoulder. "Did you get the livestock out?"

Alarm snaked through Zach at the sight of his boss's unconscious form. "Yeah, they're safe. Come on, let's get him out of here."

What if Terrance hadn't seen Mr. Harris there?

The thought pummeled his diminishing confidence as he led the way through the mass of thick dark smoke. He pressed on into the fresh night air, nearly running smack-dab into Ivy.

"What happened?" she cried above the flame's goading crackle.

"It's your father," Zach explained then coughed as he braced a hand on her shoulder, leading her and Terrance a safe distance from the barn.

The smallest whimper came from Ivy as she knelt where Terrance was laying her father on a bed of soft pine needles beneath a towering Ponderosa.

"I was just riding up from the back pasture when I heard the horses and cattle inside causing a stir." Terrance's hands trembled as he yanked off his hat and swiped at his brow. Coughed. His eyes shuttered with apprehension. "I rode as hard as I could. Didn't even know anyone else was here, and then I happened to see your father lying in the tack room."

"Thank God," she breathed, panic breaking in her voice. "Thank God you saw him there." When Ivy's face contorted with raw emotion, Zach bent down beside her and set a hand gently on her shoulder. "Is he going to be all right?" she asked, her eyes begging him for a hopeful response.

"Let's hope so." Zach gave her shoulder a squeeze and stood. "I'm g-going back to try and save the barn."

"I'm right behind you." Terrance shoved his hat on his head and trailed Zach to the growing flames.

"The buckets are all filled," Ivy called after them.

Zach waved to let her know he'd heard as he ate up the distance with long strides. He grabbed one bucket after another right alongside Terrance. They raced back and forth dousing the angry flames. Zach's face and hands seared from the fire's intense heat. He grabbed a thick wool saddle blanket from the tack room and began beating at the flames leaping over the straw-littered ground.

His eyes and throat burned from the concentrated and unrelenting smoke.

With each sputtering sizzle of the dying flames, he thanked God that Terrance had shown up.

And he prayed. Prayed that Mr. Harris would be all right.

When he abandoned the blanket and went after more water to douse the flames licking up the walls toward the ceiling, he found Ivy at the pump again.

"You're doing great," he offered on a panting burning breath. "We're definitely m-making headway."

"Really?" She pumped a little faster.

"Just keep it up." Heaving the three-gallon bucket she'd just filled, he rounded the barn and strategically doused another spot.

He and Terrance carried one bucket of water after another after another into the heart of the fire. When finally the flames had been quenched and every last glowing hot spot whispered a mere trickle of smoke, Terrance shuffled outside while Zach lit a lantern and surveyed the damage.

His office and its contents were a total loss. The tack room next door had sustained enough smoke damage that they'd be making a heavy investment in new equipment. The rest of the barn would take hours of hard work to clean, but they'd been fortunate it hadn't been worse.

Spotting one of Buddy's feathers on the ground near the barn doors, Zach reached down to pick it up. He closed his eyes, sick at the thought that Buddy had died. "Buddy," he called softly, longing to hear the owl's sweet screeching call in return.

Nothing.

On a heavy sigh, he turned and began searching for clues as to what had started the fire, the weight of responsibility hovering over his hard-won confidence. When his gaze landed on a broken and charred lantern lying on the ground just inside his office, instant dread tightened around his stomach. He was sure he'd turned out the lantern when he'd left earlier this evening.

But what if he'd forgotten?

Overwhelmed, Zach forced one foot in front of the other to where Mr. Harris still lay beneath the tree with Terrance resting against the trunk and Ivy at her father's side. He dropped to his knees beside her, fighting for a full breath of the crisp night air, and for a full measure of thanksgiving that they were all safe.

But if Terrance had not noticed Mr. Harris's silent form lying in the tack room, the man might not have made it. Guilt's enormous weight and shame would've burdened Zach for the rest of his days.

"How is he?" he asked, the three words scraping over his throat.

"He's resting." She sniffed then peered up at him, her expression a heartbreaking display of tender vulnerability. "We need to get Ben, Zach. Something must be terribly wrong with him because he still hasn't come to."

"Of course. I'll go right away." As he made to push his weary body up to standing, she reached out and stopped him.

"Zach, are you all right?" Ivy whispered her warm breath fanning into the cool October night.

"I'm fine." He struggled to drag himself beyond failure's taunting flames, but they were there, singeing his confidence. He was foreman here. What transpired on this ranch was a direct reflection on him and his ability to handle things.

"Thank you for what you did." She lifted a corner of her cloak and gently wiped his face. Her touch and care made his knees that much more weak. "You were very brave."

Ivy turned toward Terrance, his eyes a blank stare. "Uncle Terrance…"

He blinked hard.

"Thank you so much for saving my father," she measured out.

"Ivy, let me tell you something," he began, his focus now fixed on his unconscious brother-in-law. "You could've been killed here tonight." He gave a harsh cough.

She swung a questioning glance at Zach as though looking for some kind of answer.

But what did he have to tell her? Even though he couldn't imagine leaving a lantern burning, that had very likely been the cause of the fire. A foolish oversight that could have cost Mr. Harris his life, not to mention the barn, along with the cattle and the prized horses purchased with a hefty price from Callen Lockhart's prime brood.

And if Ivy hadn't gone with him to Joseph's home, who knows what could have happened.

"You really should think about going back east," Terrance said.

Ivy swept her confused gaze back to her uncle. "I can't leave my father when his health is so bad, Uncle Terrance," she reasoned on a ragged whisper. Her moist gaze dropped to her father. "Especially after tonight. He must've been so ill that he lost consciousness in there. Think of what would've happened if he hadn't been found." She looked over at her uncle. "If you hadn't come along, Uncle Terrance. And Zach," she added.

"You need to give this some serious thought, sweets." Moving over to Ivy, Terrance braced a hand on her shoulder. "You know what your mama wanted for you. She'd be sick knowing that you could've been killed here tonight. With the scent of fear and smoke filling the area, why, she's probably struggling to dig out of her grave right now."

Ivy's expression filled with confusion and hurt.

"Terrance," Zach warned, sending an admonishing look the man's way. Even if Terrance was family, he didn't have the right to lecture her when she was clearly upset about her father.

"I've got her best at heart, Drake," Terrance growled, then drove his point home once more. "Do right by your mama, sweets, and leave."

Chapter Ten

Ivy's eyes stung from total exhaustion, and from the tears she'd held in check. It was well past midnight, and the entire time Ben had been here checking on her father, her emotions had ricocheted all over her soul. Now, while she sat at her father's bedside, watching his slow even breaths, all she could seem to do was pray.

For God to mend her relationship with her father, and for God to mend his body.

A deep resounding chord had been struck in her soul. Was the past repeating itself? For three years she'd prayed that her mama would be healed, and her mama's health had only gotten worse. Her father had searched high and low for a doctor who could help, but they'd all said the same thing...*there was nothing they could do.*

Her father had grown more and more distant in his desperate search. Now, she felt the same motivation to help him.

"How's he doing?" Zach's voice filtered into her thoughts as he entered the bedroom.

She felt undeniably moved by the fact that he was here with her when she felt so very alone. "Ben said that he'll be all right in a few days—at least as far as the smoke exposure goes." Glancing at her father, sorrow plagued her heart. "But beyond that, he's sick, Zach. Very sick. And Ben doesn't seem to know what is wrong with him."

Like a whispered prayer, Zach's hushed sigh settled in the room. "I'm sorry, Ivy. I wish there was ssssomething I could do."

She could think of several things, none of which she cared to share with him. She longed for the comfort of his strong arms. And for the strength of his touch. But she was in this alone. He couldn't possibly undo years of hurt. He couldn't possibly unravel her layers of guilt and shame. She wasn't sure anyone could tackle such a feat.

She hugged her arms to her chest. "I don't know why he was out there if he wasn't feeling well. Do you think he was going to try and come to the dinner celebration?"

"Maybe. I g-g-guess you'll have to ask him."

Violet padded into the room and smoothed a hand over Ivy's shoulder. "I'll watch over him now, dear. You go. You've had a horrible night." Featherlight, she touched her fingertips to Ivy's father's cheek then adjusted the cool cloth at his forehead.

The whisper of a *knowing* smile Zach shared with Ivy in that moment gave her a small measure of joy. The very second Violet had returned from the party and discovered what had happened, she'd launched into a flurry of activity, giving Ivy's father exceptionally tender care. Ivy would like nothing better than to see her father love again. And she could not think of another woman better suited for her father than Violet.

Her eyes glistening in the dim lantern's glow, Violet peered over at Zach. "Take Ivy out of here, Zach, and make her a cup of tea, will you? You know where to find things, right?"

"I sure do." He set a hand at Ivy's back as she stood.

A protest was right on the tip of her tongue, but for some reason she just didn't have it in her to argue. Besides, his care and concern and his warm strong touch at her back felt so very good.

She'd spent six years being strong. She'd likely spend many more doing the same, but she couldn't help but indulge herself in the warmly satisfying sensitivity in this man's touch.

When Violet wrapped Ivy in a quick hug, it nearly pushed her emotionally raw state, teetering on control's precarious ridge, right over the edge. "You're so good to my father, Violet. Thank you."

"You sure are," Zach added as he slid Ivy a private wink.

"Well, he's good to me." Violet pulled her mouth tight as though to keep from crying. "Now, you go relax, Ivy, before I have to see to you myself."

Ivy turned and walked with Zach downstairs and into the generous living area. She'd always loved this spacious room with its cushiony comfortable furniture, rough-hewn woodwork and large stone fireplace that flanked one entire wall.

"Sit here." Zach gently eased her into the overstuffed leather chair. "I'll g-go and make you that tea."

"You really don't need to, Zach." She diverted her focus to the torn hem of her skirt. "I'm absolutely fine."

"Do *you* want to cross Violet? B-B-Because I sure don't." He snagged her gaze and gave her a certifiable cowboy kind of wink on his way out of the room that sent a shiver of delight cascading through her.

Zach had a way of making her feel like she was the most important person in the whole world—even though he did seem to be uncomfortable around her, at times, anyway. And he had a way of making her feel like maybe everything was going to be all right.

Even when she wasn't so sure that it would.

Ben had said that her father's health had definitely grown worse since last he'd been summoned to see Mr. Harris, almost three weeks ago.

And what of Zach? Would he be all right?

He'd risked his life to save her father's prized horse stock, cattle and the barn. Then he'd gone to fetch Ben. He had to be ready to drop from sheer exhaustion. The concern and distress she'd witnessed in his gaze after the fire had taken her aback. And the protective way he'd jumped to her defense when Uncle Terrance had pressed his opinion a little too deeply…that had made her feel wonderfully cared for.

It'd taken several minutes to get her bearings about her as she watched him head to town for his brother.

But when Hugh had stumbled back to the ranch a little bit ago, her heady feeling had been yanked down to earth. She'd been unable to miss the accusations he'd thrown at Zach. While Ben was checking her father over, she'd been sitting on the porch when Hugh's menacing tirade pierced the night air. The stinging, albeit slurred, accusations he'd speared through Zach had jarred her thoughts. Hugh had blamed Zach for the fire. Saying Zach was incompetent. Inexperienced. Too prideful to know when he was stepping out of his element.

Closing her eyes, she sighed and sank a little deeper in the chair, wishing she could know the truth of things. Wondering who she could trust. And what trust looked like.

Love…
Belief…
Faith…

Like a gentle calling wind, the words had whispered, unbidden, into her mind then settled into her heart. The smallest sense of hope swirled and swayed like a feather carried on the breeze.

She pressed a hand to her chest, feeling an odd yet calming weight there. And a tangible, if not fleeting, peace she hadn't felt for a very long time as she gathered her courage and prayed.

Sensing a strong presence beside her, she opened her eyes and found Zach standing there, staring down at her with the most endearing and kind expression on his face.

"Tired?" He handed her a steaming cup of tea.

"A little," she uttered, transfixed by his intense gaze. "Actually, I was just praying."

"A good idea." Dragging an ottoman over, he sat down in front of her.

"I haven't done that much over the years," she confessed.

"I wondered."

"You did?" Could he really be so attentive to catch on to such things?

"At the p-p-party, when Katie mentioned praying, I couldn't help but notice how you grew all t-tense." The fatigued slump of his shoulders pricked her instant concern.

So honorable, he'd forged on after the past few hours. In the room's dim golden glow she could see that smudges of smoke and ash still marred his skin and clothes, and yet here he was, wholly attentive and caring about her soul. "After all you've done tonight...*I* should be the one serving *you*."

"I'll be f-fine. You, on the other hand, have had a very rough night." He draped his forearms on his thighs and rested his weary gaze on hers. "Like V-V-Violet said."

She cupped the fine bone china in her hands and sipped the steaming tea, the soothing flavor satisfying her dry mouth. After all of her furious water pumping, every muscle in her arms, neck and shoulders protested. "What happened out there? Do you know?"

His intriguing blue eyes gazed at the floor. "I'm not sure yet, but I think I may have spotted the cause of the f-f-fire. Once daylight breaks Brodie is c-c-coming out to help me inspect things."

"I heard Hugh say—"

"Hugh needs to ssssleep off his liquor and t-try for a more civilized tone." He fisted his hands between his knees.

Confused, Ivy sat a little straighter. She wanted answers. "What does he mean by saying that you're *incompetent?*"

"Hugh is a thorn in my flesh." He raked a hand through his tousled hair. "You'd d-d-do well to avoid him."

"He's a friend, Zach," she reasoned.

"Not much of one." Pushing himself up, he stalked over to the large stone fireplace where confined orange flames flickered. When he grabbed the poker and adjusted the logs, a spray of sparks shot up the chimney in a harmless threat.

She couldn't help but wonder why the two men couldn't seem to see eye to eye. It really wasn't any business of hers, except for the small fact that Hugh had dragged her father's holdings into question with his accusations.

"Why does he mistrust you? Is there a reason he should?" she asked, believing that openness and honesty was the best policy.

Every muscle in his body tensed as he stood facing the fire. "What do you think, Ivy?"

Exasperated, she gave a sharp exhale. "*Why* is it that you always do that?"

"Do what?" he asked, pivoting toward her as she set down the china cup on the end table.

She nailed him with a frustrated look. "Respond to a question with a question?"

He shrugged. "Why d-d-do you do *that?*"

"*See!* There you go again," she accused, throwing up her hands in the air. *"You're infuriating, Zachariah Henry Drake."*

He eyed her, his brows raised over his sparking blue eyes. "And you, *Miss Ivy Grace Harris,* are nosy." Reaching back, he rested a hand on the mantle and stared at his boots. "Listen...I'm doing the b-b-best I can here."

"Then can you tell me why he would think you were responsible for the fire?" She tucked her feet beneath her as she tried to come up with one instance that might support Hugh's claims of incompetence. "I mean, in the nearly three weeks I've been here, I haven't seen you do one thing that could be interpreted as careless. You work as hard as anyone I've ever seen—even my father."

"You've been mmmmonitoring me?" he half accused.

"I've been keeping an eye on my father's holdings," she reasoned. "Even if he doesn't seem to want me around, while he's sick it's the least I can do."

The weighted silence that stretched between them undermined that small bit of peace that had touched her minutes ago.

"I'm sorry I'm being so defensive." He shuffled over toward her, each weary step challenging her insistence to press him for information. "And I honestly d-d-don't know what to make of Hugh. God knows I've t-tried to get on with him." He leveled his focus at her. "I guess you're going to have to trust one of us."

"Yeah," she agreed, those words…*love, faith* and *belief* whispering through her thoughts again.

Zach eased down to the ottoman. "Ivy, what happened between you and your f-father?"

Feeling suddenly very vulnerable, she fingered the row of brass nails tacked onto the rounded chair arms. "It's nothing."

"It's sssomething. And I want to help, if I can." Resting his forearms on his knees, he leaned toward her. "What created such a wedge b-b-between the two of you?"

She avoided his gaze. "It's more than I want to talk about."

"It's apparently more than you sh-should carry," he said, touching her fingers for a brief moment. "Alone, anyway."

"You're one to talk," she shot back, clinging to some measure of control even as it seemed to slip between her hands. "I asked you about your stuttering tonight and you shut yourself off as firm as a slamming door."

He turned his face away. "It's a ssssore spot for me, all right?"

"Well this is a sore spot for me." She smoothed a hand over her dirty skirt.

When he snagged her attention and held it so very, very gently, she could have sworn the chair beneath her swayed on rockers. "Please, let me help."

She opened her mouth to protest, but nothing came out.

"I care," he added, swallowing hard. "About you. About y-your father…."

His tenderness reached down into the deepest, darkest part of her heart, touching the gaping wound.

"I'll say this much…if he'd died tonight—" Her voice broke on a muffled and a *very unexpected sob*. Yanking away her focus, she scrambled for composure as another sob threatened at the back of her throat. Her chest grew tight. Her eyes burned. Cradling her face in her hands, she willed herself to stay strong. "If he'd died tonight, I don't know what I would've done. It would've broken my heart to lose him with so much unresolved." She faced Zach again. "The chasm between us is so wide and so deep that I sometimes wonder if it's too much to overcome."

He leaned a little closer. "Nothing is t-t-too much to overcome, Ivy. You have to believe that."

"I want to."

Was this one of those times when she had to ignore the things she saw around her and just believe?

"Believe me, then." He reached out and took her hands.

He'd been so tender, caring enough to walk with her in facing her fears. He'd gently introduced her to his owl, earnest to help her overcome her fear. At the thought of his feathered friend, living out in the barn, her stomach pulled up taut.

"Buddy…was he in the barn?" She searched his eyes, finding an instant veil of hurt there. "Did you find him?"

Zach sighed. "N-Not yet."

"Oh, Zach…I'm so sorry," she said, holding his hands in hers and swallowing hard. She'd never, in a million years, have dreamed that she'd get choked up by a bird. "I know how much you care for him. He really is sweet," she admitted, sniffing.

She was sure his eyes misted over just then as he looked at their joined hands. "Thank you for th-thinking of him."

When she lowered her focus, she gasped. "Oh, Zach, your hands…they're burned."

"They're fine." He tugged them away.

"How can you say that? They're blistered." Trembling, she reached for his hands again and peered at his skin, blazing all red and angry. He'd sacrificed his own comfort to save her father's barn, and now he was denying himself for her. "Did you have Ben look at them when he was here?"

"No. I ssssaid, I'm fine."

Determined to help, she popped up from the chair and pinned him with a resolute look. "Stay there. I'll be right back."

Before he could voice another protest she whisked out of the room, returning in short order with two clean towels, a small pan of water and the box of medicinal supplies Violet kept stocked. Setting things on the end table, she sat down again. "Give me your hands, cowboy," she teased in an effort to lighten his subdued mood.

He gave his head a resolute shake. "I can see to them later."

"Goodness, Zach! Would you let someone help you once in a while?" she scolded with more boldness than she'd intended. Unwilling to take no for an answer, she spread one towel over her knees then dipped the other towel in the pan of water. "Please. Let me see?" Patting the dry towel, she motioned him to give his hands over.

On a defeated sigh, he slid his large burnt hands forward and perched them on the towel.

While she examined the blisters, unshed tears once again burned the backs of her eyes. "These look horrible, Zach, and you haven't complained. Not even once."

"Tough as iron," he dismissed with a pulse-skittering smile.

She was shaken at the steady strength etched into his face. "And your face…" she breathed, noticing for the first time the way his skin seemed all tight and red beneath the smudges of soot. With the gentleness of a butterfly's wing, she drew the wet cloth over his forehead and over the distinctly masculine planes of his face and his slightly crooked nose.

"What happened to your nose?" she asked, intrigued by every single little nuance about this man.

He swallowed hard, his concentrated gaze flitting for a second to her mouth. "A fight."

"Long ago?" She trailed the cloth across his upper lip then to the right side of his face.

He watched her hand from the corners of his eyes. "Not that long ago. I was about n-nineteen."

"What happened?" she urged, barely finding her voice as she continued her ministrations. The heady awareness bubbling up inside her was a new sensation.

She really must be beyond the point of exhaustion.

"Two fellas were over their heads, soused in liquor," he explained, his gaze locked on her every move. "They were mistreating a woman in a back alley. I sssstopped them," he said as though he'd saved a mouse from drowning, not a woman from God-knew-what.

"What did you do?"

"I fought them, providing a long enough distraction for her to escape. In the midst of it all, they were pretty amused by my ssss—"

"Your stutter?" she finished for him, her heart heavy.

When he said nothing, she scolded herself for finishing his sentence, and determined *never* to do that again. Knowing how proud and self-sufficient this man was, it was highly unlikely that he appreciated that kind of goodwill.

"Yes. My stutter."

She could only imagine how humiliating that must've been for him. How humiliating it must've been all those years growing up when he'd been teased.

And on an occasion or two, she'd been among the teasers.

"Oh, Zach that must have been terrible." The very idea that she'd caused him grief slapped her with fresh stinging guilt. Her throat grew thick with emotion. She sniffed, struggling to get control, but regret just kept cascading over her in relentless forceful waves.

"Darlin'? What's wrong?" Grasping her knees, he dipped his head.

Sniffing again, she patted the wet cloth she'd smoothed over his face to her eyes, knowing that if she looked his way, she just might fall apart. "I—I feel so bad."

"Well d-d-don't, all right?" Pulling his hands back, he clasped them between his knees. "I may have taken a p-p-punch or two, but you should've seen them," he honestly boasted, apparently not understanding just *how badly* she really felt. His reflective gaze drifted to hers as she continued to cleanse his face. "Really, I have them to thank."

"For what?" Her focus was helplessly drawn to his firm mouth, where the most heart-stopping grins would form.

"That was the last sssstraw that shoved me toward overcoming this thing."

Her breath caught. "Except with me," she whispered, tracing a quivering fingertip down the length of his nose—perfect as far as she was concerned.

His eyes grew intense and dark.

Did he feel it, too, the draw between them?

But how could this be? She was going back to New York. Back to a life where she'd been a strong fortress, and where she'd often comforted herself with the fact that being alone wasn't all that bad. Not when loving hurt so very much.

Did he feel it, too? She had to know.

His eyes shuttered then. His chest rose and fell with every shallow breath. His lips parted. He stilled her hand against his face, his trembling sensitive touch blanketing her heart with promise.

The warm fire blazing in the hearth sizzled and popped, and for a moment, a very wonderful, a very raw and vulnerable moment, she felt free and whole and—and loved.

Zach ached to wrap his arms around Ivy. He held her gaze. Held her hand against his face. Her touch, and the tenderness in her concern, had caught him completely off guard.

Until now he'd felt like he'd done a fair job at holding his emotions at bay, but in the last few crucial, out-of-control moments, he'd as much as given himself up.

Where could he go from here?

There was no denying the sparking attraction between them. Surely she felt it every bit as much.

But there wasn't a thing he could do—or *would* do—to act on it.

Even if he managed to climb above whatever it was about her that provoked his stutter, he could never stomach a woman who didn't believe in him.

Especially when he sometimes wondered if he believed in himself.

Lowering her trembling hand from his face, he gathered in a steadying sobering breath. He slowly stood, desperately scrambling to reinforce the wall around his heart she'd just scaled.

Chapter Eleven

The next few days dragged by, but not a single minute had slipped past Zach where his thoughts hadn't drifted to Ivy.

Drifted?

More like raced. Headlong.

He'd tried to scrub any thought of her from his mind, just like he was scrubbing any hint of the fire from the barn walls. Hunkering down, he tackled the last section of wall in the tack room as he reasoned that it was *definitely* for the best that he hadn't seen Ivy for the past three days. He'd had to put aside his promise to help reacquaint Ivy with the ranch since he'd been working from before the sun rose until way after dark cleaning and repairing the barn along with all the other daily chores.

Brodie had confirmed that the fire had most likely started from the lantern. *How* was the pressing question.

After giving it some thought, Zach was absolutely positive he'd not left the lantern burning, and Mr. Harris had no recollection of what had happened that night. He didn't remember going out to the barn. Or if he'd been carrying a lantern. Or if he'd gotten sick and lost consciousness.

As much as Mr. Harris protested being down since

then, Zach was pretty sure he had no choice. Ben was insistent. Violet was insistent. And from Mr. Harris's gaunt look, it was for his best. Zach had assured his boss that he'd take care of things, and that all was well.

Was all well? With the cattle getting sick and then the fire, Zach had to wonder if he could honestly make such a promise. The ill cattle not only made it through the fire, but they were now the picture of health, and he'd personally seen to repairing and cleaning every damaged nook and cranny of the barn. He'd done his best to do right by Mr. Harris. But was his best enough?

The very bright spot he'd stumbled upon today was discovering that Buddy was safe. Early this morning when Zach had gone out to the barn, his heart had skidded to a halt at Buddy's familiar call. Just as soon as Buddy heard Zach calling back, the owl flew in that silent graceful way of his, landing on Zach's shoulder and giving him a peck on the cheek.

Gratefulness had flooded Zach's soul as he'd greeted his friend. Emotion had clogged his throat as he'd silently thanked God for keeping Buddy safe.

Just then Hugh sauntered around the corner and peered into the tack room where Zach was scrubbing. "Thought you might want to know...the fence has been cut," Hugh dished out as though he delighted in delivering the unpleasant news.

"Cut?" Weighed down by instant dread, he pushed himself up to standing and crossed to Hugh. "Where? What fence?"

"In the north pasture." He wiped a finger along the thick wood beam Zach had scoured earlier. "You missed a spot, Drake."

The beam could not have been cleaner, and Hugh knew it. Zach took a long slow breath, determined not to allow

Hugh's evasive description and pricking comments to un- ravel his thin patience. "*Where* in the north pasture?"

Hugh leaned a bony shoulder against the beam. "Near the trail leading down to Gulp's Canyon. They cut clean through the barbed wire like it was butter," he announced, making a snipping gesture with his right hand.

Zach bit off a ready curse and set his back teeth. With far more calm than he felt, he picked up the scrub brush and bucket and walked to the barn entrance. He wiped his hands on an old towel and shrugged into his sheep- skin coat. "So, did you fix it yet?"

"No." Hugh snorted as though Zach had asked if he'd fixed every fence from here to California's coast. "How do you expect me to do that when I don't have the right tools?"

"You could've wrangled up branches or something to plug the hole so that the cattle don't file on through." Stepping outside, he dumped out the water to the side then set the bucket on a shelf. "If they wander off, we may never get them back."

Hugh rolled his eyes. "They were nowhere near the break."

Unwilling to spar with Hugh, Zach held his tongue. As argumentative as the man had been in the past few weeks—especially since the fire—he'd probably say any- thing just to hold a position opposite Zach. "Did you spot any hide on the barbs?"

"Didn't look close enough," Hugh spat, standing back and monitoring Zach.

After a tense pause Zach turned and stalked back into the supply room, returning with a small roll of barb wire and two hand tools. He untied his mare from the hitch- ing post and opened the thick leather saddlebag to load the items inside.

"So...what are you doing?" Hugh asked.

Closing his eyes, Zach grappled for any amount of patience he could find. "I'm going to fix the break before it gets too dark. And before we lose any cattle—"

Just then he caught sight of Ivy jogging toward them from the house. "Hi there," she called, her sweet voice whispering over his senses. "What are you two doing?"

Zach glanced at her for a brief moment, his heart doing an unwelcome flip-flop. Turning, he took great pains to fasten his saddlebag.

"Well, Zach here is taking care of *another* incident. Seems like there's just one after another after another." Hugh eyed Zach in a clear I-told-you-so fashion. He crossed to meet Ivy, the instant pleasure beaming from his long face pricking Zach's unease. "Hi there, Ivy."

"Hi, Hugh," she responded with a weak smile. "So what's the matter, Zach?"

Forcing away his agitation, Zach met her questioning gaze. He wasn't about to let Hugh's jabs affect him, and he wasn't about to allow Ivy's presence to unsettle him, either. He had a ranch to run. "I'm on my way to fix f-f-fence," he said, cringing at the sudden jarring sound of his words. "And to make sure n-n-none of the c-cattle are gone."

"Gone?" she echoed.

"Part of the fence line has been c-c-cut," he forced out.

"*What* did you say?" Perching his hands at his waist, Hugh inclined his head toward Zach.

From the mocking sneer tempting the man's mouth, Zach was sure that Hugh was probably glorying in Zach's awkward stutter almost as much as Zach was embarrassed by it. So far, he'd managed to avoid situations where both Ivy and Hugh were in the same place, except shortly after she'd arrived. And then he'd not said a word.

But having Hugh standing here, listening as Zach stuttered, pierced like a jagged arrowhead straight through his chest.

Taking a deep breath, he willed his neck and face muscles to relax. "I said…p-p-part of the fence line has b-been cut."

Hugh nailed Zach with a triumphant smirk. "Stuttering all of a sudden?"

Zach ran a hand down his mare's thick neck, trying to calm himself with the feel of the steady and restrained power of this creature.

"I don't think I've heard you stutter since what…four or five years ago?" Hugh jabbed.

Gathering a small bit of control, Zach shut his bag and tightened the saddle strap. "Two."

"Hmmm." Hugh heaved himself up and sat on the hitching post. "You're not buckling under the weight of things here, are you?"

Zach swung up into the saddle, reined his horse in a sharp circle and stared down at Hugh. "The stalls need to be mmmucked. After that, I'm sure you c-can find *something* to keep yourself busy."

"I'm going with you," Ivy announced.

He felt oddly cornered by these two. "If someone's after our cattle then it's not safe out there, Ivy."

She whisked over to him, her taffeta skirt swishing with each determined step. "Perhaps I should bring my smelling salts," she retorted indignantly, her full lips forming a tight line. "In case I succumb to the vapors."

Zach heaved a sigh. "That's n-not what I—"

"Pull that foot out of your mouth, Drake, and maybe you'll speak a little better," Hugh said with a snort.

"Hugh," Ivy chided, only furthering Zach's growing frustration.

He sure as shootin' didn't need Ivy coming to his rescue. Not now. Not ever.

"If someone *is* after our cattle, then I need to see what's going on, Zach," she reasoned, smoothing a hand down his mare's neck. "I'll manage just fine."

"It's m-m-my responsibility to t-take care of it. I can do this just ffffine on my own."

Hugh jumped down from the hitching post and came to stand beside her. "Don't you know…he has something to prove."

"This really isn't something you c-c-can help with, Ivy," Zach explained, trying to sidestep Hugh's taunts. "But th-th-thanks for the offer."

She peered up at him, her gaze weighted with an odd desperation. "But I want to make sure things are being taken care of."

"They are. Trust me."

"I'm saddling my mare." When she turned and ran into the barn, Zach dismounted to go after her.

"I'd say you're getting in a little too deep, Drake," Hugh spurred, positioning himself in front of Zach. "Seems to me that when you've got the boss's daughter breathin' down your neck to make sure you do things right, that ain't a good sign." Snatching his hat from his head, he tapped it into some semblance of form. "Course, any *living* man would gladly have a woman like Ivy breathin' down their necks. Right, Drake?" A curling sneer tipped his paper-thin lips.

Zach grabbed Hugh by the collar. He fixed a sharp unrelenting stare on Hugh, struggling to tamp down the frustration, circling just below the surface. "If I hear you talk like that again I'll—"

"You'll what? *Fire me?*" Hugh mocked, his mouth

twitching. "I do believe that's Mr. Harris's call, not yours."

True. Mr. Harris had the final say, but if Zach made any recommendations, they would be taken very seriously. But were Zach's concerns based on years-old bitterness? Vengeance for the decade of teasing and tormenting?

If he made any suggestions, they had to be based *solely* on the here and now, or Zach would never be able to stomach himself.

"You *will* watch your tongue," he warned tightening his grip. "And your step."

Letting Hugh loose, he turned and stalked into the barn, fuming from the interchange. The man knew just what triggers to pull that would undermine Zach's control. Ever since Ivy had returned, Hugh had seemed determined to trip up Zach at every turn.

Shoving the frustration aside, Zach found Ivy in the cleaned and repaired tack room, struggling to wrestle down a new saddle. He grabbed the gear and lifted it from the board.

"I could've done that," she challenged.

He could've disputed her claim, but he didn't have it in him to wound her stubborn pride.

She was so resolved. Headstrong. Determined. And set on proving herself.

He could well appreciate an adventurous and spritely woman. But in his book, gallantry should be a man's guiding force, and when it came to this little lady, he couldn't help himself—he was just doing what came natural.

"I can saddle a horse, you know," she argued again, lugging a saddle blanket from the shelf. She scurried to keep up as he carried the saddle to the waiting mare, then she made an unsuccessful attempt at heaving the saddle blanket over the horse's back.

He took it from her. "Let me help."

From the corner of his vision, he could see her pulling up her chin a notch. She looked nowhere near ready to head out on the range on this chilly afternoon.

"If you insist on g-going, aren't you going to need to change?"

The fancy New York fashions she'd brought back with her touted streamlined skirts with far less flounce and flourish than you usually saw in Boulder. Skirts that would burst a seam if she were to straddle her mount.

"I'll be fine." She tugged at her jacket as her worried gaze darted from her skirt to the saddle.

He eyed her chestnut-colored skirt and matching jacket edged with black velvet cording, trying to ignore the innate awareness he felt as he took in the natural beauty she emanated. The truth was...she could be dressed in the crudest garment, and he'd still be taken aback at the sight of her.

"Oh...all right," she conceded, holding herself erect. "I'll be back in no time. Don't leave without me."

"I won't," he agreed, wondering what would possess him to make such an assertion.

Leading her horse out to wait beside his, he had to tamp down his instant and growing apprehension. The range was no place for a woman when there were cattle rustlers in the area. He'd have to stick close to her to make sure she stayed safe.

When Ivy returned ten minutes later in a dark blue split skirt for riding, and a matching cropped jacket with no more substance than a flimsy shawl, he had to hold his appalled expression in check. She looked more like she was heading out to England's lush green pastures for a leisurely summer jaunt than to Colorado's rough and tumble ranges to repair fence.

"Ready." She stood on tiptoe and grabbed the saddle horn. Struggled to stick a daintily booted foot in the stirrup. After several failed, albeit gracefully dogged attempts, Zach circled his hands around her waist and lifted her effortlessly into the saddle.

He couldn't miss the small gasp that passed through her rosy lips. Or the way her faltering glance fell over him, featherlight. Or the way her hands trembled as she fiddled with her skirt then clutched the saddle horn.

"When's the last t-time you rode?" he asked, mounting his horse.

"It's been a while." The uncertainty in her gaze whispered otherwise.

"Well, stay close then, and let me know if you need me to sssslow down."

"I will be *just fine,* Zach," she assured, tension bunching her shoulders. "I grew up here, remember?"

He remembered. He just wasn't so sure that she recalled the nuances of riding. The awkward way she pitched back in the saddle was his first clue. And the white-knuckled grip she had on the reins was another.

In spite of the sun dipping down in the western sky, he kept his mount to a fast trot and headed toward the north pasture. After a hundred yards or so, he glanced over to see her struggling to keep the horse from veering to the left.

"Ease up on the reins," he instructed. He slowed his horse and sidled up beside her. Reaching out, he grasped her left hand and urged her to release her death grip. "You're pulling too hard t-t-to the left. The mare's just doing what you're telling her to."

"Oh, right." Her face puckered in concentration.

"Sorry, I forgot. I guess I'm a little more out of practice than I thought." She flashed him an anxious look.

Reaching over, he set a hand on her arm. "Don't worry about it. You'll catch on f-f-fast enough."

Zach kept an eye on her as they forged on. "That's it. You're doing a fine job," he encouraged.

"If I remember right, we don't have too much farther to go."

At this slow rate, he'd be mending fence in the dark. "We'll get there soon enough."

Worry etched her brow as she peered at the western skyline. "Is it going to be light enough for us to work?"

He had to grin at the way she'd included herself in the endeavor. "We'll be all right."

"Let's go a little faster. Can we?" She glanced at him, her ivory skin shimmering in the golden light.

"Are you up to it?"

She nodded then urged her mare into a gallop over the hard-packed earth.

Smiling at her resilience and courage, he caught up to her. The tempting way her riotous auburn waves danced just above her waistline, and the invigorating look of fresh delight on her face arrested his complete attention.

Shoving his focus to the expanse stretching before him, he reminded himself that he had no business nurturing any desire residing in his heart for Ivy.

The distance passed by, and with it, day's promising light. When a distinct chill settled over the range, Zach's concern for Ivy grew. She'd never stay warm enough.

"Are you cold?" he asked as they reached the general area Hugh had reported. He scanned up and down the fence line, searching for the breach.

"Not at all." Her hands were already ghostly white and her lips were bordering on blue.

Moving down the line, he inspected the fence, eager to make the repairs so that he could get Ivy back home where it was warm. "There's where the wire's been cut," he said, pointing toward the gaping hole, thirty feet away. Leading his mare to the breech, he dismounted and unfastened the saddlebag as he glanced at Ivy. "It's going to take me a while to mmmmmend this. Are you sure you're going to be all right?"

"Would you stop worrying about me?" she insisted. Before she knew what was happening, he had his hands around her waist and was helping her down.

His strong and settling and *strongly unsettling* touch sent her thoughts spinning fast and out of control straight to a church altar. That alone should be enough to shake her back to reality, but for some reason, she couldn't seem to get there.

"Just stay here with the horses." He swept his gaze toward Gulp's Canyon, visibly concerned at the prospect of the cattle wandering down that way.

She hugged her arms to her chest. Now that she was here, she wanted to help. "I didn't come all this way just to pick wildflowers while you worked."

He gave a short chuckle as he glanced around. "Well that's good, b-b-because there isn't a wildflower to be seen this time of year," he teased, gathering his supplies in his arms. "Come on, then." He motioned her to where he'd hunkered down at the fence.

She did an awkward leap over a generous pile of cow dung, nearly losing her footing and stumbling into him. "Do you think any cattle have escaped?" she breathed, thankful he didn't have eyes in the back of his head.

"It doesn't look like it." He surveyed the cut lines of

barbed wire. "More than likely there'd be fur or hide s-snagged on the barbs if that were the case."

"Just tell me what to do," she instructed, perching her hands on her hips.

"Hold on…I've got to make sssense of this mess first." Stepping through the snarled breach, he tugged each of the three lines from the tangle of wire. "If you could give me the hand shovel I laid over th-there."

She passed it to him. "Do you want me to look for a thick branch to use for a post?" She peered nervously at the low-slung cluster of trees nearby. Where there were trees there were birds. And where there were birds, Ivy would rather not be. But she was determined to help Zach.

"I can get one," he offered, studying her with his ever observant gaze.

She scrambled to fend off her fear. "No. I'll do it."

"Are you sure?"

"Zach, I said I'd do it."

Gathering her courage, she set her shoulders and marched that direction. Each step seemed to wrench from within her a very real and raw fear. "This is silly," she whispered to herself as a branch cracked beneath her foot. When a low limb snagged her hair, she clamped a hand over a stifled gasp.

She listened for chattering or cackling or chirping, but any sound she heard seemed distant—thankfully. That didn't mean the feathered *friends,* as Zach would refer to them, weren't lying in wait.

"Ivy…" Zach startled her nearly out of her skin. He grasped her arms as though to steady her. "Are you all right?"

"Yes." She winced at the squeaky sound in that one syllable.

"You're going to be all right. They won't hurt you." He

glanced up at the dark and looming branches where God only knew *how many* birds called home. "In fact, they're probably nesting with the sun going down."

"They are?" she asked, struggling not to shudder. But it was no use. Her fear was so real and so raw that she couldn't seem to control her shaking. *And* she was cold.

He was right. She was no more prepared to traipse out here with him than she was to go on some African safari.

Zach shrugged out of his coat. "Come here, darlin'."

She loved it when he called her that…*darlin'*…even though she knew the term likely slipped from his cowboy-tongue like the words *lasso* and *cattle* and *Stetson*. Regardless, she tugged the endearing term about her even as he wrapped his warm coat around her shoulders.

"You'll get cold," she lamely protested, frustrated with her lack of preparedness. Grateful for his noble gesture.

"No chance." He tugged it together at the front, his gaze darkening for the briefest second, just like it had that night outside his brother's house.

"There has to be more to this than a harmless mmmama bird attacking you, darlin'," he said, his genuine care and concern like a warm embrace. "Tell me… what happened?"

She'd never spoken about this with anyone.

Not Violet.

Not her friends in New York.

Certainly not Neal—conversations with him could barely constitute as *surface*.

Strong…that's what she'd been. Strong and hard. But the harder her heart had become, the more she disliked herself.

"Do you *really* want to know?" she asked, bracing herself for him to grumble about the fence needing to be fixed. After all, Hugh had as much as painted Zach as some high-strung, work-hardened boss who didn't know how to have a little fun.

But he did know how to relax, right? He'd set up that beautiful birthday celebration for her.

"Why do you always assume that I d-don't care?" Picking a small piece of twig from her hair, he twirled it between his thumb and forefinger.

"I don't know. I guess because—"

"Well, I do care, Ivy." He touched her hand. "I do care."

Peering over at the breached fence, guilt overwhelmed her. "Zach, you don't have time for this now. Not with the fence needing to be fixed."

Tugging her over a few feet, he eased her down to a thick tree trunk lying across the ground then sat down beside her. "I have time, Ivy. All the t-t-time in the world."

How could she deny his genuine concern?

"Do you remember my mama being sick?" she began, recalling how sadly separate she'd felt from the rest of life in those last few months. She'd wanted to be with her mama every moment of the day, but sometimes she missed the voice of a friend.

He nodded. "Of course, I do."

Folding her hands in her lap, she tried to ignore the pitted feeling in her stomach. "Well, she'd been so ill, and I wanted to do whatever I could to brighten her day, so when she pleaded for me to take her to see her favorite stand of golden aspens, I did." At the look of sympathy etched in Zach's face, Ivy felt a corner of her control give way. Hurried to set it right again. "She always loved the aspens come fall, but the days were passing so quickly, and their color was sure to start fading. I just couldn't deny her. Even when my father had firmly instructed me to make *sure* she stayed in bed."

Warily, she peered at Zach, wondering what he really felt. Was his compassionate expression merely a mask? Would he blame her, too?

"I'll never forget the panic I felt that day," she continued, plowing through the memory just to get through. She held his coat closed, half wishing it was Zach's strong arms wrapped around her, lending her courage. "It was late September, and an early fall snowstorm had blown in suddenly. The snow was coming down so hard, and I headed back home just as soon as it started, but with how heavy it was, I could hardly see, and with Mama being so frail I didn't want to go too fast."

When he reached out and took her hand, her eyes instantly burned with the threat of tears. Swallowing hard, she went on, the memory playing out in her mind's eye as though it was all happening right here, right now. "I became distracted by a flock of birds sitting on low-slung tree branches near the narrow path." The same terror that had gripped her then, gripped her now. Haunting shame and guilt were close behind. She peered over at Zach, thankful, *oh, so very thankful,* that he was here. "I drove off the road, Zach, because I was so scared of those birds."

"Aww…darlin'…" His low voice seeped into her heart like a warm balm. He smoothed a hand over her shoulder. "You must've been terrified."

More, she was ashamed of herself for allowing her fear to distract her. "One of the wagon wheels got wedged between two rocks. It was horrible. The horses were working so hard, but the more I tried to right what I'd done wrong, the worse it became. Those poor horses were wild with fright," she confessed, rocking back and forth on the log as she held her hands to her face.

She would never forget the frantic pleading look in

their big brown eyes. Or the facade of calm her mama had tried to plaster over her wan face. Never would she forget.

"I'm ssso sorry, Ivy." His voice filled with emotion.

"Mama was too weak to walk any distance," she went on to say. She pulled her hands away from her eyes then looked at Zach. "I didn't want to leave her, but no one knew we were out there."

"You didn't have a choice," he uttered, wrapping a hand around hers. "You did the right th-thing."

"I left Mama out there, exposed to the onslaught of snow and wind. Mama never woke up once my father got her back home and in bed. She passed away two days later." Things were never the same again.

She was never the same again.

She couldn't bear telling Zach that, in her father's grief, he'd so much as accused her of her mama's death.

"I'm *so* sorry, Ivy. I had no idea."

She shrugged, battling to hold on to her composure, but something about Zach just left her so undone. Stripped her of the control she'd worked so hard to tack in place.

"It's not your f-fault, you know...."

"I make no excuses for myself, Zach." For six years, Ivy had carried the condemning weight of her father's grief and the heartrending load of her own deep sorrow. She'd continue to do so because she simply *could not* imagine shrugging free from what seemed her just reward.

Years ago, she'd begged, pleaded, prayed. Prayed for God to forgive her and for her father to forgive her, as well. But it seemed that the heavens were just as silent as her father, and she'd learned to live, chained to guilt by her careless action. How could she possibly forgive herself without their forgiveness, too?

"This g-guilt isn't yours to carry," he urged.

She just stared at him, dumbfounded. How could it not be hers to carry? She'd been the one to blame.

"It wasn't your fault, Ivy," he insisted, giving her hand a squeeze.

She was desperate to believe those words, but how could she? Her father had blamed her at the time, and he obviously still did. If he had any other feelings on the matter, then he would've attempted to bridge the wide gap between them by now, or at the very least accept her feeble advances toward reconciliation. Her hopes for restoration had grown paler with each passing day.

As much respect as Zach had for her father…if he knew how her father had condemned her, then surely he'd condemn her, too.

Chapter Twelve

Zach's heart had weighed heavy ever since Ivy had poured out her troubles to him, yesterday. Popping into his mouth the last bite of warm pumpkin bread Violet had brought to him, he glanced at the house in the off chance of catching a glimpse of her.

The sorrowful image of her huddled under that tree, her gaze shadowed by silent and profound torment, her body shaking uncontrollably as she recounted what had happened to her mother, would be something Zach would *never* forget. The brave and stoic way she'd held back her tears had struck him like a power-packed punch to the gut. The memory had been seared into his mind and heart.

Zach would do whatever he could to help. She'd told him plenty, but he sensed that she'd not divulged everything. That there was still something she'd kept locked away.

"By the way, Zach..." Violet measured out, holding out a glass of milk to him. "The harvest celebration is tonight," she continued as he nodded his thanks and took his time swallowing the creamy milk. The coy way she'd just seasoned the conversation with that information was unsettling. He had a feeling that there was more to this than just try-this-new-pumpkin-bread-recipe. "Did you hear me?"

"Yeah, I think I remember something about that." He took the napkin she held out to him and wiped his mouth.

The grin tipping Violet's mouth reminded him of Shakespeare, right after he had swallowed a songbird. "Well, *I've* decided that *you* are going to accompany Ivy."

"*Really? You've* decided that, huh?" he challenged, setting the glass and napkin in the basket draped over her arm.

"Except for that lovely little party you arranged for her, that girl has barely stepped foot off this ranch since she arrived home over three weeks ago. She needs to get out and see folks. Mingle some."

"And you think that I'm the one to see to her socializing?" He gave her an incredulous look. "Have you heard the way I talk around her?"

Nodding, she cradled the basket in front of her, her gray shawl nearly falling from her narrow shoulders. "I have. And there's not *one* thing for you to be ashamed about, either. *Not one.* So you just get any thought like that out of your head."

He shrugged off his unease—after all, this was Violet. He could trust her as much as he could trust his brothers. "I don't feel ashamed. Not so much anymore."

Mortified...yes.

"I did *not* fall to the birthing straw just yesterday, Zachariah Henry Drake. I know when you're uncomfortable," she said, adjusting her shawl. "It is pure nonsense to feel embarrassed. You need to hold that head of yours high. Do you hear?"

"I hear."

"Now, I asked Ivy last night if she was going to be attending, and she just gave me an earful of hemming and hawing."

"Maybe she doesn't want to go."

"Well, now…I don't know about that," she challenged with a thoughtful shake of her head. "I *do* think I heard her mentioning *something* about Hugh."

His mood suddenly turned sour. "Hugh?"

"Yes. I can't say as I know the details, *exactly,* but I remember hearing his name in the flurry of it all." She hooked the basket in the crook of her left arm, patted at the thick knot of hair she'd loosely fastened at the back of her head. "Maybe it's just me, but I think it would be a shame for that girl to traipse off to the celebration with him."

It would be a shame, all right. "I'm sure that she can probably make up her own mind."

"Oh, you're right. I sometimes forget that she's all grown up." She pushed wayward wisps of hair from her face. "I guess I'll just have to put my concerns out of my mind."

"What *concerns?*" If there were concerns, then that was something altogether different.

"Oh, it's probably nothing but innocent fun." On a sigh, she waved a hand in casual dismissal.

"*What's* innocent fun?"

"Oh…just that Hugh's been snooping around the house, peering in windows and calling out after her."

Anger, instant and red-hot, boiled in his veins. He fisted his hands. "Where is she now?"

"I believe she's up in the kitchen making broth for her father," she said, smoothing a hand down her flour-dusted apron. "Why?"

He peered toward the direction of the kitchen. "I'm going to ask her to be my guest at the harvest celebration."

"What a lovely idea, Zach." Violet's sweet smile only confirmed that he'd just fallen into her trap. But if Hugh had been snooping around then Zach had *plenty* to be concerned about. "You accompany Miss Ivy to the celebration and enjoy yourself."

He folded his arms at his chest, eyeing the basket to make sure he hadn't forgotten a lone slice of bread. "I'll take her, but as far as enjoying myself...I can't promise you anything."

"It's all up here." She tapped a fingertip to the side of his head. "And here," she indicated, pressing her hand to his chest. "God...He'll see you through this."

Zach met the woman's earnest gaze. He'd prided himself in doing this on his own. If God had been so intent on Zach overcoming, then *why* did He make the road so difficult?

"*You* just need to listen to Him from your heart. And when you get it figured out there, then you can be more certain of things *here*," she added, tapping his head again.

Violet... How could you not like the woman? She was as motherly as they came, and the backdoor means she had of getting things to go her way was a constant source of amusement.

"So, what about you?" he inquired, remembering Ivy's prodding that he act as a matchmaker. "Are you going to be attending tonight?"

"Yes, I likely will be there." She nervously fiddled with the glass and napkin in the basket. "Mr. Harris must go since he is chairman of the Ranchers Association, but I just don't feel right letting him attend alone when he's not been feeling well. I can recognize the signs when he's feeling poorly. He might need me."

Zach smiled. "Well, it's a good thing he has you."

"I doubt that he sees it that way, most of the time,

anyway. I'm like a slow leak, constantly reminding him of what he should and should not do with as ill as he's been. That fire…and him almost dying in it, was enough to scare me half out of my wits."

It'd scared Zach, too.

"That man would jump into the saddle and tear off into the sunset if it weren't for me pinning him down," Violet asserted.

Zach grinned at the image of this petite, albeit lively, woman pinning any man down—let alone Mr. Harris. "How are you managing that, anyway?"

"He's been sleeping quite a bit, but when he's up I keep him occupied with paperwork and the like," she noted, tapping her fingertips against the basket. "And then there's the Bible reading we've been doing together."

That gave Zach pause. He'd never, for a second, doubted that Mr. Harris was an upright honest man, but he'd never known him to be a man of faith, necessarily.

"He's so close to finding true peace, Zach," she choked out, snatching the used napkin from the basket and dabbing at her gray-blue eyes. "And joy," she added with an insistent nod. "I tell you, I'll rest a lot easier when I know he's found those things."

An overwhelming yearning for the same gripped Zach's heart so suddenly that he struggled to hold his expression in check.

"And it will be a glorious answer to my prayers the day he can embrace that sweet girl of his again." She patted her eyes, her usual sunny demeanor shadowed over as she peered into the barn. "Harsh words can never be taken back. *No, sirree.* Once they're out, you've just got to be man—or woman—enough to deal with the mess." Sniffing, she shifted her focus back to Zach. "But there's nothing says a new beginning can't just wipe a slate clean.

Right?" Her distressed expression brightened some. "Isn't that what God's mercy is really all about?"

Zach wanted to agree, but he hadn't necessarily found that to be true in his own life. He'd made a grand effort to wipe the slate clean after years of difficulty, and then Ivy had shown up.

But something had changed in him, hadn't it? Where before, he would've shrunk back when faced with his stutter, he hadn't this time. Where before, he would've avoided speaking one word to Ivy, he'd plowed through the embarrassment.

Something had changed.

But that didn't mean that he was ready to jump on Violet's celebration wagon. He had too many reservations in his heart, and the recent stress of ranch-related problems had only aggravated things.

He'd take Ivy to the harvest celebration. He'd try and make Ivy fall in love with the ranch again. And he'd do whatever he needed to in order to help her in her journey home because if what Violet had said was true, then the chasm between Ivy and her father went far deeper than just a simple misunderstanding. It could very well steal any true and lasting peace for the rest of her days. And that pierced Zach's heart more than any cruel and teasing word had. Ever.

Zach had left Ivy's side to speak with her father for no more than ten minutes and where did that get him?

More accurately…where did it get *her?*

He fisted his hands, staring at where Hugh was wrapping an arm around Ivy in a waltz, pulling her so close that the golden light bathing the big town hall had been blocked out between them. As far as Zach was concerned, the man was *way* too close.

Zach made his way that direction, edging around the table-cleared wide-plank floor as the dancers swirled and twirled. Forcing a halfway pleasant look on his face, he nodded to several townsfolk, but the whole time he kept one eye peeled on Hugh, and his every suspect move.

His ire pricked at the familiar and compromising way Hugh had slipped his hand down Ivy's back, inching toward her bottom. Zach itched to haul out and slam his entire body into the man, knocking him clear across the dance floor, but he wouldn't embarrass Ivy in that manner.

Up to this moment, their evening had been surprisingly pleasant. They'd sat at one of the long tables with the rest of his family during dinner, and Ivy had seemed to truly enjoy herself, talking and laughing right along with everyone else who'd shown up for the annual celebration.

But from the minute Hugh had arrived, Zach had been on edge. Hugh had hung back in the shadows like a vulture perched in a barren tree, his beady eyes fixed on Ivy. Zach had had no problem ignoring the man's taunting glares, and he'd done his best to keep Ivy occupied so that her evening wasn't spoiled by Hugh's uncomfortable fixation, but he'd been acutely aware of Hugh's every move.

"Step aside, Hugh," Zach said, forcing an even, no-room-for-question tone to his voice.

"Uh...I don't think so, Drake. I was—"

Cutting in, Zach assumed the waltz position, then whisked Ivy around the dance floor. Far from Hugh.

Struggling to keep his building anger from rupturing into an all-out expression, he flashed Ivy a half smile.

She peered up at him. "What did you do that for?"

"He was dishonoring you, Ivy," he said, a little exasperated at her seeming naivety.

"Hugh?" Her brow creased in confusion.

"Yes, *Hugh*," he confirmed, turning her around the dance floor.

When they twirled by Ben and Callie, he couldn't miss his brother's approving look or his sister-in-law's triumphant smile while she unabashedly stared their way.

"Hugh is *just Hugh*." She glanced behind her at where Zach had left Hugh stranded, but he was nowhere to be found. "He makes mischief, like a schoolboy, but he doesn't mean a bit of harm."

Zach recalled the coarse jest Hugh had made regarding Ivy that day outside the barn, and what Violet had shared about Hugh peering in the windows and calling out after Ivy. He definitely *wasn't* an innocent young schoolboy.

In fact, Zach had a hard time believing that he was ever so innocent.

"Do *not* fool yourself. He's a mmmman." His tone came a little harsher than he'd intended. Softening his demeanor some, he expertly wove in and out of the other dancers. "And *you* are a *very attractive young woman*," he boldly admitted, holding her gaze.

Although he seriously questioned the wisdom of saying such a thing, he couldn't deny how he enjoyed the slightest rosy blush that instantly colored her ivory complexion. Or the way her long eyelashes fluttered down over her eyes.

She dipped her head, as though aware of the telltale signs. "He's as harmless as a—"

"Do I n-need to explain this in more *detailed* terms?" Zach challenged, catching her nervous gaze and holding it as he moved and swayed with the lilting music. When he noticed the hint of embarrassment dawn in her gaze, he gave her a slight nod. "Well, I'm glad for that."

"You're a lovely dancer, Zach," she breathed, closing

her eyes for a few seconds as she relaxed and let him lead her around the scarred wood floor. The suppleness in her expression, and the trusting way she'd allowed her dainty hand to be swallowed in his, melted his heart.

A smile tipped one corner of his mouth. "Only as good as my dancing partner."

"Now, you know that's not true," she countered, glancing around the dance floor. "All three of your brothers have quite a knack, though they haven't danced much tonight. Still, it must run in the family."

"The night's young. I'm sure they'll be out there plenty. Joseph and B-B-Ben will probably stick to waltzes, though—with Katie and Callie expecting."

"They must be thrilled," she commented. "You are a wonderful uncle to Libby already, Zach. She loves you."

"We'll see how I rate the sssecond and third time around," he teased, slicing in a breath. "You n-never know."

"You'll be every bit as good, I'm sure." She smoothed her left hand over his shoulder for a brief second.

"I'll say this much…I llllove being an uncle to that little girl." He'd love fathering children of his own someday, too, but he was beginning to doubt it would ever happen, especially being twenty-four years old and not having a prospect in sight.

His heart surged. *Oh, there was a prospect in sight.* In his arms to be exact. But Ivy was less attainable than the moon was to man. He could never marry someone who didn't believe in him.

"Speaking of love…" he said, eager to change the subject. "Have you noticed your father and Violet t-tonight?"

The shiest smile tipped her lips. Ever so faintly, she gave his hand a gentle squeeze as he twirled her around the worn floor. "He does look fairly well tonight. Don't you think?"

He followed her drifting gaze to her father sitting off to the side with Violet and a table full of ranchers. "I thought so myself."

"And Violet," she added. "She certainly is a sight to behold."

"That, she is," he agreed.

"I've never seen her look so—so lovely." Her gaze grew very tender.

As one waltz wove seamlessly into another, Zach followed right along instead of peeling away from the dance floor like some of the other folks. He enjoyed having Ivy in his arms too much to let her go. Yet.

"You know...the more I ssssee them together, the more I'm c-c-convinced they're in love." He swallowed hard, the acute awareness of his own void staring him in the face.

Ivy shifted her attention that way yet again. "My father does look very happy—at least when he's with her."

Zach's heart swelled just seeing the gratefulness in Ivy's gaze. With every lilting chord in the stringed instruments' song, he guided her across the floor, enjoying the way she felt so perfect in his arms. "Love has a way of d-doing that to a person."

Her focus shifted suddenly back to him. Her brow pinched. "Do you really believe that, Zach?"

"Well, sure, I do." He could list off a thousand different instances growing up when his entire day would appear brighter by just seeing Ivy. His brothers had always thought he'd held a deep appreciation for learning, when the truth was that he would've gone to school from sunup to sundown, *year-round,* if it meant seeing Ivy.

Without a doubt, love had a way of doing all kinds

of things to a person. Making them foolish. Vulnerable. Naive. He'd been all of those things and more, so many years ago, when he would've given his life for the woman he held in his arms right now.

And if he didn't try to rein in his growing attraction for this young lady, he could well find himself stripped of the confidence and life he'd worked so hard to gain.

"I wonder if I've ever glowed like that," she considered, her words whispering over him and stirring every nerve ending to life. She stared up at him as if trying to see her own reflection in his gaze. "I mean…maybe I've been in love and have never known it."

He swallowed hard. Struggled not to trip—*over her words.* That earnest and honest depth in her eyes knocked him off kilter.

Dragging in a steadying breath, he willed his voice to stay even. "I'm pr-pretty sure you'd know if you'd b-b-been in love, Ivy," he finally said.

Her expression grew contemplative. Worried, almost. "There was a man…Neal…. I went on several outings with him in New York." She met Zach's gaze. "Maybe I feel more for him than I'm aware."

Zach's hands itched with an instant and untamed urge to hit *Neal* square in the jaw. His blood boiled hot and red with jealousy.

But how could he be jealous of a man he'd never met?

More, why would it matter *what* Ivy felt for *Neal?*

Honestly, it would be better if she did feel something for the man. Then Zach could just leave well-enough alone and get on with his life. Maybe he'd stop stuttering again. Maybe he'd finally keep his thoughts wholly focused on his job. Maybe he'd rid his mind and heart of Ivy for good.

Maintaining his hold on her right hand, he twirled her

in a circle then tucked in behind her as some of the other practiced dancers had done with their partners.

She peered over her shoulder, her beautiful gaze faltering for just a moment, her body quivering slightly in his arms.

"Do you think about him often?" he measured out, grateful for every solid word.

After what seemed like a small eternity, she gave her head a slow shake. Caught her lower lip between her teeth. "Almost never."

He could've let loose the biggest and longest sigh of relief just then, but instead, he schooled his expression and twirled her back around to face him as the waltz waned to a restful close. He held her still, captivated by the vulnerable look in her beautiful eyes.

"Then I would v-venture to say that you—that you don't love him." His chest tightened with unresolved longing. He may not be able to carry love through to a happy ending for himself, but he knew well what it did to a person.

What it'd done to him.

"When you f-find your thoughts consumed by someone..." He gave her hand a gentle squeeze then let her go. Taking one step back, he made a graceful bow. "*That's* when you know you're in love."

Chapter Thirteen

That's when she'd know that she was in love?

When she found a certain someone consuming her every thought?

Since the harvest celebration last night, Ivy's world had been knocked completely off balance.

If that was true then she could very likely be _in love_ with Zachariah Henry Drake, because his face was forever in her mind's eye. When she woke, when she slept, almost every minute of the day.

But _how_ could that be?

Tugging closed the way-too-big jacket she'd found in the mudroom to ward off the October chill, she headed into the barn. She could not deny that in spite of her wishes to stay unencumbered by anything or anyone here in Boulder, her thoughts had been increasingly captivated by Zach. His warm and winning smile. His wonderfully masculine touch. And his very sincere concern.

Ivy marched down the barn's long corridor to where her father's prized mare was getting ready to foal. Violet had encouraged her to get out here just as soon as possible. After Ivy had raced upstairs and changed into appropriate clothing, grabbed the overly large jacket for warmth and was on her way out the door, only then had Violet mentioned that Zach was tending the mare.

Sheer pride had kept Ivy's feet moving one in front of the other. Each step closer to Zach spurred her heart into an odd and rapid rhythm—as if she really was *in love*.

But that simply *could not* be.

He was a longtime schoolmate from her childhood. Stubborn and strong like her father. He threatened to undermine the strong woman she'd worked to become, simply by his presence. Every time she was with him, it seemed that she'd spill her heart or grow unusually vulnerable.

She could not afford to lose her footing any more than she already had, but she'd be hard-pressed not to reflect on the beauty of the previous twenty-four hours. The sweet and tender way Zach had asked her to attend the celebration with him. The wonderfully warm way he'd bantered with his family, including her as though she were one of them. And the graceful, magnificently masculine command he had about him as they'd danced…it'd made her knees weak and her stomach all aflutter.

Standing on tiptoe, she peered over the stall door to where Zach was hunkered down against the thick wall, his arms draped over his raised knees, his attentive gaze locked on the buckskin.

The horse shifted in the fresh bed of straw and swung her head back as though sensing Ivy's arrival.

"Hello there," Zach greeted on one of those captivating half grins of his. Shoving himself up to standing, he crossed the morning-sun-bathed stall and unlatched the door, his slightly rumpled hair and whisker-shadowed face begging to be touched. "I didn't expect to see you here."

"I didn't, either," she said, avoiding his gaze. "But Violet told me Annie was laboring, and I didn't want to miss it." Edging around Zach, her pulse skittered to acute awareness of Zach's every move. He commanded her attention without saying a word. In spite of the morning chill, his sleeves were rolled up to reveal muscle-roped forearms smattered with dark hair. His unshaven ruggedness did nothing to quiet her fluttering attraction. "How is she doing?"

He gave the mare's wide girth a gentle pat. "She's all right and the foal's in the right position. I'm hoping she'll have as easy a labor as the last t-t-time."

"That would be good. She certainly looks like she couldn't get much bigger." Ivy lightly touched the mare's massive neck, the pleasingly familiar aroma of fresh straw and horse wafting to her senses along with Zach's piney woodsy scent.

"She'll probably be f-fine, but just in case…I'm keeping a close eye on her." Zach crossed behind her to stand at the mare's head, his caring and tender touch just what she'd expect from a man like Zach. She never could stomach a man or woman who'd heartlessly dominate an animal.

Spotting Shakespeare in the corner of the large birthing stall, she had to smile. "Aww…cute kitty…."

"Shakespeare's always rrrright in the middle of things," he said, nodding to where her cat had wound himself into a huge ball of fur.

"He's just a nosy neighbor." Scooping him up, she nuzzled her face into his warm fur. "Aren't you, big boy?"

When she glanced up to find Zach's expression blanketed with endearing warmth, her heart skipped a beat.

She cleared her throat, forcing her thoughts to the mare. "So, how can I help? As you can see…I came dressed for work, this time."

"I see that." If he kept up with those pulse-pounding

half grins of his, she might just turn around and march right out of here. Apparently, he had *no* idea how they unraveled her composure.

Or *did* he?

"Nice jacket," he commented, arching his eyebrows.

She draped Shakespeare over her shoulder and held one arm out, allowing the sleeve to plunge almost to her knees. "I found this ratty old thing hanging in the mud-room."

"It looks g-good on you," he said, with an approving nod.

She gave a soft laugh at his sweet compliment. "I almost get lost in the thing. I look like I'm wearing a giant's coat."

"Nope," he responded with a breath-stealing wink. "Just mine."

Speechless, she stared at him, her face flaming hot. Without warning, she had an undeniable and strangely innate urge to bury her face in the coat and breathe in Zach's woodsy masculine scent woven into the fibers.

His coat...warm and comfortable, just like him.

Goodness, what was happening to her? Was she tossing aside every bit of decorum she possessed, and all over an old coat?

Swallowing hard, she finally found her voice as she patted Shakespeare's back. "I'm sorry, I thought it was—"

"It's all right." His grin did nothing to ease her flip-flopping insides. "C-C-Consider it yours."

Desperate to gain control over her rebellious emotions, she crossed to the small window and peered outside. "I sat in on several births with my father when I was young, you know."

"Did you now?"

"I did. My father was always so good at recognizing

the signs of labor." Turning, she set her focus strictly on the mare, while her cat purred and sniffed at her hair. "He would point them out to me."

Zach raked a hand through his slightly disheveled, but oddly perfect, hair. "I wish he was here for this one, but he left early this mmmmorning and even if I could track him down, he'd probably not make it back in time."

"He'll be disappointed. But he'll understand."

When the mare nudged Zach for some attention, he stroked a hand down her nose. "I think he was glad to finally be b-back in the saddle again."

Ivy reached out and touched the mare's velvety soft nose.

"Violet said that he was feeling so much better."

He sighed. "It looks like those d-days of strict bed rest were just what he n-n-needed. He loaded up his saddlebag with jerky and was on his way before the sun rose."

When the mare suddenly shifted in the hay, then thumped her hooves against the ground, Ivy grew concerned. "Looks like Annie's having another contraction."

Zach ran a hand beneath the mare's belly. "It sure does. But it'll be at lllleast another couple hours, probably more, before she delivers."

"Why don't you let me sit with her then?" she offered, setting Shakespeare down. She pushed up her coat sleeves till her hands peeked out. "Maybe she'd be more comfortable since I'm a woman."

He smiled. "I doubt she much c-cares."

"Well, *I* certainly would, if I were her."

"Yes. You probably would," he agreed.

"I'm sure you have a lot to do. Let me stay here with her," she offered again, eager to get rid of him so that she could gather her senses. There was just something disabling about Zach that made her nearly forget who she was. "You can check back in periodically."

He folded his arms at his broad chest. "I don't know."

"I've done this before, Zach," she argued. "And contrary to what you may think, I am *well able* to handle things."

In those few weeks before she'd gone east, after her mama had passed away, Ivy's father would not allow her to see after one thing. He wouldn't let her help with the chores, do things around the house or even run a simple errand. The idea that she'd lost his trust had wounded every bit as deep as his blame.

Maybe she deserved it.

But what about second chances? Was there room for her to make up for her mistakes? She could never bring her mama back, and though the doctor had said that it had only been a matter of time before her mama would've passed, Ivy still felt responsible.

"It's not that." He raised his hands, palms out. "It's j-j-just that if something went wrong I'd feel horribly rrre-sponsible."

Frustrated, Ivy jammed her fists at her waist, but not before her coat sleeves slipped back down. "You cannot be accountable for every little thing that goes wrong. As much as you seem to think otherwise, you cannot control all that happens on this ranch, Zach."

His focus dashed to her floppy sleeves for a second. "I don't think that—"

"And besides…*nothing* is going to go wrong," she defended, feeling reasonably comfortable in her experience. "I was at my father's side for dozens of births."

He paused as though pondering. "You're getting more and more c-comfortable here, aren't you?"

She peered at him for a lingering moment, the past

three weeks plus, racing through her mind. She'd gone from helping on the ranch out of sheer duty and deference to her father, to actually looking forward to being here and working. The earthy scents, the lowing sound of cattle or the nickering of a horse, the visual splendor of the mountains hemming the ranch in on one side…she'd missed these things.

"As difficult as it has been coming home, I can't deny that I do love it here. Sometimes it feels like I never left." She shoved up her sleeves again, with no lasting success. "Other times I can't wait to get back to the city."

"You're going back, then?" Reaching for one of her arms, he gently rolled up her sleeve.

"Well, yes. Of course I am." She nearly lost his question due to his undermining, warmly tender, incapacitating touch. "I have a job awaiting me."

"That's what you've said." With great care he tended her other sleeve, seemingly enjoying the slow and strategic way he was unseating her poise.

She swallowed hard, grappling for some strand of control. "Oh, I'm *definitely* returning, but until then I plan on being as involved as I can here. That said…you need to go on about your day." She made a shooing motion toward the door. "We'll be just fine, won't we—"

"Zach! You in here?" one of the ranch hands called from down the corridor.

"We're fine," she said, before he could protest.

"Wait out here," he instructed, nodding toward the corridor. "I'll b-be right back."

"Don't be silly."

"Laboring mares can get t-t-testy," he warned.

"I'll be fine. Take your time." She gave him a blandly triumphant smile. "I'll do what I can to keep her comfortable."

On a puffed out breath, he opened the stall door and jogged away, leaving Ivy with the mare and her cat.

She scooped up Shakespeare into her arms again and held him like a baby, just the way he liked it. "I suppose you came to watch this joyous event, too, didn't you, Shakespeare?" she asked, touching her nose to his cute pink one as he squeezed his eyes shut in that adorable way of his. "Zach's right. You always have to be right in the mix of things."

In spite of her attempt to tamp down her wayward emotions, her stomach still flip-flopped from Zach's touch.

Turning her attention to the mare, she stepped closer and brushed a hand down the side of the nickering horse. "You can do this, Annie. Don't be afraid. Take it nice and easy," she encouraged.

Just then a shadow wafted silently into her peripheral vision. The hair on the back of her neck rose as she turned to find Zach's owl perched on the stall door, staring at her with his big golden eyes.

"Oh, my…. Not you," she breathed, forcing herself to remain calm even as she recalled how sad she'd been at the thought of Buddy perishing in the fire.

She edged away from the door and closer to the mare's head, keeping her eye on the owl. Knowing how astute horses were, she struggled to keep her fear from getting the best of her. Had she not promoted herself as fully capable of sitting with this laboring mare, she would've found some way around the owl and out the barn in no time flat. Even if she had to dig her way to safety.

The owl moved its head from side to side, like he was bringing her into better focus. Peered at her as though he was ready to fly over and roost right on her shoulder.

"Be nice. Please," she begged the winged creature.

She edged back another step. She tried shifting Shakespeare upright to face the owl so as to ward off the bird, but the way her full-bodied cat draped like a rag doll in her arms didn't give her much hope. "I would like to give you the benefit of the doubt here, Buddy, but it sure seems like you strategically chose to show up when I was here alone."

The owl eyed her. Blinked.

Ivy's neck and face burned with raw fear. She pressed back against the wall. "I know Zach has said that you're friendly, and I'm very glad you were unharmed in the fire, but I'm sorry. This is a horse-only event—and maybe cats, too. Owls must leave."

Feeling the completely content and comfortable way Shakespeare purred loudly in her arms, made her slightly indignant. "Shakespeare, don't you know that cats have an animosity toward birds?" she scolded, keeping her eye on Buddy. "Don't you want to *at least* show him who is boss?"

"Are you trying to t-talk your cat into eating my owl?" Zach appeared at the door behind Buddy.

Wide-eyed, she shook her head. "I would *never* do that."

"Well...then *stalking him,* maybe?" he probed, inclining his head her way as he unlatched the door and entered the stall.

"Of course not," she defended, though she did feel a small prick of guilt. "I was just reminding Shakespeare that he rules the roost."

"Words don't lie, darlin'." Setting his fists to his taut waist, he gave her a wry grin. "I'm sorry to say, b-but it'd be no use, anyway. Shakespeare and Buddy have an agreeable relationship. Most of the time, th-th-they leave each other alone."

"Well, that's good of them." She gave him a forced smile, then whispered down at Shakespeare, "You're a spoiled kitty."

"I heard that." When she peered up at Zach, he gave her a mock glare, his eyes sparking with good-natured fun. "Don't play innocent with me."

"Me?" She pulled her head back.

Reaching out, he smoothed the backs of his fingers along Buddy's downy chest. "Listen, I came back t-t-to lllet you know that there's been another section of f-fence cut just west of here. Apparently several head of cattle have gone through. Since I'm short on help I m-m-might need to—"

"Go," she said, nodding. "Absolutely, go ahead. I'll take care of things here."

He stepped closer and ran a hand over the mare's belly. "I'll be g-gone just long enough to help Hugh herd the cattle over to Harris land. I'll be back within th-the hour."

"We'll be fine," she assured. She patted the mare's neck. "Won't we, Annie?"

"I'll take Buddy outside with me," he said, shoving his hands into his pockets.

"Oh, don't be silly. I'm fine."

"Are you sure? Because last time you—"

"I said, *I'm fine,* Zach. He'll probably get bored and fly off soon enough, anyway."

"If you have any problems just holler for one of the hands."

"I can manage," she assured, pushing him toward the door.

When Zach finally left she found herself wishing that he'd taken his owl with him. But she hadn't wanted to seem like a ridiculous child. For some reason it mattered very much what he thought.

Too much, for her comfort.

"All right, Mr. Buddy, you stay over there, and I'll stay here. Deal?" she measured out, wary as could be, and yet trying to keep her trepidation at a minimum so as to not spook Annie. "And *you,* you big spoiled cat, probably don't care about much else but your next tasty meal served on a silver platter." She ruffled the thick fur on his belly. "Apparently you don't have to work around here, but that big guy over there," she accused, pointing at the owl with her cat's paw, "likely snatches the mice right in front of your cute little nose."

The mare shifted again, nervously throwing her head from side to side. Concerned, Ivy set down the cat well out of hoof reach, then smoothed a hand down the mare's muscle-twitching neck. "It's all right, girl. Are you having another contraction?"

The horse shifted around in the generous birthing stall, as though uncomfortable.

"You can do it," Ivy encouraged, avoiding eye contact with the owl. "Just remember what it was like the first time around."

For the next half hour or so, the horse grew increasingly uncomfortable and visibly irritable with each contraction. Ivy found herself praying that Zach would return, especially seeing the mare's eyes grow wild with anxiety and pain.

Her heart sank. She'd seen a mare react like this at least twice before, and each time the foal had been breech. But how could she possibly manage a breech delivery on her own?

Zach had said that the foal was in the right position. He hadn't thought the mare would deliver for a couple hours. Had the labor taken an unexpected turn? Although she'd never found anything to support Hugh's claims that Zach was incompetent, maybe this was a small bit of proof. Maybe he really wasn't as capable at ranching as what her father or Violet had said. Maybe he couldn't recognize a breech foal even if he felt one.

Ivy could at least check over the mare as her father had shown her years ago, then she'd know if the foal was breech, and just as soon as Zach returned, she could give him an accurate analysis of the situation.

Shrugging out of his warm coat, she rolled up her brown wool sleeves in spite of the cool air hanging in the barn. She rubbed a hand down the mare's face and neck, trying to ease the animal some even when fear nipped at her own soul. What if something happened to her father's prized mare?

She could go after Violet for help, or one of the hands, but she didn't dare leave the mare alone.

Where was Zach?

Surely an hour had gone by already....

"It's all right, Annie. I'm just going to check you over," she whispered, trying to ease the animal's growing panic. In spite of the trepidation seizing Ivy's heart, she kept one hand on the giant beast and moved slowly down to the mare's backside.

"That's right," she soothed as much to herself as to the mare. "Easy now, girl. I'm just going to see where things stand." Ivy watched the mare for signs of an abating contraction then dragged in a deep breath and slid her arm inside, feeling for a breech foal.

The mare immediately flinched. Sidestepped, once, twice. Kicked.

Ivy slid to the side, but didn't dare make any fast moves. Slow and steady she pulled her arm free. The mare kicked again, thrusting a hoof into Ivy's leg.

She slammed back hard against the door, hitting her

ribs and head. She slumped to the ground, dazed. Her head swirled.

Ivy bit off a scream as white-hot pain seared her leg. Bit off another scream as she peered up to find the owl, staring down at her, his big eyes looking at her as though she was his next prey. On a hitched breath, she scrambled to move away from the skittish mare. And from Zach's owl.

Agonizing pain shot through her head and back and just below her knee where she'd been kicked.

"I'm sorry, Annie. I didn't mean to upset you," she whispered, fighting to hold back tears that threatened to fall. Pulling herself up to standing, she took in her bedraggled appearance. Sniffing, she grasped for her faltering courage.

She'd been around horses for years. She knew that, no matter how docile they seemed, their mass alone could pose a very real danger—especially that of a mare in labor.

When the horse neighed and peered over at Ivy as though to apologize, Ivy's heart clenched tight.

"It's all right. I know you didn't mean to." With reasonable caution, she hobbled over to the mare's head, her leg throbbing with each step.

The normally compliant horse shifted nervously, as though she was picking her way through a snake-infested field. After several more minutes, the poor horse gave a ruffled snort, folded her front legs then flopped uncomfortably onto her side.

"Aww…you poor girl…." Ivy was scared to death that the mare was in serious trouble. The minutes ticked by and with each one, Ivy's heart sank a little more.

Where was Zach?

She listened for the sound of pounding hooves above

the pounding in her head. Ignoring the throbbing pain in her shin and head and ribs, she inched down to sit at the mare's head.

"God...please don't let Annie die," she pleaded, recalling how many times she'd prayed the exact same prayer for her mama.

Tears sprang, unbidden, to her eyes as images of her mama, lying so still and gray with impending death, passed through her mind. She'd done everything she could to ease her mama's suffering, but it hadn't been enough. Death had come. Slow and with stinging finality.

"Please, don't let Annie or her foal die. I'll do whatever I can to help, but please don't let them die," she entreated.

The thought of seeing her father's prized mare perish at her hands left her completely undone. The guilt she would feel, added to the guilt she still carried over her mama's death, would surely be more than she could bear.

As much as Violet had said otherwise, Ivy could not help believing that her father felt the same way now as he had six years ago. In the more than three weeks she'd been home, their conversations had barely skimmed the surface. She'd tried to make eye contact with her father, desperate to see something other than disappointment in his gaze, but he'd seemingly avoided her attempts at this, as well.

Did she belong here? She had to wonder.

Uncle Terrance's words flashed through her mind. That she belonged in the city, not on the ranch. A month ago, she'd have unhesitatingly agreed.

Maybe it was already too late. Maybe she'd overstayed her welcome. Maybe the very thing she'd hoped to find here, closure and healing, would forever elude her desperate grasp.

The thought of causing her father more grief nearly broke her heart right in two.

For now, she simply *had* to help poor Annie. For the horse's sake. The foal's sake. And for her father's sake.

"We're going to make it through this…you and me, Annie." On a sniff, Ivy shoved herself to standing and hobbled over to the mare's backside again.

"And you," she said, glancing over her shoulder at Zach's curious winged creature. "*You* are going to stay right there. Do you hear? We don't need to cause this poor girl any more anxiety than she already feels."

Just then the sound of boots racing down the corridor caught her attention. Relief, sure as the rising sun, overwhelmed her so much that it was all she could do to stay standing.

"Ivy?" Zach called as he slowed then slid to a halt at the birthing stall. He opened the door, his breath catching at the sight of her standing there, her face etched with obvious pain and definable sadness.

One desperate glance from her stopped his heart cold. She obviously wanted to appear well in control of the situation, but with her quivering form, straw-sprinkled wool dress and the pained expression creasing her brow, she was completely unconvincing.

"Wh-What in the world happened to you?" He took a tentative step forward and tenderly grasped her shoulders.

"It's nothing." All stubborn, she shrugged from him. Winced.

"Darlin'…you look like you got dragged b-behind a horse," he went on to say, dipping his head to grab her attention. "What happened? Tell me…."

"Never mind me. Annie needs our help." The sorrowful way she knelt at the mare's head, seized his compassion. "I'm horribly afraid that maybe her foal is breech."

"I checked her earlier. Everything was fine," he assured. Grabbing his old coat from where Ivy had cast it onto the ground, he draped it over Ivy's shoulders.

"Are you sure?" she asked, her eyes misting over.

"Yes. The f-foal was in a perfect position, and from the way this mama's laying down, it won't be long n-n-now before she gives birth." Gently hooking his forefinger beneath her chin, he inched her gaze to his. "What happened? Did she kick?"

"It wasn't her fault," she sweetly defended on a sniff. "I was worried that maybe the foal was breech. I was trying to check her like my father had shown me years ago."

What was she thinking getting so close to a laboring mare? He swallowed back the scolding words that were on the tip of his tongue.

"Where did she get you?" he probed calmly as he helped her up to standing and led her over to a small stool in the corner of the stall.

"On my leg," she said after a long pause.

While he gently lowered her to the stool, the sorrowful way she kept looking over where Annie lay nearly broke his heart.

"It's nothing, really. What about Annie, though?"

"I'll see to her in a minute. F-F-First I want to see to you." He set a hand on her shoulder and hunkered down in front of her. "I can tell that th-this is more than nothing. You're wincing with every m-m-move you make. Will you let me have a look so that I can make sure nothing's broken?"

"I'm sure I'm fine." She sliced in a breath.

"Please…"

When she finally gave a tentative nod, he felt a small measure of relief. "Where is it?"

"Right below the knee." Inching up her skirts on the right side to just above the injury, she peered down at her leg.

Guilt, sure and strong, assaulted him as he took in the unsightly swelling bruise. Had he not left her alone, this never would have happened.

"It's already turning b-b-black and bl-blue." He tenderly palpated the knee and her leg. "And it's swelling pretty good already. I'll go after Ben just as soon as I can."

"Unnecessary." She captured his hands and shoved them away, but not before he noticed how severely she trembled. "Completely unnecessary."

"It'll do my mind worlds of good to have him look you over," he reasoned.

"I'll be fine," she argued, stubborn as an unruly horse. "Violet will see to me."

Looking her straight in the eye, he searched for some element of doubt, but he saw nothing but stubborn bravery. "You're d-definitely cut of your f-f-father's cloth."

"*You're* one to talk," she retorted, incredulously.

He gave his head a slow shake. "I should've n-n-never left you alone with the mare. This never w-w-would have h-happened," he forced out, his words coming noticeably more broken when he was so shaken up around her.

"Don't be ridiculous," she dismissed, fluffing and adjusting her wool skirt to cover her leg. "Where *were* you, though? You said you'd be back within the hour."

"I know I did." Standing, he lifted his hat from his head and raked a hand through his hair. "And I rrrraced back here as f-fast as I could, but it was more than a c-c-cut line. Far more."

"What do you mean?"

He pulled a hand over his scruffy jawline, taking a long steadying breath. "Several head of c-c-cattle are missing."

"How? Where did they go?" On a wince, she slowly stood up.

"I don't know. B-B-But we scoured the area and there were at least a d-dozen missing. We rounded up f-forty on the other side of the fence breach, but the rest are gone."

"Could they have wandered off?"

"There's always that ch-chance, but usually they stay together. The ones we d-did herd back were spooked, to be sure."

Ivy's gaze pinched with apprehension. "Cattle thieves?"

"Looks like it." He was sick at the very thought of this happening right under his nose.

"Why would someone want to steal my father's cattle?" she muttered, clearly shocked.

"I don't know, b-b-but I will track down the c-culprits," he promised. "I'll g-get the cattle back."

He'd always tried so hard to do right by Mr. Harris. With a sick sense of dread, he had to wonder if he was letting his boss down.

Chapter Fourteen

"Lucky you," Uncle Terrance said, startling Ivy from her silent reverie as she watched the new foal standing beside his mama, his long legs all wobbly and knobby.

"Uncle Terrance...you scared me," she breathed. "I didn't hear you approach."

In spite of Zach's insistence that Ivy have Violet look over her injury, she'd stayed right there in the birthing stall. She'd watched as the mare delivered a healthy and spunky foal less than a half hour after Zach had returned. The newborn was the spitting image of his proud mama. And had been delivered without incident.

She couldn't seem to take her eyes off the sweet scene before her as Annie proudly nuzzled her newborn. Zach had been back here several times over the past hour, stroking the foal, letting the little guy get used to his smell and touch and the gentling sound of his rich deep voice.

Terrance peered around the opened stall door, his rank scent of sweat and dirt invading her senses, nearly causing her to gag. "You were lucky she didn't hurt you any worse than she did, sweets," he said, nodding to the mare.

"I'm fine, Uncle Terrance." Ivy stepped back. "I just should've been more careful."

"But we care, dolly." Hugh popped around to her other side and poked her in the ribs.

She bit off a wince, trying to ignore the way her entire body ached—especially where Hugh's long pokey fingers had just jutted into her flesh.

"Terrance is right," Hugh persisted. "You were lucky."

"I don't know why the two of you are making such a fuss about this. You know how accidents can happen." Closing the stall door, she moved down the aisle. "I was simply in the wrong place at the wrong time."

"This just proves my point," Terrance said, coming around to face her.

"Mine, too," Hugh added, shuffling around to stand beside Terrance. Yanking his hat from his head, he hit it against his leg.

"What *points?*" Confused, and feeling cornered, she peered at Hugh first.

"That Zach's too green around the edges to know the ins and outs of running a ranch," he began, his thin lips disappearing in a grim expression. "He about got you killed by leaving you with a laboring mare. Not to mention the fact that he let several head of cattle get ferreted off this property right under his nose."

Zach's nose… She'd never forget that night she'd noticed the slight crook in his nose, how she'd traced a fingertip down it, marveling at just how handsome he was, soot covered and all.

"Your claims are ridiculous," she argued, shaking her head.

"Are they?" Hugh challenged with a not-so-friendly grin. "Those kinda things *never* happened with your father's old foreman."

Peering out one of the small stall windows, she noticed how the western sky was starting to cloud over. "*I'm* the one who insisted on staying with Annie."

With an annoying amount of smugness, Hugh settled his hat back on his head. "Like I said—"

"And *what* is your point, Uncle Terrance?" Ivy shifted her wary attention to her uncle. She hugged her arms to her chest, wishing she was still wearing Zach's worn old coat, but the day had warmed up to the point that she would've been too hot.

Terrance's expression softened. "My point is that you have no business being here."

"I wouldn't go so far as to say that," Hugh put in, waggling his eyebrows at Ivy in a way that made her want to brush herself off. "I like seeing her around the place. Makes my days a whole lot brighter," he said on a wink.

Her pulse definitely didn't skitter at Hugh's wink like it did Zach's. In fact, she rather disliked the gesture coming from Hugh.

"Your mama wanted bigger and better things for you," Uncle Terrance went on to say, grasping her arm gently. "She'd be worried sick to know that you were almost killed today."

Ivy sighed. "To say that I was almost killed is a bit overly dramatic, don't you think, Uncle Terrance?"

"That's Terrance...*overly dramatic*." Hugh made a deferential bow to the man, but when her uncle glared at him, Hugh flinched just as dramatically.

"Get outa here, Bagley!" Uncle Terrance grabbed Hugh's hat and pulled it down over his eyes. "I believe the boss-man said you've got some cattle to feed."

Hugh popped his hat off and backed away, scowling. "Don't get your nose so out of joint. A fella has a right to put in his two cents." He dodged forward for a brief moment and gave Ivy one of his rough and tumble hugs. "See you around, dolly."

"Bye," she responded then turned back to her uncle. "Honestly, the injury is nothing, Uncle Terrance. I'm fine." She would be—in a week or so, anyway.

Terrance's expression grew grim. "It hurts me to say this, especially seein' as how nice it's been havin' you around, but you really need to question what you're doing here. Have you gotten what you came here for?"

She had gained nothing of what she'd come for.

And yet, she'd gained so much. She'd gained a friend—a very good friend in Zach. A man she'd shared some of her deepest secrets with. A man who'd gone to great lengths to make her feel special for her birthday. A man who'd made her *feel* for the first time in a very long time.

Terrance grasped both of her arms, his concerned gaze not quite landing on hers. "You need to take a good long look at why you'd want to stay. This is rough territory, and now with cattle thieves cutting in on your daddy's herd, there could be even more trouble," he warned, sending an ominous chill down her spine. "It'd make me feel a whole lot better knowing that I didn't have to worry about you, sweets."

It'd make her feel a whole lot better knowing that she didn't have to worry, either, but was that the right thing to do?

Desperate for an answer, she sent up a silent prayer. She prayed that God would make her way very clear.

"I can guarantee you this much…your leg is going to be hurting you even more tomorrow," Violet stated, tying off the wrap that held a medicated compress to the hideous looking swollen bruise. "Now, you keep that cool compress on, do you hear?"

"I'll try. But I'm going back out there with the new foal and his mama."

Hands at her waist, Violet shook her head. "Stubborn. Just like your daddy."

Ivy gave a wry chuckle. "I've heard that once already today."

"From Zach?" the woman asked, inclining her head in an overly inquisitive but endearing way. "He's a very smart man, Zach. *And* he's worried sick about you."

"I know." Ivy popped the last bite of molasses cookie in her mouth.

Violet crossed over and retrieved the stone pitcher from the counter. "He's so worried that he wanted me to invite Ben and his family over for dinner tonight, so that Ben could take a look at your injury." She poured another glass of milk for Ivy then set down the pitcher.

"He didn't," she said, incredulous.

"He did."

"That is a downright—"

"*Caring*…wasn't that what you were going to say next? A downright *caring* thing to do?" Violet adjusted her already perfectly positioned apron.

"Yes. Of course," Ivy amended, realizing that her accusation would've been too harsh. But for some reason, she felt so very undeserving of Zach's warm and tender concern.

"Let him fuss over you," Violet urged, as though she'd just heard Ivy's thoughts.

Ivy's heart beat wildly. Her face flushed hot. Her entire body trembled in an odd, but not exactly unpleasant way, as though somewhere deep inside, those words had answered the most profound longing in her heart. The longing to be cared for, cherished, respected, loved…

"A wire came for you right before lunch, Ivy," Violet said, gently tugging Ivy from her thoughts.

"Oh?"

"I'm not sure who sent it, though." She crossed to the long row of beautiful new pine cupboards her father had ordered from Joseph and rifled through one of the drawers. "Here it is."

Ivy stood and took the envelope, trying not to appear overly eager, but she'd been awaiting word from *The Sentinel* regarding when she'd be starting her new job as assistant editor.

"Thank you, Violet." Slow and steady, she moved out of the room, willing herself not to limp as she made her way to the front porch.

She opened the door and stepped outside where Shakespeare had claimed the porch swing. He peeked at her through a slit in one eye, gave a long and languid stretch, then curled up in a fluffy ball again.

"Sleep tight." Smiling, she breathed in the unseasonably warm air, glancing toward the western sky where threatening storm clouds were building. "Oh, my…you're not going to like what's coming, Shakespeare. You used to hate storms, and I would venture to guess that you still do."

She eased down to sit on the top step then opened the cream-colored envelope. She pulled out the small slip of paper and read each word carefully, her heart sinking.

If she didn't report to work by the middle of next week, then the job she'd worked so hard to earn would go to another.

Closing her eyes, she gave a frustrated sigh.

She couldn't pass on the opportunity of a lifetime.

It would take a week by train to return to New York, which meant that within the next three days, something had to change with her father or she'd leave with a hole the size of Colorado in her heart. Not just regarding her father, but Zach, too. She'd grown to care for him and she'd found herself cherishing his every tender touch and word. But she had a life back east.

This isn't the way she'd expected things to transpire. She hadn't thought that she'd come back here with any great or grand expectations, but maybe, deep down, she had. Maybe she'd hoped for something in return from her father? A hand of friendship? Forgiveness? Love?

Those things weren't too much to ask, were they?

Not more than an hour ago, she'd prayed that God would show her the right and the best thing. Was this His answer?

For a brief moment, Ivy would've liked to give up on finding a peaceful resolution, pack up her bags and board the next train east. But she couldn't. Not yet.

She had to have some kind of closure with her father— even if it was difficult and painful. Surely, that would be better than nothing at all. Ivy would just press the subject with him. She'd corner him, not forcing his love or his forgiveness, but she'd finally tell him exactly what had happened that fateful day six long and hard years ago.

Zach shrugged out of his coat and threw it over the birthing stall door. He leaned back against the thick wood wall, looping one ankle over the other as he watched the peaceful interaction between the mare and her new foal.

The air had grown unnaturally moist and warm this afternoon. He could smell the distinct scent of a storm hanging on the horizon.

He could smell one in his soul, too. He felt pressed from every side. Knowing that cattle thieves had struck on his watch had taken his legs right out from underneath him. Brodie and Aaron had been out already, offering their help in tracking down the thieves, but Zach had turned them away. He'd do this. This was *his* responsibility.

And then his interchange with Hugh had been anything but reasonable. Hugh had thrown all civility aside and had given him a thick dark piece of his mind, accusing Zach of putting Ivy in harm's way, and of being too dense to realize when cattle thieves were sniffing around.

It'd been all Zach could do to hold his tongue. To keep his tightly fisted hands at his side. Arguing with the man would get him nowhere.

"He's a nice-looking foal," Mr. Harris said, snagging his attention. "Isn't he?"

"Yes, he is. Fine looking." Zach pushed away from the wall and shook the man's hand as he entered the stall. Although Mr. Harris was a little peaked, he still had an undeniable authority about him that commanded attention. "Sorry you didn't make it back in time for the delivery."

His boss slowly crossed to the mare and gave the new mama an approving pat on the neck. "I wish I could've seen it. Her last foal has been a pure pleasure to work with. This boy's probably going to be just as fine, right girl?"

Nickering, the mare nuzzled him. Dipped her head to where her foal was plastered to her side, his big brown eyes wary. "Yes, I see, Annie. He's a fine-looking fella."

When Mr. Harris eased away, Zach couldn't miss the wince that crossed his face. Or the way he clamped an arm over his stomach for a brief moment.

Concern immediately flooded Zach. "Are you feeling all right?"

"I'm fine." Dragging in a deep breath, he stood a little

straighter. "You did a good job with the little guy. You're getting him used to your scent and touch, right?"

"I've been in here every hour."

"Good work."

Zach had to wonder if he'd be so approving once he found out about Ivy getting injured. And all because of Zach's decision. "Sir, I need to let you know…"

"About Ivy?" Mr. Harris set his unwavering focus on Zach.

"Yes, sir."

"Violet already informed me." He yanked a kerchief from his back pocket and swiped it across his face. "Whew… It turned out to be a warm one today."

"It sure did," Zach agreed. Although he knew Violet meant well, Zach was half frustrated she had taken out from underneath him his right to own up to his mistakes. "Sir, I can't tell you how sorry I am that Ivy was hurt."

His boss pulled his black hat from his head and grew pensive. "I understand you were in a bind, but it wasn't the best idea to leave her alone with a laboring mare. No matter *what* she told you." Setting his jaw, he stared at the mare and foal. "Knowing Ivy, she probably shot at you with a healthy dose of that I-can-do-it-myself attitude. Am I right?"

A dressing down, he'd expected, but not this.

"I should've thought better than to leave her alone in that situation." Zach grabbed the bucket of oats from the shelf and crossed over to let the mare feast.

"You know what you did wrong, Zach—that's why I trust you. But I know how Ivy can be. And I know you." He settled his hat back on his head again, his hand drifting to his trademark bolero. "I asked you to make her fall in love with things here again. How's that been going?"

How could he tell his boss that Ivy had every intention of returning to New York? "I'm still trying."

Mr. Harris moved closer to the foal, down to eye level with the little guy. A thoughtful silence filled the stable. One corner of his mouth tipped in the slightest grin. "Violet said that Ivy even went so far as to check to see if the foal was breech," he recounted, wincing as he stood. Reaching to the side he grabbed for the wall then moved toward the small stool in the corner. "Is that right?"

"I'm afraid so." Zach moved a little closer just in case his boss collapsed. "That's how she took a hoof to her leg."

It was of little comfort now to know how much better Mr. Harris had felt just this morning. Not when he was almost as bad as Zach had ever seen him, right now.

Mr. Harris folded unceremoniously onto the stool, his face beaded with perspiration as he closed his eyes for a long moment. He leaned forward, his arms on his legs. Dragged in several hitching breaths. "She's something, that daughter of mine. She'll do most anything—even if you tell her not to," he stated, peering up at Zach, his eyes shadowed with pain beyond his apparent physical condition. "I think that's what I appreciate most about her."

"Sir…" Zach began, knowing that if he was going to help Ivy reconcile with her father, it had to be soon. Because from the looks of him now, he might not be around much longer.

"What is it, Zach?" Mr. Harris winced again.

"Have you told her that—lately, I mean?" He didn't really expect a reply, but gave ample time for one and sadly, heard nothing. "I don't mean to pry or stick my nose in your personal affairs, but I think—I *know*—it'd mean the world to her to hear you say those words."

"That's not likely to happen. There are just too many years and too much hurt that's run over what we once had."

"I don't know, sir.... I have to believe that there's always hope." He felt almost hypocritical in saying such a thing when he knew full well that he struggled to embrace the idea himself. "And I know that she'd love to talk over some things with you. If you could find the time—"

"I'll think on it," Mr. Harris said, giving Zach a glimmer of hope for helping Ivy truly find her way back home.

But would it be soon enough? If he never did another bit of kindness for Ivy, he was given to encouraging her toward reconciliation with her father.

Chapter Fifteen

Ivy sat outside her father's office, waiting. And waiting.

He'd gone in there over a half an hour ago—alone. What in the world could he be doing? She held her hand over her side pocket, where she'd stuffed the wire. With this news pressing down on her, she was tempted to fling open the big wooden doors, charge in there and insist on digging into the past in order to build some kind of future. But something held her back.

While she sat in the overstuffed leather chair, she found herself praying for guidance and wisdom. Left to her own stubborn will and wounded pride she might never know the beauty of reconciliation.

Shifting in the comfortable chair, she glanced outside as the storm clouds rolled over the horizon, steady and menacing.

Unsettled, she perched on the edge of her chair and peered at the chunky wood table anchoring the furniture in the living room. It was scattered with books and papers and a token almanac. A leather-bound book off to the side caught her eye.

She picked it up, held it to her face, breathing in the distinct scent of leather and paper and ink. She fingered the worn edges, the smooth cover. With a certain amount of reverence, she set the book in her lap and opened it, slowly turning through page after page of beautiful poetry, lovely sentiments—even a rough sketch here or there. Her heart swelled.

Had her father penned these words? The artistic looping scrawl looked nothing like his tight and exact penmanship. Flipping to the front of the book, she searched for the author's name, but found none.

She turned to an entry somewhere in the middle of the book and carefully read the words, her breath catching at the longing she found there. The true love. She could almost feel its mysterious power seeping down into the farthest reaches of her heart, beckoning her to care.

To trust.

To believe.

Just then a brilliant bolt of lightning illuminated the room followed by a resounding clap of thunder. Hugging the journal to her chest, she stood and crossed to the long window, peering outside at the colorful October landscape blanketed by the gray sky. When movement in the corral caught her eye, she turned to see Zach struggling to get a lead rope around a frenzied horse. She scanned the area, but there was no sign of the ranch hands anywhere.

Spinning around to face her father's office door, her heart dropped. As much as she yearned for some kind of closure, she'd have to put her plans on hold. Zach needed her help.

Setting down the journal where she'd found it, she whisked out of the house. Picking up her skirts, she raced toward the barn, ignoring the sharp jolting pain rendered by every step.

The wind-whipped rain was coming down hard, pelting her with brutal force. She'd be soaked clear through in no time. When she entered the barn, she darted to the entrance leading to the corral.

Snatching another lead rope from a hook by the door, she raced out toward Zach.

"Ivy, get back," Zach called as he saw her approach. When the massive horse reared up, kicked then tromped down hard, Zach barely dodged a direct hit.

Her insides balled into a knot. "I want to help!" she yelled above the angry rumble of thunder that shook the ground.

When she moved a step closer, he pushed out his hand to ward her off. "Don't come any closer. You'll get hurt."

"But *you're* going to get hurt."

"Ivy…I mean it," he warned, his voice containing no hint of doubt. "Stay back. He's going to hurt himself if I don't get him in the barn," he measured out, every one of his words unbroken in the intensity of the moment.

"I'll get the roan." She headed to the roan trotting nervously over by the fence, frantic for a way out.

"No!" Zach yelled, glancing over at her for a quick second. Long enough for the stallion to throw its massive head and neck, knocking Zach on the ground.

Ivy gasped, then raced toward him. "Zach! Zach, are you all right?" she called. Blinking against the driving rain, she came to a stop when he suddenly shoved himself out of the mud.

Through his soaking wet shirt, she could see every muscle bunch, tense with determination. He closed in on the seemingly untamed mass of horse, looped the lead rope around the stallion's neck then tugged him toward the barn.

"Just get inside," he growled, glaring at her as he stalked toward the barn, the stallion in tow, still restless, but no longer lethal. "I'll get the other two."

Ignoring his command, she made her way to the roan, quivering when another bolt of bluish-white lightning pierced the ground. "Come on, now. Did you see how your friend finally came to his senses?" Slowing as she neared the skittish horse, she brushed the rain-plastered hair from her face. "We'll get you tucked in all safe and sound in the barn."

When the roan sidestepped himself into a corner, Ivy closed in on him. He was smaller than the stallion, but still, she'd barely be able to loop the lead rope around his neck if he wasn't feeling cooperative.

After several tries, and a litany of warnings from Zach as he bolted from the barn toward her, she finally had the roan secured. She jogged through the rain toward the barn, passing Zach on the way and giving him the sweetest, most triumphant smile she could afford in spite of the assaulting rain.

He rewarded her with a firm scowl that left her yearning for one of his warm and spine-tingling smiles.

After all of the horses were stabled, Zach emerged from the tack room, an old blanket in his hands. "Here," he said, handing it to her.

"Thank you," she acknowledge, taking it from him and wiping her face and arms down, and ruffling the dripping moisture from her hair. When she finally peered up at him, her breath caught at the stomach-fluttering intensity in his ardent gaze.

His throat convulsed with a swallow. After a lingering moment, he turned and walked over to the open barn door leading to the corral. He grasped the door, his knuckles growing white. "You sure d-don't listen very well, do you?" His voice was low, his stutter once again apparent.

"What was I supposed to do?" she asked, appalled

and strangely flattered by the audacity of his accusation. "Stand back and applaud your efforts?"

With a shake of his head, he pinned his focus to somewhere out on the stormy horizon. "Well, that would've b-been better than throwing yourself in harm's way."

"I grew up here, remember? Stubborn horses don't scare me." Lifting her drenched skirt, she moved over to stand beside him. She couldn't help but notice how Zach, too, was soaked through. "I'm very accustomed to being around *all* things stubborn," she threw at him.

He drew his mouth into a firm line as the rain battered the barn roof. "Listen, lady…when that b-brood of horses is like that, they're almost too much f-f-for me to handle, let alone you. That black stallion has so mmmuch influence on the rest of them that whenever there's a bad s-storm, he stirs them up into a regular frenzy."

"Can you blame him?" she questioned, feeling a sharp sting of remorse as images of Zach getting tramped by the stallion flashed through her mind. Had her stubborn pride almost gotten him killed? "I mean…it can't be very comforting being out there when bolts of lightning are sizzling around you."

Just then a cat's loud and mournful cry echoed in the barn.

"Did you hear that?" she asked, peering over at him.

"What?"

"I heard a cat. It sounded like it was coming from up in the loft." She tugged Zach toward the center of the barn that vaulted all the way through the loft to the roofline. She peered up just as Shakespeare snagged his front claws into one of the tallest crossbeams in the barn and scrambled to gain his footing after nearly plummeting to sure death.

She gasped, raw fear seizing her heart.

"Whoa… That was close," Zach noted.

"He's stuck himself way up there." She pointed to her cat yowling loud and strong as he clung to the beam. "I'm coming, sweet kitty. Don't worry." Grasping the sides of the ladder, she scampered up to the hay-laden loft, ignoring the searing pain in her leg and side.

Zach followed right behind her. "Hang on, Shakespeare."

Once she was on the loft floor, she peered up at her cat, her heart clenching at his mournful cry. "He's scared to death."

"He hates sssstorms." Climbing over a mound of stacked bales, Zach made his way toward the front of the barn. "Tends to lose all of h-h-his courage when it's bad like this."

She scaled the hay behind him, nearly tripping on her rain-soaked skirt, to stand beneath her cat. Her eyes misted and throat constricted at the tortured sound of his yowl. "Oh, Zach, look at him." She glanced over to where Zach had pushed open the loft doors, allowing more light into the room. "The poor thing. He'll be stuck up there forever. It's all right, Shakespeare. I'll help you."

Another crack of thunder shook the barn, sending her cat darting away from the front wall as though he was about to jump from twenty feet plus, into her arms.

"Shakespeare, no!" she screamed. Her heart thudded furiously.

The cat came to an abrupt stop. Shrank back a few feet. Yowled so loud that Ivy was sure he could be heard from miles away.

"What are we going to do?" She desperately hoped Zach had a plan even as she scanned the barn looking for some way she could reach her cat.

When Zach grasped her shoulders and turned her

around to look at him, it was almost her undoing. His gentle yet firm touch, the warm compassion in his gaze and the strength he offered simply by his presence were nothing if not overwhelming. She struggled to hold her tears at bay.

"I'm going to g-g-get him down," he assured, lightly rubbing her arms with the pads of his thumbs. "*You* will—"

"Stand here and applaud your efforts," she quickly answered, so overcome with relief that she almost wrapped him in a hug right then and there. At the doubtful look on his face she added, "I promise."

He gave her a tentative nod, followed by one of his pulse-pounding winks. "Good. I'm glad that's settled."

Turning her attention to her cat again, tears stung the corners of her eyes. Her kitty's distraught expression broke her heart. "William Shakespeare…you be a brave kitty. Zach's coming for you."

"No f-fast moves, Shakespeare. You hear?" he cautioned, stepping over to the wall.

"How are you going to reach him?" Ivy followed close behind.

Zach nodded toward the rungs marching up the side of the barn. "I'll ssscale these, then work my way to the crossbeam on that outside ledge," he explained, pointing to horizontal exterior timber butting up to each of the crossbeams spanning the large barn.

Apprehension slithered up Ivy's spine as she peered at the narrow ledge. "That looks terribly dangerous, Zach."

"Don't worry." Grasping the rungs, he made his way up. "As long as he d-doesn't tear me to shreds on the way down, it sh-should be easy enough. You hear that, fella?" he added, as the cat warily peered at his rescuer, his golden eyes as big as Ivy had ever seen.

She craned her head back and watched Zach climb up to the ledge. "I'll be right here if you need something."

"Good to know."

"Hang on, Shakespeare," she called, scrambling over several bales to stand beneath her cat in case he decided to jump. "Zach, are you doing all right?"

"I'm fine." His face to the wall, he edged across the ledge. "Believe me...this isn't the first time I've had to go after him."

Moved by the very idea that Zach had risked his life for her cat before, she swallowed hard. "He's been stuck up there before?"

"No. Not here." He stepped around a vertical timber. "But he's been f-f-forty feet up in a Ponderosa, caught on top of the old b-barn and stuck down a dry well."

"He hasn't," she breathed, nearly speechless.

"He has," Zach confirmed, reaching the beam. He stepped onto it, shuffling one foot in front of the other to where her cat clung frantically to the beam as though it was shaking beneath his paws.

Ivy's heart beat madly as she watched him make his way to her cat. He hadn't given his own comfort a second thought. If not for his bravery, she didn't know what she'd have done.

Hugh hated cats. Even if she'd tracked him down and begged, pleaded, he wouldn't have put himself out for a feline.

"Easy, now, Shakespeare...." With impeccable balance and real compassion, Zach eased down next to the cat. He carefully pried all four of Shakespeare's claw-slung feet from the beam then slowly lifted the cat into his arms and stood. He even took the time to scratch her cat on top of his head, as though to soothe him. "I'm just here to give you a ride down. Okay?"

Watching each calculated movement as Zach shifted the cat to the crook of his left arm, facing outward, Ivy felt desperate to help in some way. "Zach..."

"What, Ivy?" he answered, pausing for a moment to peer down at her.

"Cradle him. Like this," she instructed, demonstrating as though she was cradling a baby. "He likes to be held that way."

"Trust me...he'll be better off if he can see where he's going." Zach continued on to the wall.

"Are you sure?"

"Positive." When Zach reached the wall, he shifted Shakespeare to one side and began edging over the ledge to the rungs.

"Zach..." she called again, nearly frantic to help.

"What, Ivy?" he answered, amused by her ill-placed, albeit innocently so, conversation.

"You're doing a fine job." The sweet gratitude filling her voice tugged a smile to his mouth. "Thank you so much."

He didn't dare glance over his shoulder at her. Not with Shakespeare all stiff and squirming at his side, and only one hand to grasp each vertical timber as he edged across the wall.

"You're welcome," he finally said, nearly losing his grip as he leaned back and stepped around a timber.

"Are you afraid of heights?" she asked.

He paused for a moment to get his bearings. And to shove any fear from his voice. "I'm not exactly f-f-fond of them." He didn't fancy being more than twenty feet above the loft floor, plastering himself against the wall as he moved across a narrow beam, but he wasn't going to tell her that.

She'd feel guilty. And the last thing she needed to cling to was more guilt.

When he finally reached the loft floor, he bit off a huge sigh of relief and handed Shakespeare over to Ivy. "Here you go. He sssseems to be j-just fine."

"Thank you so much, Zach." She cradled her cat in her arms. The vulnerability and deep appreciation glistening in her gaze made every treacherous step he'd taken worth it. "Really, I don't know what I would've done if you hadn't been here."

Struggling to calm his racing heart, he raked a hand through his wet hair. "Glad I could help."

She reached up and gently brushed a thick lock of hair from his face, sending a strong current racing through his body. Her nearness, and the beautiful hesitation in her tender touch, almost knocked his resolve off its axis.

"Not everyone would risk their lives this way, Zach." Her warmth seared straight through to his heart.

He could barely even find his voice enough to speak. "Just doing what is right, that's all."

"Well I am very, *very* thankful." Smiling and apparently oblivious to *just how much* her touch affected him, she held up her purring cat. "And so is this fluffy fellow, aren't you, Shakespeare?"

Carefully avoiding Ivy's hands, he gave the cat a scratch on the head. "You're more than welcome, Mr. Shakespeare."

Desperate to right his resolve to keep his head around her and to find some kind of evenness, he moved away from her and sat down in the loose hay piled in front of the open loft doors.

She eased down right next to him.

His blood thrummed through his veins at record speed. His throat grew tight. His arms ached to hold her. Rooting his gaze to the stormy horizon, he struggled to quiet the unwelcome responses.

"The view from up here is stunning, isn't it?" The gratefulness threaded through her voice held him rapt.

Mutely nodding, he stared out at the gray horizon, torn by the avid beat of his heart for Ivy and the avid vow he'd made regarding her. He looped an arm around one of his knees, and swallowed hard.

"I can't tell you how much I've missed the mountains," she revealed, her voice infused by wonder and appreciation and…longing.

Was she having second thoughts about her return to New York? What would that mean for him?

"Th-Th-Things are different in N-New York, huh?" Turning to Ivy, all rain-soaked and rosy-cheeked and far more breathtaking than any mountain scenery, he felt his resolve slip a little more.

Ivy….

She'd been a perfect and spritely upset to his well-ordered life. A stunningly beautiful challenge to his conquered world. And a lovely beckoning call to the hopes buried deep in his heart.

Never, in a million years, had he thought he'd cross paths with her again. He figured she'd come back to Boulder to visit, but he'd never imagined that her return and the prospect of her staying would mean so much to him.

She peered up at him, that dazzling spring green gaze of hers searching deep, as though seeing him for the first time. "A lot different. I've loved the city and all it has to offer, but…"

"But it's n-not home?" he finished for her, hoping that what he said was true.

What if he followed the age-old beat of his heart? What if he took one giant risk, far bigger than the risk of getting struck by lightning, getting trampled by a fearful stallion or scaling a narrow ledge to rescue a cat, and laid his heart out for her to see?

The slow and tentative way she leaned into him made his breath catch in his throat.

She shuddered slightly, as though cold. Hugged Shakespeare to her chest. "New York doesn't feel like home to me anymore than this place does."

He longed to draw her close, to lend her warmth. But he was scared to death that holding her, feeling the perfect way she'd mold to his side, and the comforting way she was sure to relax against him, would give him a false hope.

"Why d-d-doesn't it f-feel like home here?" His stutter barged into the moment with all of its abrasiveness and ugliness.

"I don't know," she whispered, peering up at him as though he might have the answer she'd been searching for. "But I'm beginning to wonder if it's because there are unsettled things. In my heart, I mean—and with my father. Maybe I'll never feel like I'm home until those things are settled."

Compassion for her had overwhelmed him on many different levels and on many different occasions. He'd prayed for her. That she and her father would find more than just a brush-it-under-the-rug kind of reconciliation, the kind that healed gaping wounds.

And when he'd prayed for her, he'd felt almost as if he was moving closer to God. The thought even now sent a knowing kind of quiver down his spine. Was it too much to hope that somehow their lives were being woven together?

"It's n-never too late, you know?" he said, touched by

the way she leaned her head on his shoulder. "To ssssettle things, I mean."

"I don't know if I'll ever find forgiveness."

"You can forgive yourself and him and go on even if your father ch-chooses not to. But *true* reconciliation— that's what I've been praying for."

"You have?" Her gaze instantly misted over.

He nodded, feeling his resolve give way. He swallowed against the thick emotion clogging his throat.

When Shakespeare pressed his paws against her as though he'd finally come to his senses, she opened her arms and let him go.

Still wholly apprehensive, the cat hunched down and belly crawled over a few feet. Far enough away to appear brave...close enough to fling himself into her arms if thunder exploded on the horizon again.

Her sympathetic smile seemed to light up the dim hayloft. "That's a brave kitty." She hugged her knees to her chest and stared outside where the torrential rain had turned to a quiet sprinkle. "The mountains are beautiful. So beautiful."

Zach was completely captivated. Not by the scenery, though. By Ivy, by the way she'd slowly begun to open up to him. By the tenderness she showed to God's creatures. By her beauty, both inside and out.

He braced a hand behind him and turned toward her. Gently grasping her chin, he nudged her gaze to his. "Ivy...*you* are beautiful."

She managed a halfhearted chuckle as though she didn't quite believe him. "Don't be silly."

She had to know just how honest and true those words were. Staring deep into her eyes, he looked past the strength and determination she wore like some mask and regal gown.

"I must look a sight," she weakly argued, fingering her damp hair with trembling hands. "All rain-soaked and bedraggled and—"

"You're *beautiful,*" he said again, simply. Honestly. He stroked the backs of his fingers down her face to her chin, her skin, so silky and smooth. "I d-d-didn't think it was possible, but you've grown more beautiful sssince you left six years ago."

"Zach, you're very ki—"

"Honest," he finished for her on a slow wink. It pleased him to see the endearing scowl she presented him, and the eye-catching way she blushed. "I'm very honest, Ivy."

She paused, then turned toward him, her slender throat convulsing on a hard swallow. She fingered the auburn velvet edging her wool sleeves. "I'm so confused, Zach."

"About…"

"About things with my father. About what my future holds." She glanced outside for several seconds then looked back at him, her admiring gaze slipping from his damp hair. To his eyes. To his mouth. She sighed, her breath lightly fanning over his face. "About things with you…"

His inhale caught somewhere in his chest as she leaned in a little closer. The diminishing space between them was charged with more energy and brilliance than the lightning-sliced skies a short time ago. He closed his eyes, memorizing it all.

Was he playing with fire? Was he setting himself up only to be let down?

There was no denying the attraction that existed between them. Or the easy way they could talk together when they were alone, when he could be himself in spite of his stutter. Had he been fooling himself, all those years, to think that he could get Ivy out of his mind and heart?

When he looked at her, at the pure and strong and lovely woman she was, he wondered if maybe her return home was by some divine design.

Just seeing the trust deep in her gaze made his heart swell. One corner of his mouth tipped in pure male satisfaction.

Her blush deepened as she stared at his mouth, her focus seemingly fastened to his grin in a way that sent a quiver straight down his spine to the tips of his booted feet.

"I know that I probably shouldn't be feeling this way about you since—"

"Shhh," he whispered, holding his forefinger to her full and soft lips. For right now, this very moment, he didn't want to hear any *buts* or *sinces* or any other words of regret. "Ivy…" he said, his voice low and tight. "I'm about th-three seconds away f-from kissing you, so if you have any obj-jections…"

With certain and undeserving reverence, she splayed one hand at his chest and one on his shoulder, and peered up at him, so beautiful, so vulnerable and *so very* trusting.

Zach tenderly grasped her arms and pulled her close. He lowered his mouth to hers, his pulse pounding at the base of his throat.

His heart skipped several beats at the willing way her lips parted ever-so-slightly. The way her soft sigh whispered across his face. And the supple way her mouth melded to his as he laid his warm claim on her lips.

He savored every single moment of this kiss. His breath came hard and fast—especially at the small whimper that came from the back of Ivy's throat as she responded so completely to him. He trailed his hands to her neck, loving the feel of her hair whispering against his skin.

Longing for more, but knowing he was nearing dangerous ground, he pulled away. Searched her eyes...fathomless with the same raw emotion that had settled in his soul.

He brushed a lock of hair from her face, hungry to uncover every little aspect of Ivy. "I've been wwwaiting to do that ever since I f-f-f-first laid eyes on you, Ivy Grace Harris."

"You mean when I returned home?" she breathed, her voice a mere whisper as he gently tugged her into his arms and embraced her.

He shook his head in response, loving the feel of her cheek pressed against his chest. Could she hear the way his heart beat sure and steady for her? Could it be that after all these years, they would be together? "Long, lllllong before that."

She leaned back enough to look at him. Her fingers trembled as she touched them featherlight to his mouth. Trailed them to his cheek and then his brow. Surely she had no idea of the innate power she had over him.

"Zach," she whispered, her gaze flitting outdoors as though needing to escape. "I'm so confused. I want to stay here in Boulder, but I have to leave."

Instant dread tightened around his stomach. "Leave?"

"I received a wire from *The Sentinel* today." Her voice quavered every bit as much as her fingertips had seconds ago. She slid back from him, the softness and vulnerability he'd just experienced in her gaze and her touch visibly falling away right before his eyes. "I'm supposed to be back in New York by next week."

Next week?

He'd just laid his heart and soul, his past and his future,

all on the line, and *now* she was telling him that she had to *leave?*

How could he have been so foolish?

Struggling to gather the pieces of himself, he edged away from her and rose to his feet.

Ivy scrambled to standing, as well. She hugged her arms to her chest, her gaze not quite connecting with his.

He'd allowed her to hurt him once.

He'd allowed her to hurt him again.

He'd been an idiot for following his heart. For believing that he could trust her with his happiness.

"So, you're g-going back?" His tone was a little harsher than he'd intended.

Her brow crimped as though she was wounded. "Y-Yes, it's what I've wanted," she answered, her voice threaded with forced confidence as she tilted her chin up a willful notch. She flattened her arms at her sides. "For a long time this is what I've wanted."

"Is it what you want *now?*" he challenged, his words as clear as his foolishness just moments ago. Zach searched her gaze for doubt, sure he'd find it there, but she'd closed herself off. "Really?"

"Of course. I'm confident enough to know what I want, Zach."

That, he didn't doubt. But was she confident enough to recognize a mistake before she made one?

Chapter Sixteen

"Come on, Ivy, just this once?" Hugh pleaded, shoving his thin lower lip out as though to push her into saying yes.

"No, Hugh," she answered, again. For the past few minutes Hugh had been trying to coax her into going on an outing with him. "It's not a good time. And besides... we're just friends."

"For old times' sake?" he persisted.

"No," she repeated, her thoughts drifting to Zach.

It'd been nearly impossible to keep her mind on anything after Zach had kissed her two days ago. Gentle and so honorable, he'd seared her very heart with the tender touch of his lips. She'd barely been able to find her next breath. Barely been able to find her voice.

But when she'd told him that she would be leaving, and he'd responded as though she'd just slapped him across the face, she'd barely held her heart in check. Surely he couldn't expect her to give up her life in New York.

Did she even have a full life back there? She had a wonderful and challenging job. Friends. And plenty of social functions to keep herself busy, but had she experienced the kind of relationship she'd formed with Zach? Deep, true and abiding?

Hugh brushed his hands down his chambray shirt as though she'd just kicked a cloud of dust over him. "Well, you can't blame a guy for trying, can you?"

Although slightly annoyed by his tenacity, she couldn't help but smile at his perseverance. "No, but you're never going to snag a girl if you act desperate."

"Desperate?" He flattened a hand over his chest. "You wound me, dolly."

"You know what I mean."

"Well, I suppose I better get back to work before the boss-man hounds me for *fraternizing with the locals.*" His tight wink fell in an oddly unceremonious way at her feet.

"He's really not so bad, is he, Hugh?" she urged, disturbed still by how antagonistic Hugh had been toward Zach—especially when she'd not found one thing to validate his concerns. "I mean really…he is as hard a worker as anybody I've ever seen. He's conscientious. And so intuitive with the livestock."

Caring, compassionate, passionate…

She could list off a hundred different attributes about Zach that had won her heart.

"It's his determination to steer the world on his own, as though he has something to prove, that rubs me wrong," he clipped off, his sharp Adam's apple bobbing with a swallow. "It's what's going to trip him up sooner or later."

Ivy reflected yet again on just how similar Zach was to her father. How similar *she* was to her father.

When she was young, she'd admired those attributes in her father, but once her mama took ill and Ivy had witnessed the way her father would throw himself headlong into life, as though he had to make up for the fact that he'd been unable to help her mama, she'd begun to disdain them.

That last outing she'd gone on with her mama, her mama had shared such touching things about Ivy's father, though. She'd loved him. *Really loved him.*

Her mama could see the beauty in all of his stubborn, headstrong, determined ways. And she'd cherished his soft and honorable and gallant heart. Her mama had said, "That is what is so priceless about my relationship with your father, Ivy. Look for these things in a man."

Had Ivy found what she'd longed for in Zach?

"He's so much like my father," she breathed, unsettled by the tender challenge in her mama's crystal clear words.

"Yep. Only your father has years of experience," Hugh dismissed as though he was some kind of authority on the matter. "How is he feeling, by the way?"

"Poorly." She peered up at the house where her father had cloistered himself in his study. "He was doing so well—went out on the range and everything—but then he fell ill again."

"Don't worry, dolly." He moved closer and wrapped his lanky arms around her in one of his crushing hugs. "Everything is going to be all right."

"Get your hands off of her, Hugh," Zach warned, startling Ivy, and Hugh, too, from the way he stiffened suddenly.

Hugh didn't loosen his hold even a little. "Relax, Drake. I'm just giving her a little hug." The provoking tone of his voice pricked Ivy's pride.

She unsuccessfully tried to push away from him, detesting the feeling of being used to make some kind of point.

"You're crossing the lllline. With her and with m-me."

When she wrenched her head around to look at Zach, he took a step closer, his unyielding focus fixed on Hugh.

"Do you see her complaining?" Hugh goaded. "Because I sure don't."

"Zach, really," she placated, trying to finagle her way out of Hugh's rigid hug. "It's fine. He was just—"

"In fact," Hugh measured out, releasing his constricting hold, "I think she was actually *enjoying* it." The inciting wink he gave Ivy infuriated her, the grin on his face crossing a line of civility that even she could see.

With stealth precision, Zach grabbed Hugh, wrenching his shirt collar into a tight ball.

"Weren't you, dolly?"

Zach hauled back and slammed his fist into Hugh's jaw, knocking him down to the rain-soaked ground.

"Zach, please," she gasped, crossing to where Hugh had angled himself up on his elbows and rubbed his jaw, where Zach's fist had just been. She was half furious at Zach's actions just now, and half heady with a sense of feeling protected. "*Why* are you acting like this?"

"What's the matter, Drake? Cat got your tongue?" Hugh shoved himself up from the mud. "Or maybe you just can't spit out what's on your mind in one piece."

"Keep your hhhhands off of her," Zach warned again, flexing his hands.

Retrieving his hat where it'd landed in a puddle, Hugh jammed it on his head. "Things haven't changed, have they? You're still falling over yourself for Ivy's attention. You're still trying to look like the big hero just to get her to notice."

"Leave it be, Hugh," Zach cautioned.

"No," she protested. Why wouldn't they listen to her? They were acting like a couple of fearsome dogs fighting over a bone. "I want to know…what is he referring to?"

"He knows what I'm talking about. Don't you?" Hugh slithered up next to Ivy as though he had some claim on her. "I warned you back then and I'm warning you now... *stay away* from her."

Zach's intense gaze never even flinched as he stared at Hugh. "Are you finished?"

"She doesn't even know you exist, Drake." The possessive way Hugh draped an arm around Ivy's shoulders just then made her skin crawl. "Didn't then. Doesn't now."

"Hugh, would you answer me, *please?*" she demanded, ducking out of his hold and pivoting to face him, her fists perched at her waist. "*What* is this about?"

"Oh, well, maybe he can tell you...that is if he can get the words out," Hugh mocked on a harsh laugh.

"That's cruel." Ivy skewered Hugh with a glare. She'd known him to be insensitive when he was younger, but she would've thought that by now he would've grown out of such immaturity.

"It may be cruel, but it's the fact, dolly."

"Do *not* call me *dolly,*" she demanded.

"Face it...you'll never have her, Drake," Hugh persisted. The hostility cloaking his gaze took her aback. "You may not be that scrawny boy you were way back when, but she's still beyond your reach."

Zach's jaw tensed. "That's f-f-for her to d-decide."

Hugh hesitated, but when a mordant smile curled his lips, Ivy knew he was up to no good. "It's just too bad that you managed to climb out of that old mine shaft, now isn't it?"

"Mine shaft?" She stepped in between them and glared at Hugh. "To what *mine shaft* are you referring?"

Grasping her arms, Hugh moved her out of his way, stinging her pride.

"Believe me...I had no idea that hole was there," Hugh

growled at Zach. "But if I had, I would've pushed a little harder…to ensure you couldn't get out."

"I'm getting very impatient here." Pivoting, she moved her gaze from Hugh to Zach. "*What* is this all about?"

Zach peered at her for a rigid moment, a flurry of emotions flashing through his heavy gaze. "Saddle up, Hugh," he finally said, his focus still set on Ivy. "We have trouble."

"*That's* nothing new, is it?" Even Ivy felt the stinging effects of Hugh's jibe. "We've had trouble out here for a while now. Ever since you took over as—"

"Leave your biases aside," Zach measured out, shoving his focus to Hugh. "This is sssserious."

Stepping forward, Ivy waved her hands to get their attention. "I am *not* invisible here. Tell me what is going on."

Dragging in a breath, Zach finally met her gaze. "Your father's prized bull, Jerky…I just found him dead in the north p-pasture—where I patched fence just last week."

Hugh snorted. "Well, *that's* no surprise."

"Dead?" Ivy gasped, instantly grieved at the news. Her father cherished Jerky, treated him more like a puppy than a two-thousand-pound bull. "Had he been one of the sick ones from a couple weeks ago?"

"Couldn't be. That animal was the picture of health." Hugh looped his arms at his chest. "He was prime stock."

"He was killed," Zach clarified, peering over his shoulder toward the north pasture where another bank of storm clouds loomed. "And whoever did the d-d-deed made a loud and clear statement, b-because they not only killed him, they gutted him."

Swallowing hard, she struggled to process the news. "But why would someone want to kill my father's prized bull?"

"I'm going to find the perpetrators." Zach's resolute gaze gave her a small measure of comfort. "Believe me, I will."

"Here we go again..." Hugh groused. "You're going to try and be the *big hero* and *save the day,*" he announced, his voice growing more cutting with every single word. "Have you *ever* thought of calling in the authorities? When are you going to learn, Drake?" Just as Hugh started to shove Zach, Zach grabbed both of his arms and held him captive.

For a fleeting moment, Ivy wanted to cheer Zach on. To applaud him for defending himself in the face of Hugh's relentless bullying, but something held her back. Perhaps it was just good old common sense. Or that Hugh was her friend...wasn't he?

"I'll do what I think right, Hugh." Zach let Hugh go then, his jaw ticking. "And you'll do well to mind your own business while you ride south to check out the herd down that way."

Ivy had been in the barn saddling her horse when she glimpsed Zach walking to the house. She ran to catch up to him, determined to have some answers—even if she had to hold him down to get them. It'd been less than a half hour since he'd delivered the horrible news about Jerky, and apart from that he'd not been the least bit forthcoming about any of Hugh's evasive statements.

He'd been focused on getting chores done so he could head out and she'd been focused on the same.

"What *mine shaft* was Hugh talking about?" She struggled to meet his long and purposeful strides.

"It's not important." Zach didn't even stop to look at her.

"Actually, it's very important. I want to know," she

persisted, grabbing his arm and tugging him to a stop. "Tell me, Zach."

He eyed her, his weighted gaze pricking her regret. "It's nothing."

"Zach, this is not *nothing*. Don't think I'm going to quietly back away from this conversation." She met his surprised gaze head-on. "Tell me what happened."

She had a horrible feeling that what he was about to say was only going to add to the guilt she already lived with, but she had to face her past. If she had any hope of finding true peace with herself, her father and with God, then she'd have to start facing her past.

He paused for a pensive moment, as though carefully considering his words. When his wary gaze met hers, her heart slipped a notch. "Do you remember that t-time years ago when several of us ventured into that old mine?"

She nodded. "Yes."

"I heard you scream," he went on to say, his strong jaw visibly tensing. "Came running up from behind the p-pack because I thought something had happened to you."

She recalled the scene. Hugh had led the group of kids into the cave, and Ivy had followed, determined to be one of the *brave*. But when the boy behind her had whispered that there was a bat swooping at her back, she'd screamed. Zach had seemingly appeared from nowhere, certain she needed rescuing. She cringed remembering how rudely and unkindly she'd responded to his gallant gesture.

"I laughed at you," she heard herself say, her throat clogged by guilt.

She held his shuttered gaze, desperate for him to know just how sorry she was to have laughed at his very noble, very Zach-like gesture. Even back then, when he was but eleven years of age, his sense of honor had shined—and in the middle of a dark and abandoned mine.

Her mama's words swirled through her mind. *Look for this in a man....*

She'd looked, all right. Had he been there for her entire life and she'd never taken the time to notice?

She searched his gaze for that magnificent sensitivity she'd grown to crave, but couldn't seem to find it for the mask of pain she saw there. Could she have wounded him so much?

"When you and the others went on ahead, Hugh hung b-back and made it *more than clear* that I was to stay away from you," he continued.

"What do you mean?" Her chest grew tight with shame. "Did he *push* you down that shaft?"

Zach said nothing. He didn't quite meet her gaze, either.

"I thought you'd fallen behind…and because you didn't have a lantern to light your way, landed in it accidentally." Could Zach have willingly carried the trauma of the event, alone, all of these years? "That's what *everyone* had said."

"That's what *I'd* said," Zach confirmed, recalling how vehemently he'd defended the lie to protect himself, Hugh and Ivy. If his brothers had known the real truth, they'd have viciously retaliated against Hugh, and they'd have shunned Ivy for being so heartless. He had no doubt that they loved him, but the mess they'd have made would've only served to make matters a whole lot worse.

Her lips quivered. "He actually *pushed* you down there?"

"He didn't know the old mine shaft was there, and ran

on ahead before he realized what had happened," Zach defended.

"Why?" she choked out.

"He was protecting what he figured was his territory—you," he reasoned, not wishing for her to feel any undo guilt. "Just like he was today."

"Zach...I had no idea. *No idea.*" Holding the back of her hand to her mouth, she shook her head. Her eyes swam with tears. "I'm so sorry."

"Save your sympathy," he quickly put in, his stomach convulsing at the very idea that she might pity him. "I didn't want it then and I sure as shootin' don't want it now."

She wiped at her eyes. Tugged at her bodice. "But your stutter...it started right after that, didn't it?"

He didn't answer. He couldn't. If he did, he risked guilting her further. More than longing for freedom from the crushing weight of his stutter, he didn't want to hurt Ivy.

When she grasped his hand, he could almost feel the overwhelming burden of guilt in her touch. "Oh, Zach. I hadn't wanted to believe that it was true. Please, you have to tell me...was I—did *I* cause you to—"

He set his index finger to her perfect heart-shaped mouth. "Nothing can change what happened."

"But I—"

"There's nothing more to say," he interrupted, determined to change the subject so that he wouldn't hurt her. "Now, I have to g-go in and let your father know about Jerky, so if you'll excuse me...."

When he turned to stride into the house, he half expected her to follow. He made it several feet before he heard her clear her throat. Stopping, he spun back around to face her, surprised by the clear look of frustration etched in her creased brow.

"You make me furious, Zach, the way you close a case when it's convenient for you." She sniffed. Brushed a hand down her skirt. "And with the way you think you're going to track the culprits down, when the situation is obviously dangerous."

"It's my responsibility."

"To get killed?" Her eyes grew wide.

"To do the best job I can for your father," he clarified, itching to get on with things so that he could ferret out the culprits.

She marched up to meet him. "Go get Brodie. Or the sheriff. *Please,*" she pleaded, gripping his arm. "Brodie tracks down men like this for a living. He'll know what to do."

"I'll handle it, Ivy," he ground out, longing for her to believe in him. Her touch threatened to weaken his resolve. "You just need to get inside where you belong."

"Kindly do *not* tell me where I belong, Zach." She tightened her grip on him.

Prying her fingers off his arm, he stepped away from her. "It's dangerous out there. Between the f-fire, the cut fence lines and now this…you have no business being out on the range."

"If you're not going to let Brodie help then at least let me," she feebly reasoned.

He gave his head a frustrated shake. "Do you wwwwant to know how you can help?"

She nodded, squaring her shoulders as though preparing for a long list of difficult tasks.

"G-Go inside. Pack. Get your things ready to go," he said, jamming his hands in his pockets. "That's how you can help—and don't leave anything unssssaid with your father."

Her face revealed palpable regret, pricking Zach's compassion. "But he's resting. When I tried to speak with him earlier, he said that he wasn't feeling up to talking."

"This may be the last time you sssee him, Ivy," he advised, trying to weed out any frustration from his voice.

Her sorrowful gaze drifted to the house, where her father was likely holed up in his office trying to ward off whatever it was that had a brutal hold on his life. "I know, but—"

"I'll make sure I'm back by tomorrow morning. I'll take you to the station," he instructed. "Now, please... for your own good. *Go inside.*"

She peered at him, a bushel full of emotions spilling from her gaze...frustration, fear, anger and—and *vindictiveness?*

"You know...maybe Hugh's right." She lifted her chin a willful notch. "You're just too stubborn for your own good, and sometimes you're too stubborn for the good of others."

He'd longed for her to believe in him instead of being swayed by Hugh. Longed to actually see enduring affection in her gaze.

He'd been such a fool. Oh, he'd believed in *her*. He'd put his heart on the line. Kissed her, cherishing every single breath that had whispered between them. He'd believed that maybe, just *maybe* she shared the same deeply profound emotions that he felt for her.

Lifting his hat from his head, he raked a hand through his hair, trying to calm the pounding in his chest. "So... you're going to believe what Hugh says?" The accusing tone flashing through his words surprised even him.

Her gaze shuttered with hurt then stubborn pride. "If the shoe fits…"

"You'll make it fit if that's what you want. Apparently you've been taking every word he speaks against me to heart." He jammed his hat back on his head and turned to leave.

"I don't want to, but what else can I think? Give me a reason to believe otherwise," she appealed, yanking him to a halt again.

"Maybe it's that I care about your well-being. And that I don't want you to get hurt."

She hesitated for a moment, slamming her focus to the looming storm clouds that threatened to dump even more rain on the already rain-soaked earth.

"One thing I've learned, Ivy…folks will believe what they want. No matter what you try to convince them of."

"You're so intent on proving yourself," she accused, folding her arms at her chest.

"I tried to prove myself to you for a good portion of my life. That's not going to happen again."

"At least prove to me that you're not so stubborn that you'd put yourself and others in danger. Because that's what you'll do if you ride out there without help."

Her words may have been delivered as a hard slap across the face for their stinging affect. She had no idea just how hard he'd worked at protecting those around him. How hard he'd worked to do right by her father. And how hard he'd worked to do right by himself, rather than settle for a dull and complacent life where his dreams were a mere figment of his imagination. And how hard he'd worked to overcome his stutter so that he could live free from its grip.

"I vowed I'd never try to prove myself to you, Ivy…a *long* time ago." He jammed his fists at his waist. A heated shudder coursed down his spine, nailing his boots to the ground. "Hugh's right, you know."

"About what?" She took a step back.

"Well, as far as you're concerned, he's apparently right about a lot of things," he spat, a good measure of vindictiveness thrown into his words. From deep within, a small voice warned him to stop while he could, but he was just so angry and hurt, and so full of regret for being so foolish with his heart. "But I was referring to the way I fell all over myself trying to prove myself to you. I wasted a whole lot of years on you."

She fell silent as thunder rumbled long, loud and ominous.

"When you showed up here it was all I could do not to slip back into the old familiar ways and try to impress you."

"You did that?" she whispered.

"Oh, yes. And I regret it to this day." He dragged in a long breath, figuring that he might as well just spill it all. He had nothing to lose. Absolutely nothing—because he certainly didn't have Ivy, her trust or her belief or her love. "I loved you. Isn't that ridiculous? I *loved* you."

Tears formed in her eyes. "You—you *loved* me?"

"More than you'll ever know," he went on to say, noticing, all of a sudden, that his stutter had not shown up for several sentences. Was it because he was finally divesting himself of Ivy?

He couldn't even enjoy the small victory, not when he knew how hurtful his words were.

"The minute I realized it was you who'd fallen in the mud, that day you arrived almost four weeks ago, I vowed I would never run to your rescue again."

"I didn't ask you to rescue me," she said on another sniff.

He eyed her, his heart gaping open, wounded by his own foolishness. "No. But you have a way of getting yourself in over your head."

She glared at him. "You're one to talk, Mr. I'm-going-to-catch-the-thieves-myself." Her lips quivered. "You are too proud for your own good."

"Do me a favor and stay out of my way." Turning on his heels, Zach stalked over to his mount. "You know what, Ivy?"

"What?"

"I never thought I'd hear myself say this...but it's a good thing you're going back to New York. You don't belong here."

Chapter Seventeen

Blinking against the rain pelting her face, Ivy tugged her hood down farther, the memory of Zach's harsh words raining on her with just as much force. It was useless to try and ward off the near-horizontal sheets of moisture or his stinging sentiments. Each second that passed sent another shiver along her spine and another doubt coursing through her mind.

How was she *ever* going to make right all she'd done wrong with Zach and her father? And how was she ever going to find the culprits who'd killed her father's bull in weather like this? She knew she should've gone for Brodie or the sheriff, but desperation had won out—and now she almost regretted it. As it was, she could barely see through the torrents to twenty feet in front of her horse. Even her mare dipped her head periodically, plodding slowly ahead as though she, too, questioned the wisdom of continuing on.

When brilliant lightning streaked across the sky, she scanned the horizon, searching for someone…anyone. She saw fencing just ahead, the same area where Zach had patched when she'd insisted on going along.

It gaped open, far wider than before.

Just like her heart. Zach's words had ricocheted through her with brutal force, tearing at every bit of strength she'd managed to hold together. He'd *loved* her so long ago? Had tried to prove himself to her for years? How had she missed it? She was certain his stutter was all because of her. It only made sense. Especially when the broken speech apparently began again upon her return. How could she have been so unkind? So dismissive? So foolish?

She couldn't believe how ruthless she'd been with her words to him, but something had driven her. Perhaps her incessant need to find answers, just like her father when her mama had been so sick.

Dread tightened around her throat as she veered toward the hole.

When another flash of lightning lit up the range as bright as day, her gaze fell on her father's prized bull.

Stiff.

Mutilated.

Dead.

Fear slithered up her spine. And sorrow for how the poor animal had lost his life. Her eyes stung, but if tears fell she'd never know. Not with the way raindrops coursed down her face.

Desperate to bring resolution to the situation, she prayed for God's help and grappled for courage. In spite of how she'd chastised Zach for being determined to ferret out the criminals himself. She had to believe that if she was able to get to the bottom of this horrible crime, her father would soften. Maybe then he'd find a way to forgive her.

Maybe then she'd find a way to forgive herself.

Shards of bluish-white light sizzled the air around her. Thunder cracked loud and harsh, sending her horse bolting forward, careening through the gaping hole. She pulled back hard, struggled to gain control.

Finally slowing the mare to a nervous trot, she urged her mount to a stop under a crop of trees—the same trees she'd dreaded being near when she'd been with Zach. And all because of her fear of birds.

The memory of his understanding and warm compassion played in her mind. She'd never felt quite so cared for or quite so cherished as she had with Zach.

And his kiss in the loft…

His kiss had sent her spiraling to the highest of heights. She'd never known a kiss could fill her with such joy. Or that his embrace could lend her such desperately needed strength. Or that his sweet words, no matter how broken, could fill her with wonderful, beautiful, loving promise.

But his words…that he'd *regretted ever coming to her rescue,* and that he was *glad she was going back to New York,* slammed into her mind, jerking her back to reality.

She might very well be in love with Zach, but her love would never find its way home. There was too much between them. She'd wounded him, greatly. She'd seen it in his eyes.

Just then the distant and distressed call of cattle whirled on the wind to her hearing. She urged her horse toward the ridge rimming Gulp's Canyon—where, a good eighty feet below, the remnants of mining had been left like telltale signs of dead dreams. When a bolt of lightning lit up the night sky, a chill coursed down her spine.

Slowing to a stop, a bright flash broke through the penetrating darkness as she peered into the canyon. Her heart sank at the sight of a large grouping of cattle huddled on a patch of ground, the canyon wall to their backs, and a makeshift fence on three sides. The rising creek churning in front of the herd threatened to drown them.

She took in the tragic sight, their frantic cries echoing off the canyon walls and straight into her heart. Knowing that someone had selfishly ferreted off dozens of her father's cattle and had heartlessly staged them here made her blood boil.

"God…if You're listening, I'm asking You to *please* help me," she prayed as she urged her horse across the ridge to the precarious slope winding down into the canyon.

She hadn't been able to help her mama when she'd gotten the wagon stuck. At least, not fast enough. She hadn't been able to help her father since she'd been home—he hadn't even seemed to care that she was around.

And Zach…she'd obviously wounded him to the point that he'd been unable to talk without stuttering around her. The very idea filled her with shame so thick she doubted she'd ever find her way out.

This was her only hope. She had to save these cattle.

For a split second, her horse hesitated at the top of the trail, as though fearing tumbling down to the canyon floor.

"It's all right, girl," she soothed, patting the mare's neck. "You can do it."

Raw fear and a sure sense of being *in over her head,* as Zach had said, nearly squeezed the courage right out of her. She grappled for bravery as she dragged in a steadying breath and sidestepped her mount down the slippery slope.

Step by precarious step, she led the horse to where the cattle were growing increasingly anxious with the swift rise of water spilling over the creek bank.

Contempt for what had been done to the cattle blasted

away all fear as she steered her mount down into the canyon.

When a bolt of lightning pierced the ground not far from them, she stifled a scream. Her horse's breathing grew heavy, the mare's sides heaving with every frantic breath. She willed herself to stay in control or her horse was sure to panic.

When she finally reached the bottom, she led her horse in a gallop over the canyon floor to the restless cattle.

The distinct sound of pounding hooves echoed behind her. She turned in her saddle and made out the faint outline of a man on horseback, his head bent low, heading her way.

Fear prickled every last nerve ending. In another flash of lightning, she tried to make out the rider, but could barely see through the wind-whipped rain.

Maybe it was one of her father's ranch hands.

But she'd left almost immediately after the horrible interchange with Zach. She knew this land as well as any one of them—surely one of them couldn't have gotten out here before her. And Uncle Terrance…he'd headed into town earlier.

Determined not to be intimidated, she swung her horse around and faced the man. "Stop!" she yelled, her voice piercing the torrent of wind and rain. "Stop right where you are!"

He sped up. Her nerve slipped a little at the sight of his long riding coat whipping behind him in the wind, looking dark and ominous. His horse's hooves hammering the rocky surface.

Just then a searing slash of white lightning pierced the air. Her horse reared back. Pawed at the energy-infused air.

She pulled hard on the reins. Struggled to stay seated.

She was trying to get control over the anxious mount when the shadowy rider all but sideswiped her horse.

He snaked out an arm at the last second. Caught her around the middle.

She screeched. Struggled against his unrelenting and painful hold as he yanked her over to his horse.

"Put me down!" she screamed, pounding her fists against his chest.

He snatched a handful of hair in one hand and drove her face into his chest, his rank scent, that familiar combination of trail dirt and sweat hitting her square in the face.

No. It couldn't be....

"Not so fast there, sweets." The man's recognizable voice, a voice she'd trusted for years, met her hearing. Her skin crawled with instant sorrow and confusion and rage.

She grew still. Swallowed hard, hoping against hope that she was wrong. "Uncle Terrance?"

"You shouldn't be out here," he growled.

She wanted desperately to believe that he wasn't responsible for this, but when he pulled her head back and peered down at her, his thin lips curled in a malicious snarl; she couldn't ignore the truth.

"What are you doing?" she demanded. "Why are you out here?"

He wrapped a wiry, but strong arm tight as a noose around her middle. "You just *had* to come sniffing around, didn't you?" he spat, his breath tainted with the putrid scent of bitterness.

"Why? Why would you do this?"

"You have no idea do you, sweets?" he hissed.

"No, I don't. So tell me," she insisted, struggling in

vain to wrench free from his grasp. "Why would you want to do something like this to my father? To his cattle?"

He neared an old piece of mining equipment that sat like some gravestone. Dismounting, he toppled her off the horse, letting her fall to the hard, unforgiving ground.

She gasped for air, struggling to grab even the whisper of a breath into her lungs as she managed to stand. In the flash of lightning she glanced around, searching for something to defend herself with.

"Your father has cheated me out of what is rightly mine for years. But it's time, Ivy. It's time for me to *have my day.*"

"What do you mean?" she implored as he snatched a rope from his saddlebag and jerked her by one arm toward the metal contraption. "What did my father ever do to you?"

"Oh, he never did anything to me, except give me the ragged scar on my head shortly after he and your mama were married, but that…*that* I can overlook. It's him taking the ranch that I *can't* see past."

"But it was deeded to him," she argued as he shoved her to the rigid wet ground.

Squatting down, he pinned her hands behind her back and around a piece of metal then began securing her to the contraption with the coarse rope. "Sure, it was in my parents' will. The folks couldn't say enough about him— thought he was the best they'd ever seen when it came to ranching. But that didn't mean that he had to *take* the place."

"I don't understand." When he jerked the rope so tight that it cut into her wrists, she bit back a wince.

"Your father came to work here as a measly ranch hand when he was still in school," he recounted, sitting back on his haunches, his face shadowed by his cowboy hat and the darkness. "Then he and my sister fell in love—it made me sick, really, watching the two of them," he sneered, his curled lips highlighted by the lightning's glow. "When they married, even though I'd worked my tail off to make something of this place for my folks, the ranch was deeded to your dear dead mama."

His heartless words stung. "But she—"

"She didn't even *want* the place!" he howled over the rumble of thunder and torrent of rain. When he slammed his palm against the metal contraption, emitting a clanging sound that echoed in the canyon, she jumped nearly out of her wet skin. "But your daddy...his eyes sparkled like costly jewels whenever he so much as *looked* over the land." He tweaked her nose, hard enough that she sliced in a breath.

"Stop, Uncle Terrance," she demanded, struggling in vain to tug her hands free from the cutting rope. "Surely you don't mean all of this."

"Surely I do," he spat, a sinister smile gleaming with another white flash. Thunder moved the ground around her. "Your mama...she'd never think to deprive your daddy. When she died off, she left the property to him."

"But he's kept you on here," she reasoned, regretting every last time she'd pitied this man for the way her father had treated him. Now, she knew. Her father had to know, too—know that he was dangerous and couldn't be trusted. "Even when he *obviously* should've just let you go," she threw out, not even caring if he was hurt by her words.

The back of his hand came out of nowhere, slamming into her face and knocking her to the side.

She struggled to sit upright as she sent a silent prayer heavenward for help. The whole left side of her face throbbed, but even so, she would've said those words all over again.

"You're hateful. Nothing like my father and definitely *nothing* like my mama," she ground out, bolstered by an unexplainable enveloping peace.

He shoved himself up to standing. "When your daddy finally eats enough of that jerky and dies, the ranch will fall to your sweet hands."

"Jerky?" Her anger had grown fierce and red and raw. "You've been poisoning him, haven't you?"

"He's a stubborn cuss. Dies slow." The evil smile he gave sent chills down her spine. "I thought the fire would finally do him in, but Zach and you showed up and saved the day!" he raged, his voice echoing through the canyon.

"You're a sick man." She braced herself for another backhand.

"I'm sure you can understand how we can't have the ranch being passed down to you." When he reached to tweak her nose again, she yanked her head to the side, denying him. "It will fall to me if you decline. Or if something were to *happen* to you."

Ivy wasn't sure *what* was going to happen to her. With the rope wet and her wrists bound so tight, there was no chance she could escape. But she could pray. Closing her eyes, she prayed that God would send someone to save her. That He'd send someone to her rescue.

Zach's heart still pumped madly inside his chest, and it'd been a good two hours since his harsh interchange with Ivy. He'd thought, *very hard,* about going back and apologizing for his hurtful words, but he couldn't. Not yet, anyway.

Maybe tomorrow, when he was driving her back to the train station he'd talk with her, iron out some of the rough creases left by his words, but right now he was too enraged to speak with any kind of civility.

He didn't want to hurt her further.

And hurt her, he had. He'd seen it in her wounded gaze. And in the decidedly defeated expression etched into her face as he'd turned to leave.

He'd been riding in the pouring down rain now for over an hour. Any hope of spotting whoever had heartlessly killed Mr. Harris's prized bull was fast fading. Tracks would be almost impossible to find. The torrential rains had washed over the hard ground, sending small rivulets of water streaming downhill.

The responsibility that weighed on Zach was more than overwhelming. Far more. He'd done his best out on the ranch to make something of himself. All he'd wanted to do was to prove—to himself, *never* to anyone else—that he was cut of the same cloth as his brothers. To prove that he wasn't some sorry excuse for a man.

But as Hugh's accusations flapped like a ragged flag in his mind, he had to wonder if there was more motivating him than he'd thought. Had the satisfaction of proving himself to others been his driving force? Had he been so bent on showing the world that he was a force to be reckoned with and not the weak and wounded boy he'd been long ago, that he'd lost sight of who he really was?

The idea cut him to the quick.

When he circled back to the bull's carcass, a chill passed down his spine at the gruesome sight. The senseless killing reeked of evil intent. He tugged up the collar of his dungaree coat to ward off the sting of pelting rain as he scanned the area. The brutality of the act was enough to keep Zach in the saddle until he located the criminals.

Dread crawled over every inch of Zach's skin as he scanned the horizon, fisting his hand around the cold hard metal of his gun. He'd strapped it to his side, *just in case,* but he'd silently prayed that the situation wouldn't warrant so drastic a measure.

Ivy's harsh words flashed through his mind as a shard of lightning split the dark horizon. Maybe she was right. Maybe Hugh was right. Maybe he was so focused on proving himself that he'd lost sight of what was going on around him. Had his stubborn pride put the ranch in more danger?

No matter what he thought of Hugh, or what Hugh thought of Zach, Zach had to make things right. Resolved to do what was right even if it meant he'd look bad, he started to rein his horse around to go for help when he spotted movement a good hundred yards away. When lightning flashed, he could see the clear image of a horse, saddled with no rider.

Fear clamped around his neck as he rode that way. Dread's hold cinched tighter when he realized that the horse was Ivy's sleek mount.

He'd told her to stay clear of the danger, and to go inside where she was safe. Had she stubbornly decided otherwise? Again, he scanned the horizon, only this time for Ivy.

"Ivy!" he yelled, cupping his hands around his mouth. "Ivy, can you hear me?" He tried again, louder, with not so much as a faint reply. The dread building in his soul threatened every last bit of his wilting confidence.

Should he turn back and go for help?

He'd been chastised, by both Hugh and Ivy, for taking things into his own hands.

But what if she was in dire trouble and needed help? *Now?*

Hugh's taunting accusation ricocheted through his mind as Zach dismounted to inspect her saddle and the horse. While he looked for any sign of foul play, he wondered if maybe he'd handled things by himself one too many times. Maybe he should just give in, lead her horse home and ask for help. For once.

Just as he was about to loop her mount's lead rope around his saddle and turn back, challenge slapped him hard in the face. His chest grew heavy with a profound kind of weight, an unfamiliar yet absolutely recognizable kind of *knowing*.

Every nerve ending grew sharp and ready with purpose. He was nearly overwhelmed with the incessant need to follow his instinct, his heart, and find Ivy.

A tangible and very raw sense of intention shattered through his soul like the forked lightning creasing the dark sky. His heart beat clear up into his throat. His breath came in shallow gasps.

"God, is that You?" he breathed, turning his face up to the sky.

He'd believed in God, had even gone to church, but he hadn't trusted Him. Why would he? When he'd needed God the most as a young boy trapped in a cave, God had seemingly left him high and dry. For at least the past twelve years of his life Zach had steered his own life, down his own path. Was God trying to get his attention?

Yes.

The purely honest and amazingly simple answer swelled in his heart like the rain that was sure to flood the rivers and streams.

Securing the lead rope around the Ivy's saddle horn, he gave the horse a swat on the rear end, urging the mare toward home. He pulled his hat down over his face and mounted his horse again, compelled to find her. While he rode toward the gaping fence line, looking for Ivy, he could easily imagine her riding all the way out here. Most women would've stayed home where it was safe and warm, but not Ivy. For every lovely and softly feminine quality she possessed, there were stubborn and courageous fibers that had been woven into Ivy.

And he loved that about her. He loved every little thing about Ivy. He'd just never be able to share that love with her.

Every thirty yards or so, he'd call her name, desperate to hear her sweet voice in reply. When he led his horse through the gaping fence, alarm tightened around his stomach. This time the hole was much broader, a tempting door to rough territory and a wide open path to danger.

Gulp's Canyon.

Everyone around knew to stay clear of the area that careened down just over the ridge. The area was rough land with a steep and winding slope leading down into the barren canyon. The small tributary invading the canyon had no way out and was a recipe for disaster in weather like this.

As he passed through the gaping fence and headed toward the ridge, the air around him sizzled with another vivid bolt of lightning. Shrugging off his anxiety, he rode hard toward the ridge.

Just then the fear-slung cries of cattle broke through the storm's gale, capturing his attention. He urged the horse faster, pulling his mount to a sudden halt at the ridge.

Lightning came bright as day across the horizon, illuminating the canyon as though it was on display. His heart skidded to a halt at the sight before him. Nearly three dozen head of Harris cattle were huddled together, with their backsides against the canyon wall, and all but surrounded by floodwater.

Fierce anger and great compassion streamed through his entire body as he reined his horse toward where the slope led down into the canyon. When a harsh and desperate cry slipped through the rumble of thunder, his heart seized in his chest. His breath came hard and fast as he slowed his horse at the trail head, straining to see through the dark.

"Ivy!" he yelled, cupping his hands around his mouth.

Alarm prickled every hair on his neck. He peered down into the dark and ominous hole, a spot of emerald green catching his eye in a flash of light.

Ivy.

He'd seen her in an emerald green cloak once or twice.

Holding his breath, he listened for her call. When lightning flashed once again and her voice wafted to his hearing, his breath whooshed from his lungs.

That was her. It had to be Ivy.

Finally, he spotted her. The small tributary had spilled out of its banks and had already filled in the low spots. The water even now pooled around Ivy, every second that passed intensifying the very real threat.

"I'm coming, Ivy!" Zach spurred his mount down the treacherous trail. Said a silent prayer for her safety, that God would help him lead her heart home.

Every single step down the steep slope was fraught with danger. Leaning back in the saddle, Zach gave his well-trained mount plenty of rein, letting the horse pick his way down to the canyon floor. When they'd finally reached solid ground, the horse bolted toward Ivy.

The canyon was fast filling with water, knee-deep on his horse in some places. When he reached the rusted piece of old mining equipment where Ivy had been tied, he catapulted off his horse and knelt down beside her.

"Zach, you came," she rasped, her voice harsh as though she'd been screaming endlessly. She inched her feet up a little farther, away from where the water was lapping at her in a dark cold threat.

"I'm so glad to see you." He cradled her face in his hands, that beautiful face that had been in more dreams than not, and looked her over. "Are you all right?"

"I'm fine," she said, a little too quickly to be convincing.

When she winced as he lightly brushed his hand over her left cheek, he pulled back and peered at her in the bright light of another stormy display. A dark bruise and swelling marred the side of her face.

"Darlin', what happened?" he implored, reaching for his pocketknife and carefully slicing through the rope. "Who did this to you?"

"Please, Zach, I'll tell you later." Once he'd freed her hands, she tugged her arms around in front of her, rubbing her wrists. "Right now we have to get the cattle out of here before it's too late."

Zach glanced over at the frenzied cattle, torn by the decision he faced. As fast as Gulp's Canyon was filling up, if he took time to herd the frantic cattle away from here, he might risk getting caught with Ivy in the overwhelming swell. "My first priority is you," he ground out. "As it is, we're going to be fortunate to get out of here."

"But they'll drown if we don't help." The raw sound scraping through her words broke his heart. He followed her focus as she peered over at the restless beasts. "Look at them. Can't you see how they're staring at you like you're their only hope?"

He could not deny her. "We've got to be quick."

"Thank you, Zach," she breathed.

"Let's get going." Scooping her up in his arms, he carried her through the knee-deep water to his horse. Despite being cold and soaked to the bone by rain and flood water, her arms wrapped around his neck brought him great comfort.

"We have to get the cattle and us out of here in case he returns."

He swallowed hard. "In case *who* returns?"

The way her anguished gaze glistened in a flash of lightning, pricked his heart. "Terrance."

"Aww...darlin'." A load of questions swarmed his mind, but now was not the time to prod for answers. The cattle were fast getting swamped by the water. And he and Ivy would, too, if he didn't take action.

"Easy now," he said, as he gently lifted her to the saddle then settled in behind her. Zach reached around her and grabbed the reins, unable to ignore the way she relaxed in his arms.

When he urged his horse toward the cattle, the experienced mount drove on with barely one protesting side-step. "That's right. Good boy."

"We'll save them in time, won't we?"

He didn't have the heart to douse her optimism. "We'll try."

Once they reached the cattle, he dismounted into waist-deep water, grabbing a tool from his saddlebag as he prayed. Danger splashed around them in every drop of rain. They could be killed by the lightning. Drowned in the flood waters. Trampled over by the nervous cattle that rushed the fence, desperate to be free.

He clipped the barbed wire, very likely the barbed wire that had gone missing from the ranch supply. How had he missed this?

"Hurry, Zach, *please,*" Ivy pleaded.

"I'm trying." Once he had the fence cut, the cattle began piling ahead into the flood waters, their cries barely heard above the storm and wind and the splashing as they surged toward higher ground. Zach mounted his horse and circled around behind the cattle. "Yee haw!

Get on now, cows!" he hollered, herding them toward the slope.

After several minutes of cutting back and forth through the rushing water, coaxing the last few head of cattle up the path, he almost sighed with relief, but something undermined any small bit of peace he could find.

Wary, he urged his mount out of the rising water and up the slope. Once they were a good twenty feet above it, he scanned the black and ominous rim looming at least sixty-feet above them, when a spark pricked up on the ridge. A resounding crack broke through the storm's gale. A bullet whizzed past them.

"Get down!" Leaning forward, Zach hunched over Ivy, raw instinct pricking every nerve ending. On the unprotected slope, they were wide open targets.

"What happened?" Her voice was muffled against his horse's neck.

"Terrance is back. He's shooting at us." Pulling his pistol from his holster, he cocked the hammer and peered up at the dark ridge. He could hear the cattle making their way to the top, their frantic moos now eerily silent as they plodded toward safety. "Stay down, do you hear?"

Her entire body quivered beneath him. "Zach, I'm so sorry. If I hadn't insisted on—"

"Not now," he ground out, his heart pounding clear into his throat.

Easing up to sitting, he held his pistol steady. Peered at the dark ridge. Lightning, bright as day overhead, illuminated Terrance. Ivy's uncle…

On a whispered prayer, Zach took aim. Pulled the trigger. The hammering action cracked the air, sending the bullet on a straight and sure path toward its target.

Terrance's fierce yowl pierced the stormy night. His gun flared again. Fractured the rumbling thunder.

A bullet seared Zach's right side. Burrowed deep. He pitched backward as pain, hot and intense, burned through him like a red-hot iron.

"Zach!" Ivy twisted around to peer at him, a look of horror on her face.

"Stay down!" He scanned the ridge. Grabbed at his ribs. Dragged in a scorching breath as he silently pleaded for God's help. His head spun. Stomach churned. Vision pulsed.

"Zach, please," she pleaded.

Willing himself to stay steady, he cocked the pistol and took aim, waiting for another bolt of lightning to pierce the dark sky.

His vision whirled and narrowed. His hearing reverberated. He felt himself pitching forward while three more gunshots sounded from on the ridge.

Chapter Eighteen

"Zach!" Ivy screamed again as Zach slumped over her. "God, please help me," she prayed, pushing upright. She quickly grabbed Zach's arms to keep him from tipping sideways. "Zach, can you hear me?"

"Are you all right?" he ground out, teetering in the saddle.

"I'm fine. Hang on, Zach," she said, wrapping his arms around her middle to keep him from falling. "Oh, Zach... you've been shot."

He sat up a little straighter, but she could feel his entire body tense in pain. "It's nothing."

She blinked against the driving rain as she struggled to see in the dark. "Where did he get you?"

"My—" His voice caught. A flash of lightning illuminated the pained expression on his face. "My side."

Guilt assaulted Ivy. She'd been the cause of his injury. If he hadn't come down into the canyon for her... "Can you hang on?"

"Sure I can. Is he still up there?" When his weight began shifting to the right, she tugged his left arm to steady him on the horse.

If she couldn't keep him in the saddle, he could very well fall to his death. The winding slope hugged the canyon wall, and apart from a ledge about halfway up—where a large cavelike hole tucked into the rock and the slope took a one-hundred-eighty-degree turn—there was no room for error.

"I thought I saw him ride off, but I can't be sure."

"I heard the sound of another gun," he forced through clenched teeth.

"I heard it, too," she confirmed. "Do you think someone's come to help?"

"We can pray that's true." When he drew in a sharp breath, his hold around her waist slipping, helplessness rained down on her with far more force than this wicked fall storm. He grabbed for his side, wobbling then struggling to right himself.

"I'll get you home. Don't worry," he promised, and Ivy had the distinct feeling that he'd die trying to do just that if she didn't take charge. He made an awkward reach for the reins.

"I've got the reins, Zach."

"But—"

"Just try and hang on," she encouraged, struggling to keep the raw fear and torment from tainting her voice.

His weight grew heavy against her back as though he was having a difficult time staying upright without using her for support. She couldn't imagine making it up to the ridge, let alone all the way back to the ranch. Determined to do something to help him, she nudged the horse on up the slope when she spotted the shallow cave not too far ahead. With the awkward way Zach, twice her size, was teetering in the saddle, she'd be fortunate to make it that far.

"Hang on, Zach. Just a little bit farther," she promised. It was all she could do to hold the reins and keep him seated behind her.

When they finally reached the ledge, she peered over her shoulder at him. His face was etched in pain. His breathing was coming in short shallow gasps that pierced her heart.

"Zach, we're going to rest for a while, all right?"

"Are we home?" he asked, clearly disoriented.

"Not yet," she whispered, emotion clogging her throat. "But we'll get there. I promise."

Tears stung Ivy's eyes as she peered down at Zach. He was shivering uncontrollably and in and out of consciousness as he lay on the hard ground. It had to be well after midnight. Over the past several hours she'd done her best to make him comfortable, but she'd had little to work with—just her cloak and his leather saddlebag and saddle blanket. Every once in a while, when lightning flashes illuminated the small dwelling, Ivy would witness the etching of raw pain over his face.

His courage and brave front left her feeling desperate to help. Somehow. Someway.

She didn't dare build a fire, though the warmth and whisper of light the flames could've provided would've been wonderful. But not knowing if Terrance was out there laying in wait, she didn't want to risk giving away their location. At this point, they had no idea who the other gunman might be. An ally, or an accomplice to Terrance?

Paging through her memory, she struggled to think of any person who might hold a vendetta against her father, but could come up with none.

Ripping another wide strip of cotton from the skirting beneath her dress, she folded it into a pad and gently pressed it against Zach's wound to help staunch the blood flow.

He flinched. Stiffened.

"I'm so sorry," she murmured. She'd done her best to tend to his injury, but in the dark there was only so much she could do. "I don't mean to cause you more pain."

"It's all right." He grabbed her hand, his fingers trembling, his grip weak. "You're doing fine."

She gave his hand a gentle squeeze, swallowing past the lump in her throat. "You're always so encouraging, Zach."

She could've broken down right then and there, but she had to stay strong. For Zach.

"Just honest," he responded, slicing in a harsh breath as he tried to move.

"We need to get you to a doctor." Having felt the warm sticky blood on her hands as she'd tended to his injury, and having seen the way the bullet had stopped him in his tracks, she could only imagine just how bad the wound actually was. "You need medical attention."

"For now, I'm fine right here."

"But Zach, it's dirty and cold and hard." She adjusted her cloak she'd covered him with. They were both soaked through, and her cape barely even covered his torso, but surely it was better than nothing. Hugging her arms to her chest, she clenched her chattering teeth and silently prayed for protection, for help and for a miracle.

Zach found her hand again, his touch lending her comfort even now. "I don't know how you managed to get me in here. But thanks."

She blinked back hot guilty tears. It'd been by sheer

force of will. "It was probably the only good thing I've done all day."

He raised his hand to her face, as though he somehow knew that a tear trickled down her cheek. "Don't say that."

"Zach, I'm so sorry," she whispered. "You wouldn't be here now, if not for me."

"You don't understand." His fingers hesitated at her mouth. "I had to come after you. I couldn't go back."

She tugged his hand away from her face, feeling undeserving of his kind and caring touch. "I've caused you so much pain."

"Ivy, stop," he rasped, coughing.

"If not for me, you never would've stuttered and you never would've been harassed all of those years," she went on to say, guilt eating away at her from the inside out. "And now this."

"Things happen for a reason, Ivy."

She shook her head. "I will understand if you never forgive me."

When he hesitated for a long moment, she braced herself, believing that he would blame her just like her father had.

"I already have," he confided.

He already had? He'd already forgiven her even when, all these years, she'd been none the worse for the wear and completely ignorant of her part in his trauma? "How—*how* can you say that so easily?"

"Believe me, all right?"

Believe him. Over the past weeks, she'd spent far too much time questioning him instead of having faith in him and believing in him.

When a shifting sound came from near the cave entrance, she bit off a gasp. Reached for Zach's pistol. Turning, she glanced over her shoulder. Her heart stuttered to a halt. Every hair on her head prickled as she remained frozen in fear, listening, watching. Then she heard Zach's horse nickering near the cave entrance.

Zach gripped her hand a little tighter. "It's all right."

She gave a small sigh, feeling silly for being so jumpy. "I almost forgot that I had tucked him away in those scrub bushes." He wouldn't fit in the cave. And she didn't dare let him loose—at least not if she had any hope of going for help.

She feared that if help hadn't come by the time day's light crept over the dark horizon, she'd have a hard decision to make. Though she didn't want to leave Zach lying there, alone in his pain and agony, he needed medical attention, and the sooner he received Ben's expert care, the better.

The thought of Zach dying broke her heart. But even when the hope flickered dim, she refused to allow her thoughts to settle there, and instead focused on belief, faith…love.

Belief… She had to believe that God was big enough to take care of things she had no control over, and that He would take care of Zach.

Faith… She felt undeniably compelled to embrace the tender strand of faith that had been woven into her heart for God and His goodness.

Love… From the moment she'd arrived back home, her heart had seemingly beat sure and strong for Zach, as though God had brought her home not only to find her way back to her father's arms but to find her way into Zach's arms, too.

Would Zach even have her after all she'd done?

He was so very good, honest and noble…just like her father. She'd trusted him with secrets she'd never told a soul. When she'd been hostage to her unreasonable fears, he'd gently helped her to step beyond them. His tender care and concern had softened her cold hard heart. His steady strength had called up courage she didn't know she possessed.

She loved Zach. *Loved him.*

When he stirred, she set a quivering hand to his clammy brow and bent over him, longing to lend him warmth. "How are you doing?" she asked, smoothing his damp hair from his face.

"Don't worry about—me." His tight voice was broken by his relentless shivering.

"Is there anything I can do to help you?" Finding his hand in the dark, she held it gently. She felt absolutely desperate to give him some kind of comfort.

He swallowed hard. "Just stay with me," he stated, his words pricking the deepest and truest part of her heart. "Stay with me."

"I'm right here," she breathed, unable to deny him.

She crawled over to his left side where she could keep a watchful eye on both him and the cave entrance. Lowering her cold and sore body to the hard and unforgiving ground, she curled up next to him. Laid her head on his shoulder. Draping her left arm over his chest and hearing the faint beat of his very big and compassionate heart, she prayed.

"Thank you." He sighed as though maybe, just maybe, he could finally rest.

Racked with fever and pain, Zach slipped open one burning eye. The storm had finally ceased its relentless howl and thundering flashes of craggy lightning. Morning's gray light was even now inching into the small dwelling as though announcing the promise of a new day.

He gathered what hope he could from that and hid it in his heart because he had a feeling he was going to need it.

He may as well have been trampled by a whole herd of cattle, as horrible as he felt. His head pounded and body shivered uncontrollably. Every aching muscle felt as weak as a newborn foal.

"You're awake," Ivy whispered, her sweet breath fanning over his face.

Trying to move as little as possible, he peered at where she'd been curled up next to him through the night. "Hi there," he rasped, his harsh voice barely recognizable.

She set her hand to his neck then forehead. "Oh, Zach…you're burning up with fever."

He closed his eyes, weary and unable to come up with a single protest that wouldn't be a lie. "Thank you."

"What?" Sniffing, she rose up on one elbow. "For what?"

"For looking after me." Zach instantly missed the comfort of her head resting on his shoulder. His teeth chattered, his whole body shuddered, only adding to the pain that seared his side. "And thank you for staying with me."

"I was glad to," she admitted, her weary gaze shimmering in the milky light.

It'd been all he could do not to let her know how horrifying it was for him to be in this cave—no matter how shallow. No matter how much daylight he could now see from where he lay. No matter how life-saving it'd been.

He hated confined spaces. Hated caves, to be exact.

From that time he'd been trapped long ago, he'd not once stepped foot into a cave. When she'd led him in here last night in the midst of the storm and after getting shot, he hadn't even realized where he was. When he'd figured it out sometime in the middle of the night, he'd had to force himself to stay calm. Her nearness and tender care at his side through the long night had eased his anguish.

Now that it was day and he could plainly see around him, fear nipped at his heels with brute force.

When she stood and stepped a mere ten feet over to the entrance and peered outside, panic constricted his throat so tightly he struggled for breath. Ignoring the scorching pain in his side, he labored to sit up. He struggled against the unseen force weighting his entire body.

"Zach, what are you doing?" She rushed back to him, kneeling down next to his side as she adjusted the cloak over his chest.

"Trying to get up and get ready to go." The site of his gunshot burned so hot he may as well have just rolled over onto glowing orange coals. "I said I'd get you to the train station this morning."

"Don't be ridiculous."

He gave her a half-wounded look. "I thought I was being thoughtful."

"Please. You need to stay as still as possible so that you don't start bleeding again," she urged, setting a trembling hand on his shoulder and another on his chest. "I have to go for help to get you out of here."

He felt ridiculous all right. Ridiculous as a child, scared of the dark. But the thought of Ivy braving her way into the unknown, and the thought of him staying alone in this cave, struck raw terror in his heart. He almost opened his mouth to insist on riding along, but he refused to add more pressure to what she must already feel.

She glanced over her shoulder to the outside. "There's no one in sight. If I don't get help—"

"Go," he insisted, before the word refused to come out. "But please...hurry."

"Zach, what's wrong?" She gently brushed her fingertips across his sweaty brow. "Is there something you're not telling me?"

He stared up at her, remembering how many times he'd expected her to be forthcoming with the memories that ate at her soul. He'd tried so hard to seem strong and in control, so he'd never reciprocated. He regretted that now. But would she think his fear ridiculous?

"Please," she repeated, brushing her hand featherlight over his cheek. "What's wrong?"

He shoved his focus over to the dark and dank cave wall for a brief moment. "I'm scared to death of caves." He swallowed hard at his confession. When he looked at Ivy and found compassion and understanding in her gaze, his heart swelled. "I'd rather lie out in the open and get picked over by wolves or vultures than to stay in here."

She touched his cheek. His neck. His chest. "But there's no way I can—"

"I know," he cut in, unwilling to let her heap on any undo guilt. He moved his arm from beneath her cloak and grasped her hand. He longed to wrap his arms around her and hold her tight, but his strength was being so elusive. "You don't have a choice."

When she bent over and gently rested her head on his chest, he felt her tremble in a quiet cry. "Zach, how am I going to leave you?" she finally asked, lifting her head to peer up at him. "This feels so much like when I had to leave mama."

"Aww, Ivy...it's all right." He smoothed her hair from her face, his arm feeling like a hundred-pound weight. His heart was heavy, too, by the desperate way she clung to his hand. "You did what you had to do then and you're going to do what you have to do now. You go. And I will be just fine." Swallowing hard, he found it hard to believe his own words.

"But you don't look like you're going to be just fine," she contended, all caring and innocent. She sniffed. "What if we never see each other again?"

"We will."

"How do you know?"

"Believe me," he said simply.

"I do," she confessed, bending over to give him a gentle hug, her face tucked into the crook of his neck. "I believe you, Zach."

"Ivy," he continued. How was it that less than twelve hours ago he'd carried her through flood waters, but now he couldn't even seem to hug her in return?

"What?"

"Can you get my saddlebag for me?"

"It's right here." She pointed beneath his head. "Do you need something?"

He managed a grin, his lips feeling all dry and cracked from fever. "There's a journal in there."

With a gentleness that meant more than a lazy soak in a hot bath would right now, Ivy lifted his head, opened the saddlebag and slid the journal from the pack. "This?"

He gave a slight nod, regretting even that small movement. "That's it."

"Oh...I've seen this before," Ivy said, slowly smoothing a hand over it as though it was some treasured possession. "It was on the table outside my father's office a few days ago."

He treasured every single word written in those pages. The sentiments echoed his life. His heart. His grief and sorrow. His struggles and triumphs. Penning the words had been a way into the darkest recesses of his heart, and sometimes his only lifeline to God.

"Did you read any of it?" Zach studied her worried gaze.

Setting a hand over her mouth, she nodded, tears glistening in her beautiful tired eyes. "I'm sorry. I didn't even know whose it was. I love books and—"

"Shhh," he soothed, touching a finger to her lips. He dropped his arm to his side, weakness assaulting him without mercy. "Listen, Ivy...if something happens to me, then I want you to have that."

Her eyelashes whispered down over her eyes. Her chin quivered as she peered at his journal. "This?"

"Yes." His voice was growing weaker by the moment. His eyes heavier. But he'd not stuttered once that he could recall. Maybe he was nearing true freedom.

Her face was full of sadness when she bent close as though to hear him better. Her eyes pooled with tears. Her desperate gaze traveled over his face. Her mouth, that beautiful perfect mouth he'd once kissed, quivered as she bowed to place a kiss on his forehead. His nose. His lips.

Without warning, a sharp pain stole his breath. He stifled a moan. "You have to promise me one thing, though."

"Anything." Tears streamed down her face and fell to his neck. Ivy's tears. Tears that he longed to wipe away forever.

He loved her. He loved Ivy.

He'd love her for a lifetime if given the chance.

Peering down at the journal she held against her chest, he gathered what little strength he had left. "Read the very last piece I wrote in there...*before* you read anything else."

"I promise," she whispered, setting the journal at his

side. Standing, she ran from the cave, tugged his horse from confinement and rode on up the slope.

Zach didn't even have the strength to call out after her. To tell her that he loved her. To warn her to watch her back.

For a spine-chilling moment, fear at being left alone here in the cave crept over every inch of his body like a whole host of spiders. He'd not felt this helpless in many long years. He could see day's light, but he couldn't seem to move enough to get there. Would he escape this time? Would help come in time?

He didn't necessarily fear dying as he had back then, but there was so much to live for. Namely, Ivy.

"God," he whispered, his solitary voice echoing in the cave and in his soul. He didn't exactly feel alone here, but instead he felt as though arms, invisible but very much real, had wrapped around him. "I've been trying hard to believe and trust You for a while now. I have to trust that You know what You're doing here."

Moving his gaze around, he took in the dark dank walls and the confining and unforgiving rock narrowing overhead. Closing his eyes, he recalled the incident that had changed his life. The haunting way he'd been humiliated in front of Ivy. The cruel way Hugh had shoved him. And the helplessness with which he'd clawed for a way out of the tomblike grave.

He shuddered at the taunting memories. At the way the incident had raked over his soul for so many years. "You were with me then, too, God," he rasped, a tangible assurance blanketing him in an undeniable way. "You had to be."

Was this what God's peace felt like?

Years ago his heart had beat with far more fervency and franticness. Now, facing the possibility of being stranded here alone, and even facing death, his heart beat slow and steady and with undeniable calm.

Maybe he'd grown numb to his circumstance. Maybe he'd matured.

Tears pooled in his eyes and a definite and warm kind of *knowing* flooded his heart.

Or maybe he'd found that which his soul had craved. Peace.

Chapter Nineteen

"No!" Ivy screamed, her heart skidding to a halt. She brought Zach's horse to a sudden stop at the top of the slope leading down into Gulp's Canyon.

Terrance didn't even bother to glance her way. He stood at the entrance to the cave, his leg visibly bloodied and his shotgun raised with stark and cold intent.

"Please, don't shoot!" She slid from Zach's horse and began picking her way down the slope and into sure danger.

She'd been gone for almost an hour, riding across the range when she'd spotted her father and Hugh, Ben and the sheriff all off in the distance. She'd motioned them this way and since then they'd been slowly catching up to her as she rode hard, back to Zach.

"Terrance, please, you don't want to do this," she pleaded, holding onto the craggy rock wall as she made her way down.

From a distance, she could hear horse hooves pounding the ground and nearing the ridge. If they spooked Terrance, he could shoot.

"Get back, Ivy," he ground out, his rusty voice echoing in the canyon. "Take another step and the gun'll be smoking."

Her heart fell as she stopped on the precarious slope. "Please," she begged, her eyes filling with tears. Her heart thudded almost through her chest. "Please don't do something so awful, Terrance. Surely you don't mean this," she reasoned.

Terrance cocked the hammer, the eerie sound echoing like death's ominous peal in the water-logged canyon.

Slow and silent, Ivy made her way closer. She reached down and grabbed an apple-sized rock from the path, praying every step of the way for God's help.

She hadn't heard Zach's voice and couldn't see him in the dark cave. Was he even aware of the danger facing him?

Terrance was probably a good twenty-five feet below on the slope. Close enough for her to see his breath coming hard and fast. Far enough that she'd never get there soon enough to knock him off balance if he pulled the trigger.

Terrance glanced at her over his shoulder. His lips curled. As he slowly turned back to the cave and steadied the gun, she hurled the rock at him and—

One gunshot.

Two.

Three.

Four.

Crouching down, her heart ground to a halt as she slammed her eyes shut. Panted. Clung to a small outcropping of rock, listening for another shot. After a moment, she slowly opened her eyes and looked toward the cave.

Terrance lay facedown on the ledge. Still.

Her entire body trembled as the seriousness of the moment assaulted her senses. She struggled to standing, her legs wobbling. Her breath coming in short gasps.

"It's all right, Ivy, honey." Her father's voice…strong and sure and tender, came from up on the ridge. "It's all over."

She turned, her eyes pooling with tears as she peered where he was perched on his mount, his gun smoking, along with Hugh's, Ben's and Sheriff Goodwin's.

"It's all going to be all right," he echoed, holstering his gun.

"Oh, Daddy," she whispered, tears streaming down her face.

For years she'd longed to hear those words from him. Longed to hear him call her *honey* again. Longed to know that he was there, ready to support her when she needed it the most.

Turning, she made her way toward the cave, her vision clouded by tears as she prayed that Zach was alive. Prayed that her daddy's words were true.

"You're going to be all right," Ben assured, giving Zach's shoulder a squeeze.

What wonderful words. *He was going to be all right.* He'd made it through a cold and uncertain night and then surgery, but he was going to be all right.

"In bed for a good week or two and plenty sore, but you're going to make it, little brother." Ben's eyes glistened in the afternoon glow spilling into the room.

"Thanks for your help," Zach responded then glanced at Ivy in a way that sent a tremor shooting through her.

"You need your rest now, Zach," Violet cautioned,

fluttering about the room, Ivy's father watching Violet's every move as though he adored everything about her. "Just like your brother said."

Her father had insisted Zach take the large bedroom on the main floor while Zach was healing. So that he could be as much a part of things as possible.

"I'm fine, Violet," Zach protested, biting off a wince as he moved. "Besides, who's going to do my job if I'm down?"

"Hugh's glad to fill in for you. I think he feels like maybe he needs to make up for his attitude with you, Zach." Her father shared a knowing look with Zach. "He'll check in with you regularly."

Obvious relief rested in Zach's expression.

He'd been through so much. He'd said that it'd been all he could do to raise his gun in self-defense. The four shots that had shattered the air had come as a complete shock. It was uncertain whose shot had killed, but Terrance was dead, taking with him a dark and deadly nightmare that had sent waves of shock through the ranch and beyond.

"You better listen to Violet, Zach," her father cautioned with a relaxed smile, more relaxed than Ivy had seen him in years. "After all, she's going to be the lady of the house before too long."

"Well, I'm glad to hear that you two have finally opened your eyes," Zach commented, smiling. "But I'm sorry to know that I'm losing my touch."

"What's that supposed to mean?" Ben said, chuckling.

"He was going to do a little matchmaking," Ivy explained, reaching for Zach's hand and giving it a brief and gentle squeeze as she peered up at her father and Violet. "We thought the two of you needed a shove."

"Well, we finally figured it out over the past day," he said, draping an arm about Violet's shoulders in such a sweet and tender way. "Violet's going to be staying in town with Joseph and Katie for now, but just as soon as you're up and going, Zach," her father said, nodding to Zach, "I'd like you to walk this little lady down the aisle for me."

"I'd be honored, sir." With slow movements, Zach held out his hand to her father. "Honored."

Ivy was thrilled for her father and Violet, but deep down she longed for the same. She didn't know where things were going to lead with Zach, but she was content to wait. To show him just how much she believed in him. How much she loved him.

She'd already wired *The Sentinel* that she would be staying right here…in Colorado. No matter what happened with Zach, she knew that this was home.

"How's Brodie doing?" Zach asked, drawing in a slow breath.

The other shots they'd heard that night had been from Brodie. Brodie had had his suspicions about Terrance, and had been keeping a close eye on him. When he'd stopped by that evening after both Zach and Ivy had left, Hugh had informed him about the recent events and Brodie had been determined to ferret out the man. Sadly, he'd been gunned down. When Ivy had come across the men heading toward Gulp's Canyon, it'd been because Brodie had pushed himself to get back to the ranch and sound a warning, the heroic feat nearly costing the man his life.

"It's hard to tell yet," Ben answered on a slow sigh. "If he makes it through the next couple days, he's got a very long road ahead of him."

"We'll be praying," Violet said, grasping Ivy's father's hand.

"We sure will," Zach added, nodding up at Ivy.

"He'll need it. I'm not sure he'll ever ride again," Ben

added with a sorrowful shake of his head as he turned to Ivy. "Thank you for all you did for Zach, Ivy." Ben snapped his bag shut and shrugged into his coat. "I don't think he would've made it if it hadn't been for you.

"And you, Mr. Harris, remember what I told you. Lots of rest and a bland diet of food until that poison works out of your system. Understand?" he said as he stepped to the doorway.

"I've burned every last piece of jerky on this ranch," her father said.

"Good." Ben clasped him on the back. "You should be feeling better in a couple days."

"I'm feeling better already, Doc," he said as Ivy and he walked Ben to the front door. "Believe me."

"Zach's just like you," Ben remarked on a wry grin. "I have a feeling he's not going to want to stay in bed like I've advised."

"Hard to keep a good man down. That's why I hired the young fella." Her father shook Ben's hand as he opened the door. "See you later, Doc."

"Take care, Mr. Harris," Ben said, waving. "You, too, Ivy."

"I will," she responded as her father shut the door and turned to her. "You hired Zach because he was just like you?"

He gave his bolero a gentle tug. "He reminds me a lot of myself when I was that age. I needed a good and honest man who would love this land. Sure, he's made some mistakes, and he'll make more, but I'd rather have him put his heart and soul into things than to just bide his time."

Ivy peered up at her father. "He is *so much* like you, Daddy. Mama told me to look for someone like you."

"Come here, honey." He folded her into a tender hug.

"You were something, you know. Zach told me what you did for him. Your mama would've been so proud of you."

"Thank you, Daddy," she said, cherishing the feel of her father's arms after so many years.

"Ivy...I'm so sorry for the pain I caused you for so long," he confessed, his chest hitching on a broken breath as he pressed a kiss to the top of her head. "I felt horrible that I couldn't do a thing to help your mama. The good Lord knows how often I wanted to talk to you about the things I said, but my stubborn pride always seemed to get in my way."

"I should've been more forthright about what happened, about how insistent mama had been about taking the ride to see the aspens. She was desperate to see them one last time and I couldn't deny her, Daddy."

"I never could, either."

"I'm so sorry."

Holding her arms, he pulled back and looked down at her, his expression gentle and kind, like it had been so very long ago. "You know that it wasn't your fault."

His words traveled to the deepest and darkest crevices of her heart, to where she'd tried so hard to bury the guilt and shame she'd felt all of these years.

"Do you—do you *really* mean that?" she whispered, setting a hand over her heart, sure it would beat right through her rib cage. Her eyes pooled with giant tears.

She'd waited a long time. So very long.

Forgiveness and reconciliation were worth the wait.

"Aww, Ivy...you and I...we were both sick at heart after losing your mama." He wrapped his strong arms around her, soothing away years of emptiness. "We both tried so hard to keep her alive. When she died, I said things to you that I never should have. Things I never, ever meant."

"Oh, Daddy..."

"For six years I've lived with the guilt. I've believed that I couldn't make it up to you. The Lord knows I prayed, but my stubborn—" He dragged in a stuttering breath, his eyes misting over.

Tears streamed down Ivy's face as she peered at her father, overwhelmed by God's absolute love and mercy. "We both have our regrets."

"Well, we have a lot of time to make up for. But I think we're on our way." He pressed a kiss to her head. "Welcome home, honey. Welcome home."

"Are you all right?" Zach asked as Ivy padded into his sick room.

"I haven't felt this good in six years, Zach," she admitted, gently lowering herself to the side of the big four-poster bed.

His smile warmed her heart all the more. "You and your father..."

She nodded, folding her hands in her lap. "We got a good start—a very good start to working things out."

He swallowed hard. "I'm so glad to hear that, darlin'. I've been praying..."

"I don't know how to thank you for all of your help," she admitted, reaching behind him to adjust the pillow bolstering him up in bed.

Zach set his earnest gaze on her in a way that gave her pause. "I have some ideas."

"What?"

He reached for her hand. "Well, for starters, I'd like it if you'd read for me." He nodded at his nightstand where his journal had been placed.

"From this?" she guessed, taking his journal from the table. She held it to her chest, remembering the crushing sorrow of thinking that he might die and knowing that he wanted her to have the journal…his words, his heart and his life.

"Turn to the last entry, will you please?" he asked.

She smiled at him and with tender care, thumbed through to the last entry. Her heart beat fast with great anticipation. She peered up at him, loving the depth of kindness and honesty and gallantry that were there in his eyes.

Looking down at the page, her heart stuttered to a halt. She began to read.

"How beautiful your gaze, sparkling with adventure yet unseen, even as tender young leaves bud joyous and spring green."

Swallowing hard, she glanced up to find his gaze fixed on her in a way that sent a tremor straight through her.

"I never could seem to get your beautiful gaze out of my mind, Ivy Harris. No matter how hard I tried," he said, that half grin of his turning her insides upside down.

"Would I, to twine my fingers with yours, to walk this fair journey, touch life's glowing destinies our eyes shall yet behold," she quoted.

"When we're together there's just something that happens," he said, his voice low and strained with emotion, his sweet honesty stealing her breath away. "Something that I can't deny."

She reached down and gave his hand a gentle squeeze, and then read the last line.

"I should then be a very happy man, a rich man, a very blessed man, indeed."

Trembling, she raised her gaze to find Zach's intense focus covering her with certain passion and absolute love.

"Facing death does something to a person, Ivy," he said. "It makes them take a good hard look at what they want—and what they don't want. And I *know* that I don't want to live another day without you by my side.

"I love you, Ivy. I think I've loved you from that very first day you skipped into grade school all those years ago." He pulled her hand to his mouth, pressing a kiss there that left her stomach fluttering.

Her eyes filled with tears as he drew her closer, caressing her face, with his work-roughened hands. Hands that had eased her pain, calmed her fears, made her feel safe and cherished. "You have?" she sputtered, blinking back tears.

He nodded. "You wore a light green checked dress that matched your eyes. And you had ribbons of the same color in your hair."

"Oh, Zach…you remember that?" she asked on a small and joyful sob.

"I'll never forget it," he said, tugging the journal from her hands and laying it on the bed. "I was convinced from that point on that you were going to be my bride. Someday, anyway."

"Even over these last six years?" she whispered, loving every single thing about this man.

"Well, give or take a year," he said winking as he gathered her hands in his. "There will never be anyone else for me, but you."

"I love you, Zach," she breathed, sniffing. "I think I've loved you from the moment you lifted me out of the mud."

The smile warming his face churned her insides. "You were adorable. Protesting, but adorable."

"I had no idea just how much I needed your help. And your love," she said, on a hiccough. "Thank you for loving me."

"Now that's an easy thing to do." With that, he pulled

her hands to his lips and pressed a tender kiss to each one. "Ivy Grace Harris, will you marry me?"

"Yes. Absolutely yes." Ivy could barely see through her tears. "Oh, I love you, Zach."

"I love you, too, darlin'," he said, enjoying every last kiss she rained over his face. "Welcome home, Ivy."

* * * * *

Dear Reader,

I hope you have enjoyed *Rocky Mountain Homecoming*. Seeing my characters through to the end of a book is always gratifying, but throughout the writing of these pages, I felt particularly connected to both Zach and Ivy, and was delighted to write them to freedom.

Liberty is one of the sweetest gifts we will ever embrace. Finding freedom from deep-seated wounds that have held our hearts and minds hostage can profoundly affect our lives—it can change the course of our thoughts, our actions, our hopes and our prayers. That kind of freedom can lead us down paths we never thought possible.

A friend of mine once said that success is merely a series of diminishing failures. How very true. Zach and Ivy's stories are woven together by their courage and tenacity to face their past and overcome. Ultimately they learn from their mistakes, and instead of allowing discouragement to make them bitter, it makes them better. This is my hope for me and for you.

Thank you for following the Drake brothers and their stories. Please watch for the next series based on the Lockhart family. I would love to hear from you. You can reach me at www.pamelanissen.com.

With love and deep appreciation,

Pamela Nissen

Questions for Discussion

1. Zach's comfortable world turns upside down the moment he sets eyes on Ivy. Have you experienced a similar situation with someone? And if so, what was your response?

2. Facing overwhelming shame and guilt, Ivy returns home. Do you remember a time when you braved through tough emotions to do what was right?

3. Zach is determined to not let Ivy's presence at the ranch destroy his hard-won confidence, but his stutter in her presence is a constant threat to his resolve. Have you experienced a similar situation? How did you succeed?

4. When Zach discovers Ivy's fear of birds, he responds by trying to help her overcome. Have you ever helped someone through a similar circumstance? If so, what did you do?

5. Ivy is impacted by Zach's strong and sure presence on the ranch, but refuses to let her guard down around him. Have you wrestled with longing for something yet pushed it away at the same time? If so, how did you work beyond that response?

6. As mishaps continue on the ranch, the weight of responsibility grows even heavier on Zach. Do you think his response to this is right? What would you say/do to ease his burden?

7. When Ivy insists on handling the laboring mare, alone, she finds herself in trouble. Have you ever insisted on doing something only to find yourself "in over your head"?

8. Believing he can only count on himself, Zach has held God at arm's length. Do you remember a time when you responded in the same way? What transpired?

9. Ivy holds misplaced guilt that she's sure God will condemn her for. Have you ever felt this way? If so, what transpired that brought you freedom?

10. When Zach faces his greatest fear in the cave, he finds God's abiding and comforting presence. Do you remember a time when you faced a fear and found God right there?

11. Zach and Ivy find ultimate healing and freedom when they let go and trust God. Have you ever been profoundly healed in doing the same? If so, what led you to freedom?

INSPIRATIONAL

Inspirational romances to warm your heart & soul.

Love Inspired.
HISTORICAL

TITLES AVAILABLE NEXT MONTH

Available October 11, 2011

MARRYING THE MAJOR
Victoria Bylin

FAMILY BLESSINGS
Amish Brides of Celery Fields
Anna Schmidt

ONCE UPON A THANKSGIVING
Linda Ford & Winnie Griggs

UNLAWFULLY WEDDED BRIDE
Noelle Marchand

REQUEST YOUR FREE BOOKS!

2 FREE INSPIRATIONAL NOVELS
PLUS 2
FREE
MYSTERY GIFTS

Love Inspired.
HISTORICAL
INSPIRATIONAL HISTORICAL ROMANCE

YES! Please send me 2 FREE Love Inspired® Historical novels and my 2 FREE mystery gifts (gifts are worth about $10). After receiving them, if I don't wish to receive any more books, I can return the shipping statement marked "cancel." If I don't cancel, I will receive 4 brand-new novels every month and be billed just $4.49 per book in the U.S. or $4.99 per book in Canada. That's a saving of at least 22% off the cover price. It's quite a bargain! Shipping and handling is just 50¢ per book in the U.S. and 75¢ per book in Canada.* I understand that accepting the 2 free books and gifts places me under no obligation to buy anything. I can always return a shipment and cancel at any time. Even if I never buy another book, the two free books and gifts are mine to keep forever.

102/302 IDN FEHF

Name _____ (PLEASE PRINT)

Address _____ Apt. #

City _____ State/Prov. _____ Zip/Postal Code

Signature (if under 18, a parent or guardian must sign)

Mail to the **Reader Service:**
IN U.S.A.: P.O. Box 1867, Buffalo, NY 14240-1867
IN CANADA: P.O. Box 609, Fort Erie, Ontario L2A 5X3
Not valid for current subscribers to Love Inspired Historical books.

Want to try two free books from another series?
Call 1-800-873-8635 or visit www.ReaderService.com.

* Terms and prices subject to change without notice. Prices do not include applicable taxes. Sales tax applicable in N.Y. Canadian residents will be charged applicable taxes. Offer not valid in Quebec. This offer is limited to one order per household. All orders subject to credit approval. Credit or debit balances in a customer's account(s) may be offset by any other outstanding balance owed by or to the customer. Please allow 4 to 6 weeks for delivery. Offer available while quantities last.

Your Privacy—The Reader Service is committed to protecting your privacy. Our Privacy Policy is available online at www.ReaderService.com or upon request from the Reader Service.

We make a portion of our mailing list available to reputable third parties that offer products we believe may interest you. If you prefer that we not exchange your name with third parties, or if you wish to clarify or modify your communication preferences, please visit us at www.ReaderService.com/consumerschoice or write to us at Reader Service Preference Service, P.O. Box 9062, Buffalo, NY 14269. Include your complete name and address.

LIH11B

Sophie Bartholomew loves all things Christmas.
Caring for an orphaned little boy
makes this season even more special.
And so does helping a scarred cop move past his pain
and see the bright future that lies ahead...

Since the moment Kade had appeared at Ida June's wreath-laden door behind a spotless, eager Davey, Sophie had had butterflies in her stomach. A few hours ago, they'd been having pizza and getting better acquainted, but she felt as though she'd known him much longer than a few jam-packed days. In reality, she didn't know him at all, but there was something, some indefinable pull between them.

Maybe their mutual love for a little lost boy had connected their hearts.

"Christmas is about a child," she said. "Maybe God sent him."

One corner of Kade's mouth twisted. "Now you sound like my great-aunt."

"She's a very smart lady."

"More than I realized," he said softly, a hint of humor and mystery in the words. "A good woman is worth more than rubies."

"What?" Sophie tilted her head, puzzled. Though she recognized the proverb, she wasn't quite sure where it fit into the conversation.

"Something Ida June said."

"Ida June and her proverbs." Sophie smiled up at him. "What brought that one on?"

Kade was quiet for a moment, his gaze steady on hers. He gently brushed a strand of hair from the shoulder of her sweater, an innocent gesture that, like a cupid's arrow, went straight to her heart.

"You," he said at last.

Sophie's heart stuttered. Though she didn't quite get what he meant or why he was looking at her so strangely, a mood, strong and fascinating, shimmered in the air.

Their eyes held, both of them seeking for answers neither of them had. All Sophie had were questions she couldn't ask. So far, every time she'd approached the topic of his life in Chicago, Kade had closed himself in and locked her out.

A woman above rubies, he'd said. Had he meant her?

Sophie senses Kade's eagerness to connect. But can she convince him to open his heart to love—and to God? Don't miss THE CHRISTMAS CHILD by Rita® Award-winning author, Linda Goodnight, on sale October 2011 wherever Love Inspired books are sold!

SHLIEXP1011

Cody Jameson knows that hiring gourmet chef Vivienne Clayton to cook for the Circle C Ranch *has* to be a mistake. Back in town for just a year, Vivienne wonders how she'll survive this place she couldn't wait to leave. To everyone's surprise, this big-city chef might actually stand a chance of becoming a cowboy's lady forever.

The Cowboy's Lady
by Carolyne Aarsen

◆ ROCKY MOUNTAIN HEIRS ◆

Available October 2011 wherever books are sold.

www.LoveInspiredBooks.com

LI87698

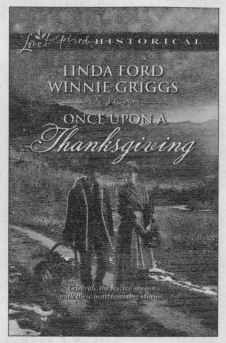